Bam-Bam's Inked Hart

Bad Boys of Beta Squad series, Book 3

Siobhan Muir

DEDICATION

Dedicated to the men and women who are injured in the course of their duties for our nation. Thank you for your service and you're more valued than you know. Please stick with us a little longer.

ACKNOWLEDGMENTS

Writing a book is never really a one person job. Keeping track of details is so much easier when you have help. Not only does it take a great deal of hard work, editing, and research on the part of the author to get things correct, but without my compatriots, there'd be a lot more mistakes. Great thanks go to Silver James who made sure the typo bugs weren't too big and my military details seemed accurate. Any mistakes made are all my own. Thanks to Cara Michaels for designing the most glorious cover art.

CHAPTER ONE

Zamora Hart leaned against her car as she wiped her eyes and crumpled the note in her hand. Two more of the men she'd visited in the hospital had killed themselves. Two more Marines became part of the nasty statistic of twenty-two veteran suicides per day. She closed her eyes and let the grief flow through her. She couldn't show it to the men she'd come to visit today. They needed her to be upbeat and encouraging so they had hope. *And won't end up the same way.*

Taking a deep breath, she threw the note back into her car and locked it before she reached for the handle of her collapsible utility wagon full of treats. But she paused as the skin between her shoulder blades tingled. *Is someone watching me?* She turned her head and scanned the parking lot of the Coronado Medical Center, but the only people she saw were patients arriving and a few medical personnel returning to work. *That's weird.*

She shrugged the unease away and marched for the entrance, still hounded by the feeling of being watched until the doors whooshed closed behind her. She let out her breath in relief and took the elevator up to the second floor. *I'm just being silly.* She rolled her head on her neck and dragged the utility wagon through the elevator doors. She strengthened her smile and waved to the attending nurses at the station.

"Hey Lisa, Mae, how are you?"

"Hi Zamora. Are you here for the general population or the rehabilitation side today?" Mae smiled as she stood and inspected the contents of the wagon.

"General population, I think, especially the new arrivals. I have a bunch of books and music to hand out." She'd brought cookies, chocolate, candy, and beef jerky, too, but she kept that to herself. Oh, the nurses knew, but they'd all adopted a don't ask, don't tell policy when it came to treats for the injured military men and women.

"Sounds good. Thanks again for doing this, Zamora. The patients and the nurses really appreciate it." Lisa winked. "We get to read some of the books after they're done with them. You bring some really good ones."

Zamora grinned. "I know a few authors online and they're always happy to send books to the troops."

"Well, it helps a lot." She handed Zamora a visitor's badge.

"Glad to hear it. See you later."

She pulled her wagon down the hallway, trying to ignore the scents of disinfectant and injury. So many lost to the war, lost to peace. With twenty-two veteran suicides each day, being home didn't seem like a safe place anymore. *Like the two I just heard about.*

Zamora swallowed against the renewed tears and shook her head, pushing away the morbid thoughts. *I can only do my part here.* She fixed a friendly expression on her face as she knocked on the door to a room, pushing it open.

Three men lay in the beds within, two with arm injuries, and one with an amputated leg. The amputee rested closest to the window and she'd found him the most cheerful despite his missing limb. He and one of the others had been here for a few weeks, but the third man was new. At the moment he rested with his eyes closed and she took her time to look at him. His arm wore a stabilizing brace that could be removed to tend the bandages and a sleeveless hospital gown covered his torso above the blankets. Golden blond hair matched arching brows over a straight nose. She'd consider him a beach-bum pretty boy except the muscles in his other arm spoke to his strength. Normally she didn't stare at the physiques of the injured men, but the curve of his smooth pectoral peaking from the gown was too beautiful to ignore. *He'd look good with a little ink there.*

"Howdy, Zamora. Whatcha got in your wagon today?" Lance Corporal Harrison's voice cracked as he levered himself up on his elbows.

"Howdy yourself, Harrison. How are you holding up?" Zamora smiled as she pulled her wagon to his bedside.

Harrison shrugged as he waved at his leg stump. "Not bad all things considered. I could still carry you home even if I am missin' half my leg." He grinned. "When are you gonna let go of your cares and run away with me?"

She snorted. "Neither one of us will be doing much running until you get your prosthetic and get good at wearing it."

He winked. "You just give me time, darlin', and I'll be runnin' circles around all them other boys."

Zamora laughed. "I'm counting on it, marine."

"Hoorah, ma'am."

"So what did you bring?" Petty Officer Third Class Sikes winced as he sat up with his amputated arm. He hadn't talked to her the first few times she'd been in the room because he'd been embarrassed by breaking his arm while trying to change a Jeep Willy's tire. He'd ignored it too long and it had turned septic. Now he had his own prosthetic to look forward to, along with her company.

"I brought that beef jerky soaked in garlic you like so

much, Sikes." She smiled as he licked his lips like a hungry toddler and pulled out the treat. "But you have to promise to hide them better. I got in trouble for bringing in contraband last time."

"I promise, Zamora." The fingers of his good hand twitched as he eyed the jerky.

"Good." She nodded. "I also brought those romantic suspense novels from that author you liked so much, Harrison."

"Aw man, how can you read that romantic shit?" Sikes groaned and rolled his eyes.

"It's not shit, it's kick-ass adventure with hot sex. What's not to like?" Harrison snorted as he accepted the books. "Beats gettin' shot at and the guy always gets the hot girl. Can't go wrong with that. Thanks, Zamora."

"Somebody getting shot and getting the girl?"

Zamora turned and met the bluest eyes she'd ever seen. She damn near fell into them, her body tingling like she'd touched a live wire, but she mentally shook her head. She didn't believe in the wide-eyed spark of love no matter what Harrison's novels said.

"Looks who's awake." She gave him a smile even if her heart thundered at his beauty. He'd been pretty while asleep, but the animation in him when awake made him gorgeous. "My name's Zamora and I bring goodies to the injured. Would you like anything from my wagon?" She dragged it closer to his bed so he could take a look.

His gaze never moved from her, though it did drop to her chest. *At least I know he's probably not gay.* Her breasts had always been large and most men noticed them before they noticed her ink. But instead of glassing over from tit-shock and drool oozing from his mouth, he returned his blue gaze to her face and tilted his head.

"What all did you bring?"

"Let's see…" She crouched to dig through the contents of her wagon. "I have some edible goodies like oatmeal cookies, rice crackers with wasabi peas, teriyaki beef jerky, and chocolate." She flipped the packages aside. "I also brought some DVDs of comedies and thrillers, a few suspense and cowboy novels, and some other romances."

"You should go for those, Killian." Harrison waved his books. "Kick-ass adventure with hot sex and you don't even have to get shot at."

Sikes rolled his eyes. "Man, if you're gonna pick a book, at least pick one of the suspenses. No mushy stuff."

"Just because you haven't gotten in touch with your feminine side, Sikes, doesn't mean the rest of us are so handicapped."

Zamora bowed her head to hide her grin. It was an old argument and Harrison was anything but feminine, but hearing him tease his roommate cracked her up. The man named Killian snorted and she met his blue gaze again, sharing a smile.

"I think I'll pass on the reading and take the oatmeal cookies." He followed her hands as she fished them out. "Are they homemade?"

She barked a laugh, but covered her lips with her hand. "No, sorry. I'm not really much of a baker. But I'm a mean shopper of baked goods." She handed him the little wax bag of cookies.

"I take it your talents lie elsewhere?" He grinned.

She lost her smile for a moment, anger kindling. Bloody hell, did he think just because she had big tits and couldn't bake she was a sex practitioner?

"What do you mean by that?" The sharpness in her voice silenced the argument of the other two men.

Killian nodded to her arms. "Your ink. Those tattoos are really good. Did you have them done or do them yourself?"

She raised an eyebrow. "How did you know I was an artist?"

He pointed to the nylon wagon. "The emblem

embroidered in the side. Think Ink Tattoos. Is that the shop you work in?"

Understanding and relief loosened her shoulders. "Own, actually. My pride and joy. Bringing permanent color to a vanilla world."

"Nice." Killian's smile turned sultry. "Maybe I'll stop in some time and get my own ink."

She tipped her head and scanned the breadth of his shoulders. "I'm sure we could find a space for some art on you." She gave him a small smile, but she didn't suffer players, and Killian struck her as a man who knew his own beauty. *And he is lovely.* "It was nice to meet you, Killian. I hope you heal up quick."

"Will we see you again?" Despite the cock-sure smile, desperation and fear sparked in his very blue eyes.

Her heart went out to him, but she shrugged with a smile. "Maybe. You gonna be here next week?"

"Same bat-time, same bat-channel."

Zamora laughed even as she tried not to encourage him. "I'll stay tuned, then." She waved to the others. "See you later, Sikes and Harrison."

She dragged her wagon out of the room to a chorus of male voices wishing her well, and headed off to make her rounds. There were too many wounded men without families nearby to skimp on visits. But Killian's hidden desperation stuck with her as she moved on.

****

Petty Officer Greg "Bam-Bam" Killian scowled at the nurse as he unwrapped Greg's arm. It hurt like a sonuvaprick even though the doc said it was healing well. Not well enough from Greg's perspective.

"Stop glowering at me, Petty Officer. If the arm looks good, the doc will clear you to leave."

The nurse shot him a scowl of his own and Greg

shoved his expression behind impassiveness. He didn't really want to see his arm after the tangos from their last op butchered it, but he could hope it had healed more than expected.

The scent of dried blood mixed with the sharp tang of medicine killed the hope. His arm slowly appeared as the nurse cut away the bandages. Some stuck to the skin and he hissed when they pulled on the stitches. The muscles used to run smooth along his bone, robustly bulging with each flex when he moved. Now they looked like they wore baseball stitching over misshapen ridges and valleys. Hell, some of the muscles were downright missing. He tried not to blanch, horrified, but a moan of disgust escaped before he could swallow it.

"It looks good." The nurse nodded.

"Good? *That* looks good?" He couldn't keep the horror out of his voice.

"It does. The stitches are clean and the skin is pink, not red. There's no sign of infection." The man gently squirted saline over the stitching to clear off the last of the dried blood and bandages. "The doc will take a look and give you her prognosis, but I suspect you should be able to take care of this on your own."

Greg swallowed back his repugnance. "Will I be able to rebuild the muscles?"

The nurse's expression turned neutral. "The doc and your physical therapist will be able to tell you that better than I."

In other words, not fuckin' likely. Another thought snaked past his shield and his gut clenched. *What if this means I'm out of the Teams?*

Before the panic could set in, a small woman in a doctor's white coat entered the room and waved to the two other men in the beds across from Greg. While she didn't pause, she did seem to know each and every man by name and had a nice word for them. Dr. Meecham even managed to give him a smile.

"Good to see you up, Petty Officer. How is the arm feeling?" While her smile remained in place, her eyes held intent observation. The woman missed very little.

"Good."

She raised her eyebrows. "Don't kid the kidder, Petty Officer. How's it really feeling?"

He wanted to break down into heartbreaking sobs like cartoon characters did on Saturday mornings, but his SEAL training nipped that in the bud. He settled for a grimace.

"It's stiff, sore, and looks hideous, ma'am."

A real smile stretched her lips. "Better. Let me take a close look at it and we'll go from there."

Dr. Meecham grasped his arm and turned it to get a better look. Greg looked away, his heart sinking as she peeled away the last of the bandage. *I'm so fucked.* The fingers of his right hand remained numb, like lead weights at the end of his arm.

"This looks pretty good." The doctor nodded as he turned back to look at her.

"That's what the nurse said."

"You don't sound very convinced."

"I'm not, ma'am. It's…" He ran out of words and just shook his head.

"The bullets tore a lot of the muscles and tendons in your arm. We reconstructed what we could and took some skin grafts from your thighs to finish." She paused and tilted her head to look at his arm. "It looks like they're healing very well and there's no sign of infection."

He couldn't look again. It was too disheartening. "When I'm out of here, how long will it take to get back performance?"

"That really depends on you, Petty Officer." She gave him a smile at his rolled eyes. "I know that seems cliché, but here's the thing. You will be able to recover with your physical therapy, listening to the directions of your doctors, and rehabilitation exercises. You'll have to go slow and take your time, push through pain, and give up your expectations. But if you do that, the arm will heal." She sobered. "My only concern is nerve damage. Because of the extent of injury here, the nerves may have sustained so much disruption that you may feel numbness and deadened sensation in your hand."

His stomach sank and his face fell. Dr. Meecham nodded.

"It's too early to tell yet, so don't panic. You need more time to heal and rest. How is the pain level? And don't man-up on me, Petty Officer. I've known too many SEALs to put up with that."

Despite his despair, he cracked a smile. He liked the doctor even if she brought hard news.

"Right now, the pain is at a six of ten, ma'am."

She nodded. "I think we can move back to something a bit more mild than Dilautid. I'm going to put you on morphine to see if that takes care of the pain. If it's not enough, we'll switch back. If the healing continues the way it looks, you might be out of here in a week or two."

"Really?" That was the first hopeful thing he'd heard in a while.

"Really. Keep focused on that goal and on healing. I'll check back on you tomorrow."

"Thanks, Doc."

The woman nodded and headed out on the rest of her rounds. Despite the ugly wound in his arm, he finally felt like things were shifting in the right direction.

He got to enjoy that warm feeling for about five minutes until someone official and serious came in looking for Petty Officer Greg Killian. The man didn't appear particularly military, but the expression he wore could be described as stoically disdainful.

"I'm Petty Officer Killian."

"You've been served, sir." He handed Greg a large

manila envelope and retreated without another word.

Greg scanned the envelope and ignored the curious stares of the men in the beds across from him. His stomach soured at the return address. Divorce court. It either meant his wife MaryAnn had countersued or it was a declaration of a scheduled hearing. Either one made anger and anxiety rise in his chest.

He slowly opened the flap on the envelope and withdrew the paperwork inside. Court documents, scheduling the hearing of the divorce between Petty Officer Gregory R. Killian and Mrs. MaryAnn L. Killian, Friday April 30th at two o'clock.

At least it'll be over once and for all.

The thought brought him no joy. He still felt betrayed and abandoned. For all his hard work protecting home and country, the one person he'd valued most had turned her back on him. He might not have been the best husband, what with the SEAL missions always taking precedence over holidays and family celebrations, but he'd always been faithful to his wife, even in the face of so many willing partners while away.

But she wasn't faithful to me.

That wound still ached more than the one in his arm. He shoved the papers back in the envelope and leaned back, closing his eyes against the pain and fury.

"Hey, man, you takin' a power nap, or what?" CPO Kevin "Rimshot" Stanton stood at the foot of the bed, a smile on his face and flowers in his hand.

Greg blinked, not sure what he saw was real. *Rimshot smiling? Has the world ended?*

"Gotta rest when I can, Stanton. What are you doing here?"

"Can't I visit my buddy in the hospital?"

"And the flowers? Those for me, too?"

Stanton snorted. "Never took you for a wildflowers kinda guy, but I'll leave 'em if it'll make you feel better."

Greg shook his head. "Nah. Seems like something you'd bring a woman. Who're they really for?"

"Jaime Hensen."

Greg frowned. "The woman we brought back? Chris's best friend?"

"Yep, that's the one." Stanton smiled again. "Not only is she beautiful, she's found my sister, Bethany."

"Really? That's great, Kevin. I'm happy for you. Where is she?"

"Jaime or Bethany?"

"Your sister."

Stanton shook his head with a rueful smile. "Wyoming of all places."

"Have you seen her yet?"

"Nope. Waitin' on Jaime to feel better before makin' the trip. I figure I'm gonna need someone to keep me from pummelin' Bethany for disappearin' for so long."

Greg knew the feeling. Maybe he should ask one of the squad to go with him to the divorce hearing. *Nah. Don't want the guys to see me that low.*

"You trust Jaime to keep you cool, eh?"

"Yeah." Stanton sighed and leaned a hip against the bed. "I was damn lucky she forgave me for shootin' her, but it was a close thing. I was afraid there for a while she'd tell me to go to hell. But she didn't. It's given me hope that she'll agree to marry me when I get around to askin' her."

"Married?" Didn't that just beat all? Here he was, laid up in the hospital with divorce papers sitting on his lap, and Stanton was talking about marriage.

Biggest fucking cosmic joke in the universe.

"Yeah. I never thought I'd go for it after the mess my parents made of it. But Jaime's the one, man. I can't imagine not havin' her to come home to."

"Yeah, that's a nice idea. I hope she thinks you're worth it enough to wait for you when you go on missions and shit."

Stanton frowned then his gaze caught on the envelope on Greg's lap. "Aw hell, Killian. Is that what I think it is?"

"You mean divorce summons? Yeah."

"Shit, I'm sorry. When?"

"April 30th. At least I have some time to heal before I'm required to be in court."

"Damn." Stanton shook his head. "How's the healing goin'? What's the diagnosis and outlook?"

Greg appreciated the change in subject, but the information didn't make him any happier. "It's going, but there's a lot of physical therapy and muscle rebuilding ahead of me. And there might be nerve damage. We'll just have to see."

"Aw, man, that's hard. But you know. The only easy day—"

"Was yesterday. Yeah, I know."

"Hooyah." Rimshot grabbed his flowers and stood up. "I'm gonna go check on Jaime. You hang in there, Killian. I'll text the others from the squad to come on by. I know they'd like to see you."

"Yeah, that'd be great. Thanks."

Greg closed his eyes again after Stanton left, not wanting to interact with anyone as he sifted through his thoughts. Anger, frustration, betrayal, disappointment. Each one zinged through his body, making him grit his teeth and catch his breath. Tears burned at the back of his throat and eyes as he allowed himself to wallow in his misfortune for a bit. Life had rarely been fair, but he'd definitely received the short end of the stick this time.

As promised, Stanton texted the squad and all the members came to visit over the weeks he healed. Hell, Rimshot came several times on his way to see Jaime. The man seemed happier and happier each visit. Even Zamora stopped by with her weekly visits offering goodies, her smile friendly and warm.

MaryAnn never came once.

CHAPTER TWO

"To fucking up and fucking over." Greg "Bam-Bam" Killian raised his glass to no one with a sour grimace.

His divorce from MaryAnn Killian, MaryAnn Wilson once more, was complete. *Not my divorce.* Not really. He hadn't wanted to split from his wife, but the idea she'd been fucking someone else while he'd been deployed made it very difficult to want to work anything out with her. He just kept seeing her moaning like she did when he made love to her except the guy she moaned with had darker hair, darker eyes, and darker skin.

Greg's jaw clenched as tight as his hand around the shot glass. *Motherfucker!*

It didn't matter that he was a highly decorated SEAL. It didn't matter that he and his squad had saved her ungrateful ass from terrorists. All that mattered to her was her fucking manicures, her perfect clothes, and her husband being around for her every stupid whim.

"Yeah, don't mind me. I was just saving the fucking world for you."

It hadn't mattered to her. She'd liked the SEAL part when he first met her, when she was just a Navy Bunny looking for some hot SEAL sex. But it was another matter when she realized he hadn't been kidding, and he really did have to leave at the drop of a hat.

Greg threw back the shot and slammed the glass down on the bar. "Another."

The bartender shot him a pitying glance and poured another shot. "This is the last one, man. I'm cutting you off."

Greg nodded, his grimace turning ironic. "Seems to be going around." Yeah, his wife had cut him off too, at the goddamned balls.

At least I still have them. All through the divorce process he'd tried to fuck his way around Coronado, taking any woman willing to suck or fuck SEAL cock. His pretty face still drew them in and they wanted the thrill. He gave them that in spades.

It only made him sick inside. And empty.

But hey, he was free.

He threw back the last shot and set the glass on the bar before digging out his wallet. He had enough cash now that the lying harlot had gotten reamed by his lawyer. She'd committed the adultery and therefore she lost out on getting half of his pay. She'd tried to suggest he'd neglected her, but the court made it very clear she knew what she was getting into being a SEAL's wife. Greg did his duty and never fucked anyone outside of their marriage, even while deployed.

Maybe I should've.

He staggered to the head to empty his bladder and his sorrows, but he only succeeded in decorating his shoes. *Shit, I'm drunk.* Understatement of the year. *No, fidelity is the understatement of the century.* Why did the Marines value it so much? *Maybe because it's so damn rare.* No one stuck with anyone anymore.

Except SEALs. Bronco never fucked around on Lindsey or his squadmates. Magic always had Ghost's back even before he married her. Hell, the entirety of Beta Squad never let each other down.

Greg zipped up his fly, washed his hands, and stumbled out of the bar into the balmy night air. The breeze off the ocean cleared some of the alcoholic haze clouding his mind, but mostly he floated down the vacant sidewalk. The alcohol dulled the pain of MaryAnn's betrayal, but it waited for him to come down off the high. As it was he strode down the street intent on finding something more to distract him.

Brilliant light flashed on his left, signaling trouble on the way, and he lurched backward to avoid the muzzle fire. He slammed against a brick wall beside a window and took stock of his location. The breeze ruffled the fronds of the palm trees and a random car or two passed on the street, but nothing else seemed amiss. Greg frowned. What had he seen?

Taking a deep breath, he peeked around the corner toward the flashing lights. A neon OPEN sign flashed red and blue in the window of a tattoo parlor, Think Ink Tattoos. The name sparked some recognition, but being a light-year from reality made it difficult to connect. He frowned hard at his boots, the sidewalk sliding in and out of focus. Where did he know the name from?

The image of a beautiful woman with short crimson hair, green-golden eyes, and a rainbow of ink on her arms filled his thoughts. *Zamora.* Despite his drunken state, the image and name of the woman who'd conquered his fantasies since he'd been in the hospital hardened his cock. Zamora, who'd brought treats and company to the wounded, owned Think Ink Tattoos. He hadn't seen her since he'd left the hospital, but he'd wanted to.

Shoving off the wall, he rolled his head on his shoulders and straightened his t-shirt. He hadn't been laid in a week and she was fucking hot. He pasted his best smile on his face and pushed through the doors of the tattoo parlor.

He expected the interior to be dingy, dark, and greasy, but the room he entered glowed with stylish recessed lighting, buffed and resined concrete floor covered in bright oriental rugs, and comfortable dark leather furniture. The walls held framed pictures of tattoos and elegant graffiti art while soft classical music played over the PA system.

A young man with enough piercings to look like an advertisement for a scrap yard looked up from the book he read with a friendly smile. Ink decorated his arms from wrist to biceps where they disappeared under the sleeves of his t-shirt, but the title on the book read *The Handmaid's Tale.* Greg smothered his smirk, he'd never been much of a reader. *Trying to pick up women, I guess.*

"Can I help you, sir?"

"Yeah, I'm looking for Zamora."

The young man scanned Greg as his smile faded. "Can I tell her what this is about?"

How did Greg explain he just wanted to get laid and Zamora seemed like a good candidate?

"About getting…inked."

He'd almost said 'fucked', but a sane voice saved him at the last moment.

The young man nodded slowly, his expression guarded. "Can I have your name so she knows who's calling?"

Calling? Oh, calling on her. Greg hadn't heard phrases like that since his grandfather told him about dating Mima.

"Petty Officer Greg Killian, U.S. Navy."

The smile reappeared. "Okay. Why don't you have a seat and I'll go tell her?" The young man patted the counter and waited for Greg to sit down before he disappeared behind the curtain wall.

Greg let his gaze fall on the coffee table in front of him and the thick photo albums laid there. He grabbed the first and thumbed through the pages of tattoo art done at the shop. The art ranged from simple to elaborate, and he admitted some of it was beautiful. The best one was of a golden-haired mermaid sliding through a coral reef. The artist had captured the marbling of the water's reflection on the long scaled tail and Greg could imagine swimming with her.

He sat back in the chair and closed his eyes. The leather creaked a little, but cradled him just like the sea always did when he went for a swim. He let his mind wander with the mermaid and he swore she turned back and winked at him before darting among the kelp. He swam after her, laughter and excitement fueling his strokes.

"Think you can catch me, Petty Officer?" The mermaid laughed as she peeked from behind a large chunk of coral. "You know where you are, right? You're in my world now." She grinned at him and disappeared. "Catch me if you can, Petty Officer."

He grinned back at her and followed her motions with his gaze, tracking her through the dim underwater world. She remained well-camouflaged, but he was patient, and when she moved again, he pushed off to give chase. Unfortunately, the kelp had wrapped around his arm and legs, and held him back. He turned to shake the sea vegetation off, but it tightened around his left arm, squeezing.

Greg snarled and jerked his arm harder, but the kelp wouldn't let go. Motion zipped past out of the corner of his eye and he caught the flash of a tail fluke as the mermaid teased him.

"Aw, are you stuck, Petty Officer Killian? Is that what you're doing here?"

The questions didn't make sense, but her derisive tone said everything he needed to know. He gathered his strength and made a herculean effort to pull free. The kelp released him faster than he thought and he jerked out of his dream to find himself on his knees on the floor of the tattoo parlor.

"What the fuck?"

"My question exactly. What the fuck are you doing here, Petty Officer Killian?"

He raised his gaze, following the feet stuck in Doc Marten's knee-high leather boots and legs tight black leggings up to the emerald green "Girls Love Ink" tank top swelling over lovely, large tits. His gaze stuck there, taking in the large nipples pressing against the ribbed fabric, and his mouth watered. *They'd taste so good I bet.*

"My eyes are up here. The tits don't talk."

Greg jerked his eyes to her face. "What?"

"The tits don't talk." Zamora gave him a flat look. "What are you doing here, Petty Officer?"

He swallowed hard around the fantasy of tasting her big nipples. "I wanted to get f—inked."

"Finked?"

He shook his head. "Inked. I want a tattoo."

"Uh-huh." She tilted her head and his world almost tilted with her. "I have a policy to avoid people who come in here six sheets to the wind before starting a tattoo. Saves on lawsuits and personal injuries to me and my staff. Come back when you're sober."

Anger kindled and he growled. "I need to get finked now."

"You mean, fucked now."

He nodded so hard his neck cracked. "Yeah."

Zamora sighed. "You came through the front door, and you can go out the same way—"

"Hell, no, I'm not going anywhere without you." He shot her his best leer, but uncertainty hit his gut when she only scowled.

"Well shit." She turned to the young man behind the counter. "Brew some coffee, Toby. It's gonna be a long night."

Toby raised a dubious eyebrow. "You're gonna let him stay?"

Zamora shrugged, her nearest breast jiggling beautifully. "I can't let him drive home and I have no idea where he lives. Might as well let him sleep it off here until he can stagger home."

Home. Greg didn't really have one anymore. MaryAnn wanted the house and he couldn't be bothered to return to the place he'd thought would one day contain his family. He was supposed to contact on-base housing to set up living quarters after his divorce hearing, but he'd forgotten and it was already Saturday. Government and military installations didn't do domestic work on the weekends.

"Don't have a home." Damn, was that his voice sounding so petulant?

"Great, a melancholy drunk. I'm gonna make coffee." Toby closed his book with disgust and strode off into the back of the shop.

"Thanks, Toby." Zamora sighed again. "Come on, Killian. Let's get you a place to lie down." She tugged on his arm to help him to his feet.

Greg swore his body had become filled with lead. Even the act of standing took almost all of his super-human willpower. God, he just wanted to sleep in a comfortable, safe place. He shuffled after her, his gaze stuck in front of his feet. The glossy concrete floor slid past him like ripples on a lake and some of his melancholy faded. Water was safe. *Gotta get back to the clear water.*

"Here you go, Petty Officer. Just sit down on this futon."

Zamora helped him keep his balance as he slumped down onto the cotton-covered day-bed.

"Would you be my clear water?" Greg had no idea where the question came from, but asking Zamora seemed like a good idea.

"Clear water?" She tilted her head again. Or maybe it was him who tilted because she caught him and pushed him back upright.

"Yeah, clear water. Safe haven, home port, port o' call…" Safe zone. Something MaryAnn hadn't been for years. Tears started in his eyes and he blinked to hold them back. Why had she forsaken everything they'd had?

"Oh, man, he's got no business using that kind of talk. You should get him a hotel or something, Zamora." Toby scowled as he shook his head. "Or better yet, let him sleep it off in the alley."

"Come on, Toby. He might be pathetic right now, but that's mostly the alcohol. He's a decorated sailor in the U.S. Navy. Have a little compassion."

"SEAL." Greg needed her to know he wasn't really pathetic. *Most of the time.*

"You're a SEAL, Petty Officer?" Her face came close to his as she grabbed one of his hands. "Here's a cup of water to start with. If you don't drink this now, you're gonna be sick and I won't get the stench out of my shop for weeks. Drink."

He could barely get it to his mouth without spilling and she had to hold it for him. The water slid down his gullet like a refreshing river and he drank all he could.

"He's a terribly pathetic SEAL at the moment." Toby shook his head. "Coffee will be done in a minute."

"I gotta hit the head." Greg tried to lever himself to his feet.

"Hell. Toby?" Zamora rubbed her face with one hand.

"Oh, no. No, no, no. I'm not dragging his ass to the bathroom." Toby backed away, waving his hands as if to ward off a magic spell.

"Well, I can't do it. You're at least his same gender."

"Same gender or not, I don't play with another guy's junk."

Zamora snorted and dropped her chin in disbelief.

"Hey, just because I'm bi doesn't mean I find all men attractive. Especially super-macho, drunk SEALs." Toby scowled. "You get to help him to the bathroom and lock him in. I'm sure he can find his dick even when he's drunk."

Greg frowned. "I can always find my dick. And the ladies can, too."

"Oh, for fuck's sake." Toby threw his hands up and stomped away.

"Come on, sailor dick. Let's get you to the bathroom before you pee on the floor." Zamora dragged him to his feet and shoved him toward what looked like a closet door covered in playbills from local drama houses. "In you go and don't come out until you're empty. Got me?"

"Not yet, but I will."

He thought the line fairly witty, but she rolled her eyes and closed the door in his face.

CHAPTER THREE

Zamora scrubbed her hand over her face and tried to ignore the disapproving scowl from Toby as they waited for Killian to get out of the bathroom. When Toby had come to get her, she'd worried one of the injured had sent for her to say goodbye. Or worse, her ex-fiancé had stopped in to demand she come home. *Yeah, like that's ever gonna happen.*

But when Toby said it was a drunk petty officer, she'd been too interested to see which one. *That's gonna get you in so much trouble.* Even drunk as a skunk, Greg Killian made her insides go all gooey.

"Don't give me that look, Toby. He might be drunk, but I'm not heartless." Thank God she hadn't mentioned how handsome Killian was to Toby after she met the injured SEAL. He'd never let her forget it.

"So what are you gonna do? Let him sleep here while we're open?" Toby shook his head. "What about when we close in an hour? What then?"

Zamora sighed and rubbed her forehead with her fingers. "What do you want me to say, Toby? He needs a place to rest until he's sober enough to get home."

"He's not your responsibility."

"No? Than whose is he? Because right now, no one else is claiming him, not even the U.S. Navy."

"Get his phone, call a buddy of his, and have the buddy come get him."

The suggestion was both smart and reasonable, but for some reason Zamora balked at the idea. *She* wanted to take care of him, if only for a few short hours. *What the hell is wrong with me?* She'd been on her own, independent for years. Any boyfriends had been short flings, or fuck buddies after her retreat from her family and ex-fiancé. For the first time since she'd secured her independence, she wanted to take care of someone.

Not just someone. Petty Officer Killian.

"That's a good idea." Admitting it didn't mean she'd agreed to do it, but Toby wore a mollified expression when Killian staggered out of the bathroom.

"Feeling better?" Her voice sounded dry even to her.

"Yeah. Empty, just like you ordered." Killian sank back down onto the futon.

"Good. We close in about an hour. Why don't you drink some coffee or water until then. You got a friend who can pick you up?"

The look he gave her made her wish she was the friend in question. *I'd pick you up, honey, and take you for a ride.* There was definitely something wrong with her if she considered a drunk Navy sailor someone worth picking up.

Killian grimaced and shook his head. "No."

"No, what?"

"No friends to pick me up. They're all…" He shot her a narrow-eyed look. "Out of town."

Relief cascaded through her and she resisted the urge to shoot Toby a triumphant look. Then it occurred to her why he'd hesitated. SEALs went out of town all the time, on training, on missions, and sometimes didn't come back. She suspected those who were injured hated to be left behind, and Killian sat here, drunk off his ass, while his squad was away.

"Sorry to hear that." She meant it even if it gave her more time with him. "Just start with the coffee and the futon, and we'll go from there."

He nodded and Toby handed him a mug, still steaming from the machine. Killian took it and inhaled as if the caffeine would provide better oxygen. *God, I hope he doesn't throw up.* Alcohol poisoning sucked and struck down even the toughest of people. But though he wobbled a little, he remained upright with a rosy glow rather than pale and sickly.

Satisfied he'd be okay for the last hour of work, she retreated to the front with Toby.

"Now what?" Toby scowled as he opened his book.

"I don't know. I'll think of something. In the meantime, I'm gonna clean the equipment and sweep the floors."

Toby nodded. "'Kay. Did you want help?"

"Nah. Just keep an eye on the front."

"Okay."

Zamora left her partner to his literature and headed for the broom closet. While she didn't look directly at him, she kept Killian in the peripherals of her vision while she pulled out the broom and dustpan. Normally she left the menial cleaning to Toby, but she wanted to keep an eye on the petty officer. *I just don't want him to be sick on my floors.*

Her thought didn't convince her any farther than she could throw Killian.

The last hour of work passed steadily and Killian remained upright. He used the bathroom twice more, but each time he came out he looked better. Still, exhaustion and stress tightened the skin around the edges of his eyes and mouth, and she wondered what had him all knotted up.

When she locked the doors and bid Toby farewell, she paused by the futon to check on Killian. He'd put the mattress into the bed position and sprawled face-down across it like a drowning man on land. A soft snore echoed off the concrete floor and she snorted with amusement. *I should take a picture with my phone and use it for blackmail.* Except he needed his anonymity as an active SEAL more than she needed a laugh.

Shaking her head, she untied his shoes and dropped them on the floor beside the futon before turning off the lights in the shop. She followed his snores back to the day-bed in the darkness and settled down with her back to the mattress. It wouldn't be a restful night, but at least she knew he'd be okay.

What about me? What if I'm not okay with him? He was a trained killer, after all. God knew he could probably hurt her without using his hands. She snorted softly. *Hell, all men can do that.*

She sighed and leaned her head back on the futon, letting her eyes close. For some reason she trusted Killian to protect her rather than hurt her. At least physically. He could definitely break her heart.

But there's no chance of that because we're not involved. She just hoped it stayed that way.

****

Greg woke in an unfamiliar place with his nose buried in soft, fragrant hair. Despite the remnants of an alcoholic haze, his senses sharpened and he stopped breathing long enough to listen. Muted traffic sounds came from some distance away as if he'd fallen asleep in a building downtown. Beyond the scented hair, which appeared crimson when he opened his eyes, he smelled ink, leather, and lemon-scented cleanser. Someone's soft, steady breathing overrode the sounds of traffic and his arm rose and fell with their breaths.

He lifted his head, careful not to jostle the person with

his arm. *What the hell is my arm doing around them anyway?* As soon as he rose he realized why. Zamora lay beside him on the futon, her head pillowed in her arms while her ass remained on the cold concrete floor. In sleep she lost some of the hard creases bracketing her mouth and eyes, the lines of wariness and defense she wore like armor.

Instead she wore elegance and beauty beyond what she showed the world, and he had the sudden urge to encourage her to show it more often.

What the hell? He was in no condition to encourage a woman do to anything but suck his cock or warm his bed for a night. Anything other than that and she'd turn on him.

He lifted his arm off her warm side and held back a moan as he rolled onto his back without waking her. Damn, the pain of moving fast still hit him at odd times. What the hell was he doing here in her shop still dressed? He frowned and tried to think back to the night before, but everything was hazy. He remembered the divorce hearing and being "free" of MaryAnn. She hadn't gotten much since they'd had no children and she'd been the one to cheat, but it had still burned like a bastard. He'd gone straight to the bar to drown his sorrows.

Then what?

He remembered bright lights and Zamora's pretty face, and hoping he'd get laid or at least naked with her. But lying here on a futon in the backroom of a tattoo parlor didn't qualify on his list of priorities. He should be at least disheveled and she should be wearing a satisfied expression.

So why aren't you? Changed your mind mid-stream?

He rolled back to look at her and tried to think past the post-inebriation fog. Hadn't someone else been there? He rubbed his face with his hand, trying to ignore the throbbing of his head. The image of a guy wearing shrapnel came to mind and coffee. No wonder he hadn't gotten laid. He wasn't into sharing.

At least Zamora had been kind enough to let him sleep off his drunk here. God knew he hadn't given her much choice. She could've deposited him in the alley behind her shop after he told her what he'd wanted, but instead she'd given him coffee and a futon.

I'm a world class jackass. No one could argue with that.

What he really needed was some water and to get his ass home. Unfortunately, he hadn't arranged for 'home' and would have to crash on a friend's couch. *Or futon.* As much as he'd like to stay with Zamora, he figured he'd worn out his welcome already.

Greg sat up slowly to mitigate the throbbing in his head and shuffled his way to the bathroom. He used the toilet then looked at himself in the polished mirror. *Fuck, I look like I lost a battle.* As a SEAL, he couldn't imagine losing any battle that didn't result in death, but he certainly looked like death warmed over.

He threw water over his face and tried to smooth down the tufts of longer hair on the top of his head, but it only made him look like a drowned rat sporting death warmed over. He sighed and straightened his shoulders before he returned to the main room.

Zamora had climbed onto the futon and sat knuckling her eyes like a six-year-old. Greg stopped, his heart suddenly full of tenderness and compassion for the pretty woman. Even with all her ink, she wore an elegance that couldn't be taken from her. *I wonder what scars they hide.* He suspected such marks weren't the more visible kind he wore.

"Morning."

She dropped her hands and shot him a look of wariness. "Morning. How are you feeling?"

He gave her a half-smile. "Somewhere between an ass-kicking and a boat ride over chop."

"That sounds like an uncomfortable ride."

"Yeah, they aren't fun." He dropped his gaze to his feet and actually shuffled like a chastised teenager. "Thanks for giving me a place to sleep it off. I was a shit-faced jackass and I'm really sorry if I said anything worse than usual guy dumbassery. Yesterday was a bad day."

"I thought the SEAL motto was 'the only easy day was yesterday'?" She leaned her elbows on her knees.

"Yeah, well, if that was the easy day, God help me through today."

"Wanna talk about it?"

He raised his eyebrows and met her gaze. Her expression said she was just as surprised as he was.

"Sorry. None of my business. I'm gonna go make some more coffee. Then I'll drive you to wherever you want to go." She stood and her full breasts bounced a little, reminding him why he might have staggered here last night.

"Nah, it's okay. My divorce hearing was yesterday. I'm free of my marriage. Yay." He twirled a finger in the air and grimaced.

"Oh, I'm very sorry." She sent him a compassionate look. "Endings like that are tough."

"Yeah. Tough." One of the worst things next to finding out MaryAnn had been fucking a guy while he'd been deployed. He should've known something was wrong, but she'd always seemed happy to see him when he got home. *So much for being the observant SEAL.*

Zamora cleared her throat as she shoveled coffee grounds in the filter of the coffee machine. "So where should I drop you? Do you have any place to go?"

He opened his mouth the whine about his ex kicking him out, but he'd given up whining when he'd gone through BUD/S, and somehow he didn't think Zamora would appreciate it.

"Yeah, I just need to get back to my vehicle."

His voice must not have sounded certain because she

clicked the button on the coffee maker and leveled a look at him. "Seriously, do you need a place to stay until the base opens up on Monday?"

He gaped at her and she snorted.

"I've lived here in Coronado for the last ten years. I know all about the Navy and their hours of operation. Anything not mission related gets relegated from oh-eight-hundred to sixteen-thirty, Monday through Friday. This would be—" She squinted at the clock on the machine. "Oh-seven-ten on a Saturday. If you didn't arrange it yesterday before sixteen hundred, it ain't happening until Monday some time. So do you need a place?"

His mind remained a bit foggy after his debauchery the night before so he was a bit slow on the uptake. "Are you suggesting I stay with you until Monday?"

She shrugged and he wished he could take the question back. A beautiful, compassionate woman offered him a place to stay and he was questioning it? *What the fuck is wrong with me?*

"I've been where you are. Friends busy, family cutting ties, no place to stay." She shrugged again, pain flickering across her expression before it smoothed. "If someone hadn't given me that first helping hand, I might not be where I am now, so I'm just paying it forward. I have an extra room at my cottage on the beach. You'd have a view of the base from there and plenty of space to run for PT. If you want it, it's available."

Greg didn't know what to say for a few moments. His mind kept serving up images of being the same space as her, day after day, and something about it made sense. *I'm completely off my rocker.* She didn't know him from any of the other sailors occupying Coronado Naval Base, yet she still offered him a place in her sanctuary.

When he tried to speak, his voice came out in an unmanly squeak and he had to clear his throat to find coherency.

"Hooyah, ma'am. Yes, thank you. That'd be really nice."

Zamora's expression smoothed into a smile and she nodded. "Okay, let me print out directions to the cottage and have an extra key made."

"You don't have one already?" He raised his eyebrows and hers lowered.

"I don't just let anyone stay at my home."

"No, no, that's not what I meant." He grimaced and pointed to his head. "Not communicating as well as usual. I mean, you don't have an extra in case you get locked out?"

"Oh, yeah, I have one of those, just not here." Her face smoothed out again. "There's a hardware store just down the way and I'll have one made at lunch today. I'll leave it up at the front counter for you in case I'm busy in the back when you stop by."

"Why would you trust me with a key to your place? You barely know me."

She shrugged as she yawned while the coffee dripped into the carafe. "I saw you at the hospital and again last night at your worst. Plus you're a SEAL with a better than likely over-inflated sense of justice."

Greg snorted. "Just because I'm a SEAL doesn't mean I'm a hero. I just came out of a divorce hearing, remember? Obviously I wasn't much of a hero to her."

"I'm supposed to be swayed by your ex's example?" She shook her head. "Yeah, following the crowd isn't my strong suit and besides, most people look at others superficially, then can't deal with what they find underneath. I haven't found the surface to be very indicative of what a person is really like."

Looking at her tattoos, he supposed that was true. Most people would look at her and say she rebelled against society, or she'd gotten into drugs and whoring. Or worse, would categorize her as a lost waif to save from the evils of ink and alcohol. *How many people have dismissed her?*

Or was that her secret defense? She lay hidden from those who would exploit or victimize her. The same self-righteous pricks who looked down their nose at inked women like her would easily see no problem with objectifying a pretty woman with large breasts and relegate her to something for them to enjoy, ignoring her intelligence and kindness.

"Tats don't make the man, nor does rank, or money." The last was said with a sneer despite her voice not changing pitch.

"Yeah, I've seen that, too." MaryAnn certainly hadn't been who he thought she was. "Who taught you that lesson?"

She shot him a surprised look then grimaced. "My family and the ex-fiancé. They all said one thing and acted the almost complete opposite. It's why I ran away from home."

"So all this is just a massive act of rebellion?" Somehow that seemed disappointing.

Zamora's lips quirked into a half-smile. "Yeah, somewhat. It may have started out that way, but in the end I actually found out who I really was and what I wanted to do. It felt good to play by no one's rules but my own. I figured out I could do all the things my family said they'd do, but didn't."

She grasped two paper to-go cups and poured out the coffee. "Do you take cream or sugar?"

"Neither unless it's real cream." He wrinkled his nose as she handed him a cup.

"You're a coffee snob?" She grinned. "I wouldn't think a SEAL would care."

"I don't get to care until I'm stateside. When I'm not on a mission, and can choose."

To his surprise, she laughed and it melted some of the disappointment at her admission. *So she rebelled? The only kids who haven't have no backbone.* He didn't think

Zamora had a problem with backbone. He sipped his coffee, the brew strong and flavorful.

"Damn, that's good coffee."

"You're not the only coffee snob."

He grinned. "Are you sure you're okay sharing your home with a SEAL? We are kinda straight-laced, at least in the eyes of the public. I wouldn't want to ruin your street cred."

"Are you sure you can handle staying in the house of a tatted, pierced, single woman with questionable morals, at least in the eyes of the public? I wouldn't want to ruin your squeaky-clean reputation."

When she put it like that, it seemed just as judgmental as his own questions.

"Touché. If the offer still stands and I haven't fucked it up with being a jackass, again, then yes, I'd be grateful for a place to stay this weekend."

"All right, then." She nodded and handed him a lid for his cup. "Grab your gear, SEAL, and let's get a move on."

He hadn't brought much with him, though he found his shoes beside the futon and sat to put them on. She sat beside him and donned her own footwear. He shot her a look when he realized she wore one black sock with a skull and crossbones stitched in white on it and one red sock with black hearts. She must have noticed his expression because she slapped his thigh after she finished tying her sneakers

"Life's too short to wear matching socks."

Then she left him to grab her keys and purse.

CHAPTER FOUR

Zamora dropped Petty Officer Killian off at his SUV just a few blocks down from the Surf N' Turf bar where he'd imbibed the night before. He'd thanked her again for the place to stay for the weekend and promised to stop by the tattoo shop sometime after lunch.

"And call me Greg. As you said, rank doesn't necessarily make the man."

She matched his grin and shook his hand. "All right, Greg. See you this afternoon."

"Let me give you my cell number in case anything comes up."

She raised her eyebrows. "Is this a crafty way of getting my phone number after we spent the night together?"

Greg threw back his head and laughed. "No, but it would be a smooth line, wouldn't it?" He shook his head. "What's your number? I'll text you mine."

She rattled off the digits and he typed them into his phone, then pecked out a few more numbers before stabbing the send button. Her own phone pinged with a new text and she fished it out of her purse. A blocked number showed a text and she raised her eyebrows.

"Yeah, it's a SEAL thing."

"All right. Thanks for your number. I guess I'll see you later."

"Roger that."

She backed out of the parking spot beside his red FJ Cruiser and made the executive decision to take care of her errands immediately. She could get herself a breakfast burrito at the Channel Island Café before the hardware store opened up and see if Toby wanted to join her before they needed to open the shop at thirteen hundred. She almost shook her head. *Why am I thinking in military time?*

It had to be the cute, emotionally scarred SEAL she'd offered to house for the weekend. This time she did shake her head as she pulled into the parking lot of the Channel Island Café. Why did she always pick the emotionally unavailable men? It wasn't like she could save or fix them. *You know, there could be a very good reason his wife kicked him to the curb.*

Now she sounded like Toby. For all his piercings and ink, he was Mr. Practicality, a quality she used to admire in him. She snorted. Still did and thank God for his abilities. He'd saved them both time, effort, and money because of them.

She pulled out her phone and spied Greg's text. A smile curled her lips as she saved the number in it to her contacts as Petty Officer G. Killian. He certainly was a pretty boy, but except for his unfortunate inebriation the night before, he didn't act like much of an entitled playboy. *Not like Stan.*

She slammed a lid on that thought and flipped through the contacts to Toby's number. It rang a few times before he picked up with a groggy, "Hello?"

"Morning, sunshine. Fancy some breakfast with me?"

"Who the fuck is this, and what have you done with Zamora?"

She laughed at his wary tone.

"Seriously, what are you doing awake at this hour? It's unnatural." He sucked in a surprised breath. "Is that SEAL still with you?"

"No, the SEAL has gone on his merry way." There wasn't any point telling Toby about her plans to put Greg up. "I just have some errands to do this morning and needed to get a jump on them. Want to join me? My treat."

Toby rarely gave up free food. He had hollow legs as far as Zamora could tell and he was always constantly eating.

"Where?" It was more of a growl than a question.

"The Channel Island Café."

"You're an evil temptress, you know that?"

"I've been known to resemble that statement." She grinned even if he couldn't see it. "So see you here in twenty?"

Toby sighed. "Yeah. See you in twenty. Order me some sourdough toast with honey. The real stuff, not that shitty syrup they put in those little plastic containers with the jam."

She snorted. "Will do."

Toby clicked off and Zamora waved at the waitress for coffee. Toby would want some, too, but she ordered the sourdough toast and real honey for twenty minutes from then. She came often enough to the café that the waitress just nodded. *I'm becoming predictable.*

She wrapped her hands around her mug and stared out the window, letting her mind drift. The scents of fried food and coffee filled her nose as the wind kicked up the palm fronds on the trees outside. Like the breeze off the ocean, her mind tumbled back to the petty officer and her decision to let him stay with her.

What's wrong with me? He could be a serial killer for all she knew. Hell, he was a SEAL. Killer came with the job description. But he didn't set off her 'manipulator' radar and he hadn't been whiney when mentioning his

circumstances. *Not that SEALs are ever whiney. I hope.*
Maybe they were when not on a mission.

The coffee revived her after her mostly-sleepless night.
Killian had been a loud sleeper when drunk, but he'd slept
hard. *I probably snore when I'm exhausted or drunk, too.*
But it wasn't his snoring that had kept her awake. *No, it
was that he'd been there at all.* He smelled good under the
alcohol and the heat of his body had kept her warm even
when she'd sat on the cold concrete floor.

She scrubbed a hand over her face as Toby walked into
the Café. How could she already be attracted to this SEAL?
He doesn't need anyone to feel sorry for him. But
something about the man stirred her instincts to help, and
she'd offered him a place to stay until Monday.

"You look like hell." Toby slid into the booth across
from her.

"Thanks. Love it when you're a little ball of sunshine."

"Hey, if you wanted 'balls of sunshine' you shouldn't
have woken me up at this god-forsaken hour."

"You're awake already. No point in being a snot about
it."

"It's far too late to avoid snotdom." Toby waved at the
waitress for his own coffee. "How'd it go with the pretty-
boy SEAL last night?"

Zamora raised an eyebrow. "Are you sure you're not
interested in him?"

"I told you, Zamora, he's too macho and robust for me.
I like men who are slender, wiry…"

"Geeky?"

Toby laughed. "Yeah, I bet your SEAL doesn't even
know who Dr. Who is."

"I didn't get the chance to ask."

The waitress delivered Toby's coffee and toast, and
Zamora ordered the short stack of pancakes with
raspberries and cream over them. Toby inhaled this coffee
as if the fumes would kick start his engines and she settled

in to enjoy her second cup.

"So why did you really want me to come out with you today?" Toby didn't look up, but she experienced the trepidation only found in victims of the Spanish Inquisition with his question.

She took a deep breath. "I wanted to let you know I offered the petty officer a place to stay for the weekend."

Toby's gaze snapped to her face. "Are you insane, Zamora?"

"Jury's still out." She grimaced and rubbed the condensation ring from her mug on the table. "I just wanted to let you know so you wouldn't be surprised."

"You mean so I wouldn't be surprised when your body ends up in a ditch somewhere with bullet holes in it?" He scowled.

"Come on, Toby. He's a U.S. Navy SEAL. An unsung hero."

"Doesn't mean he's not dangerous or a nice guy." He sighed and rubbed his face. "Look, you weren't there when he first came into the shop. He was a playboy, a guy looking to get laid, and he remembered you from somewhere, so figured he could hook up with you."

"You're right, I didn't see him when he came in, but I did talk to him this morning." She smiled at the waitress who brought her pancakes and the check. "Thanks." Zamora spread the raspberries and cream around the cakes. "He was genuinely contrite and in need of help. You remember where I was when I first started out?"

Toby grimaced and nodded. "Yeah, I remember."

"If it hadn't been for the kindness of others when I needed help, I wouldn't be where I am today."

"Yeah, but a Navy SEAL? These guys are professional killers, and you're inviting one into your home." He shook his head. "You might as well put out a sign that says 'cover me with raw meat and let the sharks have at me.' While that's very Lady Gaga, it's not conducive to a long life."

"Well, at least I don't writhe and shake like Lady Gaga. And no one should be subjected to my singing."

He sighed. "Seriously. Why did you offer it to him?"

"Because he needed it, and right now he has no one else." She laid her hand on his arm. "Please, Toby. I just wanted you to know so you were aware. I have a feeling about him."

Toby scanned her expression, questioning her veracity without using words. *Damn, I bet he'd be an asset to the interrogation teams.* She resisted the urge to squirm as she dug into her meal. *I know I'm right, though. Something tells me the SEAL needs my help.*

"Okay. I think you're crazier than a shithouse rat, but okay."

Relief cascaded through her. "Thanks. I'm headed to the hardware store to make up an extra key for him that I'll leave at the front in the shop, then I'm going grocery shopping and fix up the extra bedroom in my cottage. I'll be back at the shop by three at the latest."

"Hey." Toby laid a hand on her arm and waited for her to meet his gaze. "If you need anything or backup or an excuse to leave, text me. I'm a great foil for assholian guys. And trust me, SEALs can be big assholes."

"Tom wasn't a SEAL."

"No, but I met a few while I was with him. Trust me, they didn't treat the others in the Navy any better than the woman flocking around them." Toby tilted his head. "I believe the term they used for the women was 'Navy Bunnies.'"

"I know, Toby. I'll be careful."

"And text me if you need to."

"I will."

CHAPTER FIVE

Greg swigged his coffee as he pulled into his erstwhile driveway. The house stood silent and vacant and he sat in his FJ Cruiser for a few moments, trying to convince himself to go in. This was the house he and MaryAnn had bought after he'd gotten his promotion to Petty Officer. It wasn't large or opulent, but it had been comfortable.

Now it stood as a glorious reminder of everything that had gone wrong with his marriage.

Better get this shit over with.

He got out and strode to the front door, ignoring the yucca flowering in the front. *They only flower just before they die.* Seemed fitting it flowered now at the death of his marriage. He unlocked the front door and pushed inside.

Most everything remained as he'd last seen it, but there were a few key differences. All the furniture MaryAnn considered his sat shoved into one corner of the living room along with what looked like boxes of his clothes. All his movie posters and framed vintage military photographs sat on the furniture and new art sporting bold colors and geometric shapes, filled their spaces on the walls.

He'd brought his own boxes to pack up the few small items he'd wanted, but MaryAnn had been busy. Anger at her selfish and deceitful actions threatened to explode out of him, but he couldn't let her win like that. She was off in some Colorado resort, enjoying a post-divorce spa weekend. *Saving grace, I guess. I wouldn't want to see her anyway.*

He grabbed his boxes and headed for the bedroom to make sure nothing of his remained. He didn't expect clothing, but there were a few items he'd inherited from his grandparents he wanted to keep. *Like Granny's jewelry.* Originally it had been intended for his wife, but MaryAnn no longer fit that description. He took some vicious satisfaction in her loss of it.

Fortunately, she'd left it behind rather than take it with her on her Colorado jaunt, and by the time Bronco and Lindsey texted they'd arrived, he had everything he wanted from the bedroom, including his grandmother's topaz engagement ring. That needed to stay in his family.

"Greg, you in here?" Bronco's voice came from the entryway.

"Yeah, in back bedroom clearing out the debris."

John and Lindsey Andrews appeared in the doorway and scanned the room with surprise.

"Did you get everything out?" Lindsey waved at the piles of things haphazardly stacked here and there.

Greg laughed. "Nah, this is what it looked like before the divorce. Some folks have junk drawers. We had a junk room."

"Yeah, I guess."

"Most of it really is junk and she can take care of it. There are only a few things here that are valuable to me." Greg shrugged. "Turns out I don't have that much here. I guess I'd moved out a long time ago."

"Hey, don't say that." John laid a hand on his shoulder. "You might not have been the best husband, but you never cheated, and you had lots of opportunities to do it."

"Yeah, I never cheated, but a fat lot o' good it did me."

Greg shook his head and set a half empty box outside the doorway. "Let's get the furniture loaded into your SUV and take it to the storage place. That way I don't keep you two too long."

"We're here as long as you need us, Greg." Lindsey gave him a warm smile. "Do you need a place to stay this weekend? We have the extra bedroom."

The extra bedroom which would become the baby's room when the little tyke arrived.

"Thanks for the offer, but I got it covered. Just need to get this house cleared out before MaryAnn gets back."

He didn't tell them he'd found a place to stay with Zamora. He knew he should take them up on their offer, but he didn't want to give up the opportunity to spend time with her. God knew he didn't need a new relationship after the last eighteen months of back and forth with MaryAnn, but it felt good to hang out with someone new, someone who didn't know his ex-wife or have a history with her.

John helped him carry out his leather couch and matching loveseat. *So much for the love part of it.* There'd been no love on that seat for years. At least he had his friends to help him now.

While the doc hadn't cleared him to go back to active duty yet, he had full functionality in his arm despite the damage it took from a thug's automatic on his last mission. But the wear and tear of lifting heavy stuff took its toll and his arm ached by the time he loaded a few boxes into his FJ Cruiser and took the first load to the storage facility.

Thank God he'd arranged that long before the divorce hearing. He already had the keys and the code to get into the yard. They unloaded the furniture and the boxes into the unit, with the exception of his extra clothes and a lock box full of weapons. No way would he leave them in a storage unit for enterprising punks to use to fund drug addictions or gang placements.

They made two more trips back to the house before

Greg nodded in acceptance. He had everything he wanted from the remnants of his marriage. He pulled the keys to the house off his ring and laid them on the counter for MaryAnn to find. She could change the locks or not as she saw fit. He wouldn't be back.

"I'm really sorry, Greg." Lindsey hugged him as they closed the locked front door. "Can we invite you over for dinner this week? We'd like to see you while you recuperate."

"Yeah, sure. That'd be good." He nodded and tried to find a smile, but his face felt stiff. "Thanks again for all your help. Would've been a bitch with the arm as it is."

"Not a problem." John man-hugged him, thumping his back before releasing him. "You sure you don't need a place to crash?"

"Yeah, no. I'm good, thanks." Greg opened his car door. "I'm gonna take this last load to storage and head on over to a friend's place. I'm set."

"Roger that. Catch you later this week." John waved and helped Lindsey into their truck before sliding behind the wheel.

Greg watched them leave then kicked his own vehicle in gear and headed back to the storage place. The house represented the past and he was saying goodbye. His mind sifted through the thoughts and emotions associated with MaryAnn and his marriage, and while anger still rose, at the moment he felt numb. His home and worldly possessions consisted of a storage unit, a couple of boxes of clothes, his gun safe, and his vehicle. *Pretty pathetic for four years of marriage and six years as a SEAL.*

He locked his storage unit and headed back toward downtown and Think Ink Tattoos. Zamora had promised to leave a key there for him and he hoped she hadn't forgotten. *Or that she'd left it with that shrapnel guy, Toby.* Greg didn't think Toby liked him or trusted him, and he couldn't blame the guy. Greg had been in a terrible place when he came in last night, and he wasn't much better now, but at least he was sober.

Despite the Saturday afternoon tourist traffic, Greg made it downtown just a little before four o'clock and found a place to park a few blocks from the shop. The wind had risen with the approach of a spring storm off the Pacific and the darkness of the clouds suggested it would be a helluva blow. *So much for the weatherman's prediction. He should've just said 'April Fools!'.* The date closed in on tax day, but the weather seemed far less predictable.

Stepping in the doors of Think Ink Tattoos provided a welcome wind-break. A pretty, young woman with her nose, eyebrow, and lip pierced looked up and smiled at him. She had no visible ink, but her hair draped around her face in pink, purple, and turquoise locks.

"Welcome to Think Ink Tattoos. May I help you?"

"Yeah, I'm here to pick up a key left for me by Zamora. My name's Greg Killian." He matched her smile and her gaze dropped to his feet before leisurely rising back to his face.

"She left a key for you?" She snorted. "You're not her usual fare. More clean-cut than most."

Before Greg could ask, Toby appeared around the half wall and his brows lowered as soon as he caught sight of Greg.

"If it isn't the guy who wanted to get 'finked.'" He didn't quite sneer, but Greg heard it all the same and grimaced.

"Yeah, that's me. Zamora said she'd leave a key?"

"She did." He reached below the counter and retrieved an envelope. "Directions to her place are inside with it. Just do me a favor."

"What's that?" Greg raised an eyebrow.

"Lose it. Or better yet, don't take it at all and find another place to stay."

Greg grunted with bitter amusement. "You don't trust me very much, do you?"

"Is it that obvious?" Toby shot him a dry look. "Look, I know I couldn't take you even with you injured, and I'm not really into pugilism. But Zamora has been hurt bad and has worked hard to get to where she is. Don't hurt her more if you can help it. Treat her like a person rather than someone to warm your bed from time to time. She certainly deserves more than a quick lay."

"I'd be happy to give you a quick lay if Zamora doesn't want to." The woman with the multihued hair waggled her eyebrows and grinned.

To his surprise, Greg wasn't at all interested. Since MaryAnn had gone to town on him, he'd been screwing almost anyone who'd agree to it. But for some reason the pretty woman with the piercings did nothing for him.

"Thanks for the offer, but I'm just here to pick up the key and head out. Some other time, maybe." He gave her his best non-committal smile and took the envelope from Toby. "Thanks. I'll keep that in mind, Toby."

"Yeah, sure you will."

Greg ignored the blatant disbelief in Toby's expression as he retraced his steps to his SUV. The wind had driven almost everyone inside and relief hit him as soon as he closed his car door. He opened the envelope and pulled out the Google Maps driving instructions to Zamora's cottage. The address did indeed put her right on the beach and Greg whistled in appreciation. Either she bought when the market was in the toilet or it had been a fixer-upper. Property in such a location cost in the ballpark of a late model F-16 fighter jet.

He threw the SUV into gear and headed into the late afternoon storm. Rain spattered the windshield and the wind carried loose fronds of palm trees across the road. The storm made the traffic light bounce and the wind pushed the SUV around as he drove. It took him a bit longer than expected to arrive at Zamora's cottage.

"Damn."

The cottage matched the house he'd left empty of his stuff that afternoon in size. It was a single story adobe and brick building with mature palms and landscaping all around it. Two small patches of lawn faced the street on either side of the front walk, but otherwise Zamora had xeriscaped with dry-weather plants local to the region. A detached two car garage sat at the end of a driveway patterned with colored local stones reminiscent of Van Gogh's Starry Night swirls. The tires rumbled over them with a comforting hum.

With the garage door closed, he couldn't tell if she was home, but light glowed from the cottage's windows in the pre-storm gloom. He turned off the vehicle and shoved the key in his pocket before he ducked out into the wind. He grabbed his duffel bag and locked the Cruiser before heading for the door closest to the garage. While he needed to bring in the weapons locker, he didn't want to show up at her door with it.

Despite having a key, he knocked on the door to let her know he'd arrived. If she wasn't home, he'd let himself in and move the SUV out of the driveway. But Zamora appeared at the little diamond shaped window in the side door and smiled when she recognized him.

"You made it." She stepped back out of the doorway. "Come in out of the wind. Looks like the Pacific is gonna be ornery tonight."

"Yeah, looks like. I wouldn't want to be a Coastie tonight." Greg set his duffel down just inside the door.

"A what?"

"A Coastie, the Coast Guard? They have to go out when the ocean is pitching a fit and save the dumbasses who think they can best it." He shivered and she blinked at him. "What?"

She shook her head. "I just don't think I've ever heard

a SEAL say he wouldn't like to go out on the ocean."

"Heh, I'd rather take on more manageable enemies like terrorists, personally. You can guess what they're going to do. The ocean has its own rules." He shuddered theatrically and she laughed. "Thanks again for giving me a place to stay for the weekend. Would it be okay if I brought in my weapons locker? I couldn't leave it in the storage unit and it won't be safe locked in the car, and since I'm in between places..."

"Oh, yes, bring it in. I think I have a place to put it so it's out of the way. Do you need help bringing in anything else?"

He opened his mouth to decline, but his arm had been complaining and the index finger of his right hand had gone numb since he moved his stuff that morning. "Yeah, that would be great. Thanks."

Zamora nodded and followed him back out to his FJ Cruiser. "Did you get all your stuff taken care of?"

"Yeah, most of it's in the storage unit, but some things couldn't be left there, like the weapons locker and my grandparents' antique jewelry."

"Oh yeah, you wouldn't want to leave that there." She waited for him to open the back of his cruiser.

To his chagrin, his arm shook when he opened the hatch and his finger had the sensation of a lump of clay. He muttered a curse and reached for the locker, but his arm failed at the last moment and the damn thing almost slid out of the back onto the ground.

"Whoa!" Zamora skidded up in front of him and caught the locker.

The locker weighed a good sixty pounds and he usually had no problem carrying it, but most women couldn't steady such weight. She gently set it on the ground and he gaped at her, impressed.

"Are you all right?" She covered his left hand on his right arm with her own. "You're shaking."

"I'm fine." Anger at his weakness rose and his face tightened into a scowl.

"Hey, I know your arm took a helluva beating, so let me help you." Zamora met his gaze, her expression determined. "I don't think you're weak, and if you do, that's something you need to work on. There's nothing weak about accepting help when needed, so don't go all macho on me. I'm not impressed with that. We'll carry the locker inside together, okay?"

He wanted to rail at her about his weakness, that it endangered the team, and let them down. But he wasn't with the squad at the moment, and he wouldn't be until he healed. And he wouldn't heal if he acted stupid. He only had to accept help, which he could, do what he came to do, and try to have a nice weekend after a shit week.

But fighting back the anger, his go-to response, took all his concentration.

"Yeah, okay." He exhaled slowly, trying to blow out all the anger with it. "Yeah, thanks. I could use the help. After all the moving stuff today, the arm is pretty shaky."

An approving smile curled her lips as she bent down to grasp one handle of the locker. "It's going to take a while to build strength back up. I know some massage and Reiki techniques that can help if you want me to rub your arm later."

Have her hands on me even if it's just my arm? Hell yeah.

"That would be great." He bent down to grab the other handle. "I think I overdid things today."

"Understandable. Let's get this inside. Do you have anything else you want to bring in before the storm breaks?" The wind had risen higher and ripped away her words, but he heard her.

"Just a couple of boxes of clothes. They need to be washed and pressed, so if you have some laundry machines and an ironing board, that would be great."

SIOBHAN MUIR

She nodded as they headed for the house. "I do, but I suck at ironing."

He laughed. "That's okay. I'm really good at it."

"Oh yeah? I knew SEALs were kick-ass, but I didn't know that extended to domestic chores as well."

"Just wait until you see my ability at dishes. I wield a mean scrub brush." He flashed her a grin and she laughed, taking his mind off his throbbing arm.

She opened the door with her free hand and backed into the house. She deftly avoided the furniture to set the locker down beside the kitchen table, a retro formica affair with the uneven boomerang design in rust and green just like his grandmother's table. Fortunately she hadn't accumulated the ugly, uncomfortable chairs that often went with the table.

"Let's get the boxes before the rain hits. I can smell it coming."

"You can smell the rain?" He raised his eyebrows as they returned to the windy driveway.

"Yeah. It's one of my favorite scents, but we better get after it." She shot a look at the lights of the base across the water. "It's comin' hard and fast."

The lights flickered as the rain blanketed them and Greg reached for a box. Fortunately they weren't terribly large and he could carry it one-handed. Zamora grabbed another one just as the rain hit the beach.

"Come on, in the house before we're in an impromptu wet t-shirt contest."

Her absurd comment made laugher break from his chest and he pretended to slow. "So, should we just wait for it then?"

She shot him a mock scowl. "Shut up."

"Hey, I'm not one to pass up any opportunity to enjoy beauty."

She snorted and ducked in the house, almost closing the door in his face. "Me either, so maybe you should stand

48

out in the rain and I can admire the beauty."

Greg laughed again and set the box under the overhang above the door then stepped back just as the deluge hit. He threw his head back and closed his eyes, trying to ignore the icy stings of the rain soaking his shirt. *Mind over water.* He'd had to do it hundreds of times in BUD/S training as well as in the field. But he hoped she wouldn't make him stay out long. *Except it was your idea, jackass.*

He heard a feminine sigh and tipped his head forward to find Zamora leaning on the doorjamb wearing a dreamy, appreciative smile. He might have been on the injured list, but he hadn't neglected his workouts, and now he was glad for it.

"Definitely pretty." She nodded toward his wet chest. "I think you might have boobs as big as mine."

"What? I don't have boobs. These are pectorals."

"They're boy-boobs. They're big, round, and they have a nipple on the end. Same thing." She arched a brow, daring him to refute her claim.

He almost reached out to pull her into the rain with him to test her theory, but stopped himself in time. *I don't know her that well.* They weren't married or even going out, but somehow it felt as if he'd known her long enough to be comfortable with her.

"Come on before you freeze. I think I have a towel big enough for you to at least get half-dry." She picked up the box and held the door open for him as lightning flashed overhead. "Do you want to take a warm shower or just use a towel?"

Can I take a shower with you? He opened his mouth, but fortunately his wiser side prevailed once again. "I'd like to take a shower. It's been a long day with packing and hauling, and while the rain helped, yeah, I'd like to be clean."

"I can relate to that." She nodded as she closed the door behind him. "Come on. I show you where you'll be staying and the bathroom you can use."

He picked up the duffel bag and ignored the twinge in his right arm. The cold rain had helped, but it still throbbed from overuse. And his first two fingers of his right hand had gone completely numb. *Shit. I gotta get that back or they'll be tossing my ass out of the Teams.*

The cottage reminded him a bit of the Tardis from Dr. Who. It seemed bigger on the inside with creamy pale ceramic tile and warm, comfortable furniture upholstered in abstract geometric shapes. A real brick fireplace made up the wall beside wide windows looking out on a deck facing the beach. She directed him down a hallway to the last bedroom on the left with a bathroom at the very end of the hall.

"Here go you. Why don't you soak that arm and relax the muscles while I put dinner in the oven and get out the massage oils." Zamora stood to the side. "I left towels on the bed, but there are more on the linen shelf just inside the door of the bathroom."

He snorted. "How many towels do you think a guy needs?"

She smirked. "I dunno. One of my first boyfriends used two, one for his body and one for his hair. And my ex had to have clean towels for every day. He couldn't reuse anything." She grimaced as she shook her head.

"Seems kinda inefficient."

"You don't know the half of it." She waved a hand to dismiss her memories and brought out her smile. "After we broke up, I found myself using only one towel for as long as I could stand, and once you go efficient, you can't ever go back."

"Unless you're in a hotel on vacation."

"Exactly." She grinned. "So enjoy your shower and I'll see you when you get out."

"What's for dinner?" He dropped the bag in the room and grabbed one of the towels set out.

"My own creation called PBS." She winked.

"Public broadcasting supper?"

She laughed and he held back a shiver. Why did her laugh make him feel so damn good?

"No, Pasta, Broccoli and Sausage. It's a mixture of bowtie pasta, broccoli florets, and Polish sausage. Good stuff and filling. I made extra because I figured you'd be hungry, what with moving and trying to heal."

"Oh, that's enough to make a man hurry."

Zamora shook her head. "Don't. Take your time. It needs about fifteen minutes to bake the flavors together."

"Sounds good. I'll be ready to eat by then."

She nodded and headed back toward the front of the house. He couldn't resist watching her ass as she walked away. Even in the rolled-up jean capris, t-shirt and flip flops, she was sexy as hell and his cock reminded him he hadn't used it in a while.

Yeah, well, as much as I want to fuck Zamora, I'm not gonna screw up a good place to stay. He threw himself into the shower and let the hot water heat the soreness out of his muscles. He closed his eyes and leaned his head back as the water beat over his shoulders. He wanted to relax, but his mind filled with images of Zamora naked and smiling up at him as she wrapped her hands around his shaft.

Said anatomy rose in salute of the idea. Fuck. He couldn't go out there sporting a hard-on when she'd put him up and made him dinner. Fantasies were one thing. Showing them off quite another.

Squirting some bodywash into his hand, he closed his eyes and wrapped his cock in his slick fist. It didn't take long for his body to get into the action, and his mind obligingly filled in the gaps with more illicit images of Zamora. On her knees, sucking his cock. On her back, taking his cock between her luscious breasts. On all fours, her pussy clenching around his thick shaft. Looming over him, her tits bouncing, as she rode him hard.

The last image sent his orgasm surging from his balls, and he moaned as his cum splashed over his hand to be washed away by the shower water. *Holy shit.* He hadn't had a fantasy that good in years, and his mind usually did a pretty good job. He'd hoped the release would mellow him out and keep him from making an ass out of himself at dinner.

Let's just hope I'm right.

CHAPTER SIX

Zamora took the kettle off the stove when it whistled and poured hot water over the tea ball in her mug. Her hands shook a little as the excitement of having Greg in her house bounced around inside her like a ping pong ball.

Why the heck was she so excited? *There's something wrong with me, that's why.*

She'd lived in Coronado long enough to have seen every type of man the Navy and Marines could hope to have. The SEALs strutted around cocky as all get-out and rightly so. They'd earned their accolades. The Marines marched along the streets, living up to the phrase, "mess with the best and die like the rest." She had no use for them or their egos. So why was she so enamored by this one injured SEAL? Why did she think she needed to rescue him?

SEALs do the rescuing. They don't need a knight in rainbow tattoos.

But her gut wouldn't let go of the idea. She imagined spending time with Greg, sharing laughs over ink and walks on the beach. *Warning! Warning. Way too early to even entertain such ideas.*

The timer on the oven dinged and she jumped, her

mind coming back to reality. She pulled the pan of PBS out of the oven and set it on the burners to cool before she returned to the dining room to light her candles. *They aren't romantic, they're practical.* On stormy nights like this, sometimes the old wiring couldn't handle the surges and the lights flickered off. The candles were a smart precaution. At least that was what she told herself.

The shower shut off and she retreated to the kitchen before she spied his mostly naked ass walking from the bathroom to the bedroom. She didn't want to get hooked on his physical beauty any more than necessary. *And he's frickin' gorgeous.* One thing she had to say for Coronado. There was no lack of male eye-candy.

She dished up the food and brought it to the table just as Greg reappeared in the dining room. He wore a clean t-shirt and dark blue sweats with big yellow letters spelling NAVY down the left leg. The injured arm showed angry red scars from surgery up and down his biceps, and she mentally cataloged the oils she'd need to help.

"Feeling better?"

"Yeah. That smells good. Can I help with anything?" He paused to scan the different dishes around the kitchen.

"Nope. Just take a seat at the table. Would you like a drink? I do have red wine and tea, too." She handed him a fork and the cheese grater.

"No, thanks. I'll just drink water."

"Huh, cheap date." She mentally smacked her forehead as soon as she said the words. *What the hell, Zamora? You're just giving him a place to stay, not a place to screw.* "Sorry, that sounded a lot better in my head. There's filtered water in the fridge. I'll get you some."

He laughed. "That's okay. I can get it. Would you like one, too?"

"No, thanks. I have tea. I need to stay sober for the rest of the night."

They made it back to the table without any further

mishaps or inappropriate comments mostly because she kept her lips tightly sealed over her teeth. The rain beat against the front windows in waves as the wind kicked up the sand from the beach. So far the lights remained steady, but she remained grateful for the candlelight.

"Damn, that storm is serious tonight." Greg sat down in the nearest chair and watched the rain. "Now I'm really glad I don't have to be out in it."

"Yeah." She followed his gaze as she settled into her chair. "But there's something kinda exhilarating about being outside in a big rainstorm. The weather does what it wants and you can either get out of its way or ride it through."

"Unless you're Coast Guard."

"Or a Navy SEAL." She shot him a look with a smile.

"Yeah, more often than not." He nodded as he reached for his glass with his right hand and flinched, the smile deteriorating.

"Still pretty bad?"

He shrugged and switched hands. "It's okay."

Zamora snorted. "You don't have to play tough guy with me. I'm not your CO or your girlfriend. If it hurts, it's okay to admit it. Healing takes time and energy." She shrugged. "And I promise not to tell and ruin your tough-guy reputation."

"That's good. Sometimes his reputation is all a man has." He gave her a smile and disappointment tripped through her.

Guess we're gonna stay at arm's length. Why should she care, though? Honestly, all she'd offered was a place to sleep. Nothing more.

"Can you really do some massage that'll help?"

His question surprised her and she swallowed the bite of food faster than she intended in an effort to answer.

"The Reiki? Yeah. It's energy manipulation, based on science."

"Based on science?"

"Yeah. You know we're all made up of energy vibrating at different frequencies, right?"

He nodded, chowing down on his dinner.

"So Reiki operates on the principle that you can manipulate those frequencies, repair damaged lines, remove blockages, and redirect things so the flow is restored." She sipped her tea to wet her throat as she nodded at his arm. "Your arm was badly injured, the regular energy lines and frequencies disrupted by damage. Now we need to rearrange the energy lines so they can work around the damage and heal it."

"And you know how to do this?"

"I'm not a master, mind you, but yeah, I've learned some of the techniques." Zamora scanned his arm. "I think what I'll start with is just rubbing the muscles gently, figure out where the pain is, and shift the energies away from it." She blinked and grimaced. "That's if you're okay with it. I just realized you hadn't actually agreed to it."

He flashed her a smile that made her shiver. "Yeah, I'm okay with it. Anything to help. It won't stop shaking. Like I said, I think I overdid things today. I kind of forget I'm injured until it starts to fail on me."

She nodded. "Yeah, I bet you're used to your body just responding to what you ask of it, and when it doesn't, it surprises you."

"Yeah. That's it exactly." He gazed at her with new admiration. "How did you know that?"

"After visiting enough guys in the hospital, I got to hear some of the complaints and frustrations." She shrugged. "After the hell you put your bodies through, I can't imagine SEALs taking injuries all that gracefully."

He snorted. "I'm very graceful. When all my body parts work like they're supposed to."

Zamora laughed. "Yeah, well, we'll work on getting your *arm* back up to speed. I'm sure the rest of you works just fine."

He waggled his eyebrows. "Are you sure you don't want to test it?"

"Not tonight, hot stuff. Besides, after I'm done with you, you'll feel like you've done hard PT carrying a Scottish caber." She waggled her eyebrows back at him.

Greg laughed and nodded. "Cabers, eh? We had to carry something like that during BUD/S training. It was a pain in the ass."

"I bet. I've seen some of the training from afar." She shook her head. "I think I'll keep my status as average."

He smiled, his gaze assessing. "I think you're anything but average."

She tilted her head. "Okay, I grant you I'm not your typical woman, but I have my average moments. It's kinda like a bad habit. We all have them."

"It's a bad habit to be average?"

"Well, yeah. Shouldn't you be the extraordinary hero of your own story? I mean, you're a SEAL. There's nothing average about SEALs."

"I can't argue with you there." He scraped up the last of his meal with his fork and sat back in his chair. "That was really good. Thank you."

"There's more if you'd like some."

"No, I'm good. I will drink about a gallon of water, though." He rose, talking his plate with him back to the kitchen. "Where do you keep your cups?"

"Cupboard above the toaster. Would you put the kettle on, please?"

"Sure."

Zamora paused and blinked. She'd asked him to start the kettle as if he'd become a long term boyfriend or roommate. *Don't go there. He's military.* She was just giving him a place to crash until he got his own on Monday. Tuesday, tops. But it had been natural to ask him to do something around the house.

Weird. She hadn't had a roommate since she'd first moved out on her own. She valued her privacy and independence. It seemed strange to love Greg's company more than her usual solitude, but she found having him in the house felt comfortable and soothing rather than an intrusion.

She cleared her plate from the table, wondering why she felt so relaxed around him. *He's a Navy SEAL. They're alpha, OCD, and arrogant. How can I be comfortable around him?*

"Everything okay, Zamora?"

She jumped, damn near dumping her plate onto the floor. "Where did you come from?"

"Sorry, I didn't mean to startle you." He tilted his head. "Are you okay? You're wearing a frown."

"Yeah, no, I'm good." She shook her head and dredged up a smile. "Let me dump these and I'll get my oils for massage." She left her dishes in the sink and made a beeline for her Reiki materials, including the calming candles. Hell, she needed them almost as much as he did.

Thunder boomed just as she came back into the living room and she shivered. Greg sat on her couch and stared out the windows at the rain beating against them. She took a moment to study him, seeing exhaustion, pain, and sorrow in his expression and the set of his shoulders. He held his right arm with his left, supporting it as if it had reached the end of its endurance, and her heart went out to him.

"Your right arm is the only injured one, right?"

He turned his head, his gaze focusing on her. "Yes, ma'am."

She nodded and set her oils and candles down on the coffee table. "All right. Let me light the candles and we'll see what we can do."

He raised his eyebrows, but said nothing, his expression curious. She lit the jasmine candle and set it in front of him as she opened up her oils. After she touched his arm she'd know which she'd need.

"Okay, so take a few deep breaths and relax. Focus your gaze on the candle flame."

He smirked. "Should I start humming Kumbaya, too?"

She dropped her chin. "If you think it would help."

He lost the smirk and sighed. "Okay."

"Think of it like the trance people get into when they're sitting around a campfire. Everyone stares at the flames, watching them dance, and relaxes. Same idea here. Just watch the candle flame and let your mind settle down."

He sighed again and resettled his shoulders, focusing his gaze on her candle. "Now what?"

"I'm going to touch your arm and see if I can get a sense of where the energy is knotted up. That'll help me know what oils to use and where I need to focus the healing energy."

"Are you sure you're not going to dance around naked, shaking crystals at me?"

"I could, but it wouldn't help your arm heal. And since that's our main goal, I think we'll just keep our clothes on." She resisted the urge to smack his injured limb. "Ready?"

"Yes." He didn't sound convinced.

"Take a deep breath like you're at the doctor's office and let it out slow."

"Should I turn my head and cough, too?"

Zamora clenched her teeth over her anger. "If you'd rather make fun of me and disdain my help, I can just head to bed and leave you alone with your pain. I'm sure it'll make you more of a man than accepting help for your injury."

She hadn't spoken loudly, but he turned wide eyes on her. *Gotta remember not to put so much venom in my voice next time.* She ignored him and recapped her oil bottles before reaching for the candle. She'd been a fool to think he'd accept her abilities after knowing her for such a short time. *Men rarely take this stuff seriously. Idiots.*

He laid a hand on her shoulder, halting her motion.

"I'm sorry, Zamora." He waited for her to meet his gaze before saying more. "I'm not used to alternative medical practices, and I'm mad at myself for overdoing it with my arm. Plus it hurts like a sonuvaprick, and I get sarcastic when I hurt. I'm sorry. I really could use your help."

She gazed at him, her anger still pulsing, and he met her stare, neither backing down nor being combative. After a few heartbeats, she nodded, but left her oils capped. She'd only open them after she knew which she needed.

"Fine. Sit still and watch the candle. If you move or make another sarcastic remark, I'll poke you in the arm with my nails. Are we clear?"

He opened his mouth to rip another remark, but stopped himself in time. "Yes, ma'am."

"Good. Deep breath, let it out slow. Anytime you're ready."

He turned his head and set his gaze on the candle, breathing slowly. *At least he listens to orders well.* She waited for some of the tension to leave his shoulders as he relaxed before she reached to grasp his arm at the triceps. She took her own deep breath and closed her eyes.

The moment she gently gripped his arm, energy zinged between them and she almost let go. *What the hell was that?* Whatever it was, it filled her with a sense of peace and "rightness" she'd never felt with anyone before. Like her earlier sensation of comfort around Greg, the energy pulsed strong, and correct as if she'd found her soulmate.

Whoa, whoa, whoa! This guy is a SEAL, plus he just got out of a horrible relationship. She didn't do emotionally unavailable men. *And I'm not about to start now.*

She mentally rearranged her focus and breathed through the electric energy, trying to ride the waves rather than offer resistance. The energy in a human body always looked like rainbow ribbons to her. Healthy energy lines appeared in blues and greens, whereas disrupted or broken lines lay in browns, grays, and blacks. White lines represented new pathways, and red or orange lines showed places where the energy fought against disease. Yellow lines meant the energy paths were out of alignment but still functioning to some extent.

Most of Greg's body held green and blue lines, but the closer she got to his arm, the lines changed to yellow, brown, and gray ribbons. A few more yellow ribbons swathed the area around his heart and she almost directed her focus there first, the urge to heal his heart the most urgent.

No, focus on his arm. That's what means most to him right now.

She took a deep breath and pictured the knots and folds in the ribbons unraveling. She started with the brown and gray ribbons, focusing healing and positive energy at them to restore their vitality. At first, nothing happened. The strands remained stubbornly dull and unresponsive. But as she focused and pushed her energy toward him, the ribbons settled into a slow vibration, shaking off some of the dull color. The grays didn't respond much, but the browns shifted into lighter shades, trending toward yellow.

Greg made a sound, something resembling a moan, and Zamora lost her focus, pulling out and away from his wounded arm. She opened her eyes, surprised to find herself bent over his arm, head bowed as if praying. She blinked and raised her head to take in her surroundings.

The candle flickered gently, sending light splashing over his face. His own eyes remained closed, but sweat beaded his forehead and temples. His jaw was clenched tight and lines of strain bracketed his mouth.

"Are you all right, Greg?"

"Yeah, I'm good." His tone of voice suggested the

opposite.

"Did I hurt you?" Exhaustion threatened to drop her eyelids closed, but she forced them to stay open as she waited for his answer.

"No, not really. There was a weird popping in my arm, like one of the ligaments snapped back into place. It didn't hurt, exactly, just felt really strange." He frowned as he noticed the droop in her shoulders. "Are you okay? You look ready to drop."

She managed a one-shouldered shrug. "It's been a long time since I've done this. I think I'm out of practice. I've forgotten how tired it makes me." She turned to blow out the candle and nearly face-planted into the coffee table.

"Whoa!" Greg caught her shoulders with his hands, his left holding her up. "I think you might be more tired than I am. Come on. I'll help you to bed."

"But I need to lock up and turn off the lights." She tried to protest, but he steered her toward her bedroom

"I can do that. I'm a security specialist in general. Come on, inkheart. Off to bed."

"Inkheart?"

"I thought it fit you better than 'sweetheart.'" He smiled as he guided her to her room and escorted her through the door. "Use the bathroom and I'll tuck you in."

She snorted, shaking her head. "I'm not ten, you know."

"Thank God for that." He shot her a grin. "That means I don't have to read you a bedtime story, right?"

She laughed. "No, no bedtime story. I won't be long."

Zamora ducked into the bathroom and commenced her usual nighttime routine albeit dressed. She stared at herself in the mirror, shaking her head at her lack of discretion. She hadn't tired herself out this badly doing energy work since her first time. Why was working on Greg so different? She washed her face and removed her bra before returning to her bedroom.

Greg stood at the window, his legs braced shoulder-width apart and his left arm cradling his right. She suspected he would've had them folded if the right arm worked properly. He turned when she headed for the bed and she stumbled at the intense look in his blue eyes. Her heart did an unusual flutter-skip and giddy excitement zinged through her. *What the hell is wrong with me?* She mentally shook her head and climbed into the bed.

"Thank you for escorting me to bed. I think I can take it from here."

He opened his mouth to comment—*probably in a classic smartass remark*—but closed it as his lips curled into a smile. *Damn, that's almost as sexy as the smoldering look he's giving me.*

"All right, inkheart. Sleep well and pleasant dreams." He retreated to the doorway and paused. "Door open or closed?"

"Open is fine."

"Open it is. Good night, Zamora. Thanks for the help on my arm."

"Does it feel better at all?"

He nodded. "A little. I'll see you in the morning."

She yawned. "Roger that."

He chuckled. "You got the lingo down pretty good, inkheart."

She met his smile with one of her own. "Copy that. Good night."

"Night." He shut off the light and disappeared out her door. Zamora snuggled down into her bed and closed her eyes, her lips still curled into a smile. She liked him, and his new nickname for her, even though she knew she shouldn't. *He's a SEAL and given his track record, probably terrible at relationships.* But she still liked him. *It's okay to like him, right?* Her smile broadened and she let the giddy excitement carry her into dreamland.

****

Greg walked around Zamora's house, locking the outer doors and turning off the lights as he went. Despite the weird popping he'd felt under her hands, the pain and numbness in his arm had faded a little. Relief filled a tiny corner of his mind for the first time since he'd woken up in the hospital. It wasn't much, but more than he'd experienced in weeks.

Once the doors were secured and the lights off, he retreated to his room and got ready for bed. He usually slept naked, but because of his unfamiliarity with Zamora's household practices, he opted to keep his underwear on. He settled down in the bed and drew the covers over his body, thinking of his hostess.

He liked her, more than he liked any other woman in a long time. She held no fear for telling it like it was, but she didn't come across as being condescending or disdainful. When she helped him with unloading his vehicle, she hadn't shown any pity or contempt at his weaknesses. Instead, she'd supported and encouraged him. *Night and day difference to MaryAnn.*

He shoved the thoughts away. He didn't want to think about his ex. She'd done enough damage and taken enough of his thoughts and time. And their marriage was officially finished. Too bad his heart and mind couldn't get on that bandwagon.

Taking a deep breath, he closed his eyes and focused his thoughts on Zamora, his lovely inkheart. The nickname had come out of nowhere, but the moment he said it'd felt right. She hadn't told him to fuck off so he guessed she liked it. The ink on her arms blazed in glorious color in his mind's eye, and he imagined her smirking at him from some tidal pool, one elegant eyebrow raised in challenge.

He wanted to take her challenge, show her he could do it and was worthy of her. *Hold up, worthy of her?* The oddness of the idea made him open his eyes. Since when did he feel unworthy of anyone?

Maybe since my wife cuckolded me and my arm no longer works. To his horror and surprise, his throat closed and tears filled his eyes. Sorrow, rage, and grief filled his body and spilled down his cheeks, great sobs thundering from his chest. He thanked whatever deity watched over him that he'd thought to close his own bedroom door because he couldn't stop the release of all his pent up emotion.

He didn't know why it all came out now, but he let it go, curling into a fetal ball as he buried his face in the pillow. No one could see him break, no one could hear him wail. He was safe, secure, and sheltered in Zamora's house. Not even his squad would know. Eighteen months of anger and frustration poured out of him in shuddering sobs as Greg grieved for his losses. Exhaustion finally set in as his grief ebbed and he slipped into sleep.

CHAPTER SEVEN

Zamora woke to pale, storm-washed sunshine and the sense that something had dramatically changed. She opened her eyes and scanned her bedroom, but everything appeared the same. She held her breath and listened hard before sniffing the air for new smells. The scent of coffee teased her more awake and she sat up, scrubbing her eyes. *Coffee.*

She slid from the bed and zombie-shuffled into the kitchen, looking for the source of black elixir. The coffeepot sat demurely silent in the empty room, but a small pad of paper rested beside it. A message had been written in precise block letters.

Went out for a run. Made coffee. Be back soon.

Greg

She stared at the note with surprise until the scent of coffee lured her into pulling out a mug. *He made coffee. And wrote a note.* She didn't know which surprised her more. He wasn't her roommate or her boyfriend, yet he acted with the consideration of both. She leaned her back against the counter and sipped her coffee, trying to wake her mind up enough to contemplate such an occurrence.

The coffee hit her tongue with a delicious, hot burn and she moaned. *Damn, he even makes great coffee.* She could definitely get used to having such a roommate. *But it's only for a few days until he gets his own place.* It was the safest option, really. She didn't know him very well. Despite her lack of familiarity, she liked the idea of Greg staying longer than just a couple days.

Zamora snorted and shook her head. "Yeah, like that's gonna happen."

She set her coffee down and busied herself around the kitchen making breakfast. She didn't know what Greg preferred, but she made bacon, toast, peeled some oranges and grapefruit, and made herself some soft boiled eggs. She'd wait until he returned to cook eggs for him. *Eggs are a personal thing.* Still, she found herself trying to guess which kind he'd prefer.

She poured herself another cup of coffee as she let her gaze slide out to the beach beyond her deck. The sand remained empty under the overcast morning and the waves gently lapped against the shore. She found the post-storm beach soothing until motion took her gaze away from the waves.

A single figure jogged along the hardened sand near the waterline, the motions easy and graceful. As it closed on her section of beach, the man became clearer, wearing tight athletic shorts she'd seen on football players, and a gray t-shirt with the letters NAVY stenciled in black across the chest. And what a marvelous chest it was. The taut muscles pressed against the sweat-stained fabric and snagged on the little nipples poking through. His legs churned in a constant rhythm, the big muscles of his thighs outlined with every stride.

"Sweet angels of mercy." The oath escaped as the glorious man ran straight for her deck, his strides faltering as he hit the softer sand. *Whoa, that's Greg.* She'd thought him handsome before, but she'd never seen him essentially outlined in clothing.

He stepped up on her deck and put his hands on his

trim hips, throwing his head back to let his lungs expand. His broad chest rose and fell in great breaths and pulled his shirt tight against the hard abs of his belly. Zamora swore her jaw dropped when he bent over to stretch his hamstrings with his back to her.

I thought their butts flattened when they worked out. Not Greg's. Each buttock sat in firm roundness and she enjoyed the flex and stretch of them as he moved. When he stood and turned, she spun her back to the window and poured a cup of coffee for him before he caught her staring. So much for being the impartial roommate.

She headed for the sliding door to unlock it so he could come in and waved when he looked up. He waved back with a warm smile and her insides did a happy jig. *Get a hold of yourself, woman. He's just a friend in need.* She was in need too, but for a far different reason. *I should contact one of my fuck buddies and take care of this.* Or buy new batteries for her personal love tool. She backed away from the door as he came through.

"Any coffee left?"

She shot him a scowl. "As if I would be so lame as to drink it all."

He grinned. "I'd hoped, but I know we're both coffee snobs, so there was some question. I'm gonna jump in the shower to wash off the sand and salt water."

"Okay. I made breakfast, but wasn't sure how you liked your eggs. Or if you do. Want some?" She waved at the fruit and bacon on the counter.

"Yeah, thanks. I like them poached, but I'll eat them over-easy, too." He pulled the t-shirt over his head and she damn near forgot to breathe. "Whatever's easiest."

She blinked and cleared her throat. "Have you ever had them soft boiled? It's like poached in the shell."

"Yeah? How long does it take to make those?"

"Seven minutes."

"I'll hurry then."

She watched him disappear down the hall and couldn't keep her eyes off his ass in those tight athletic shorts. *Dear God, he shouldn't wear those in public. Women would fall at his feet in supplication.* Or she would.

Instead, she forced herself to focus on making eggs for her guest. She hoped the chains would hold on her attention or she was liable to ruin the one day she had with him before they went on with their respective lives. He'd go back to being a SEAL and she'd run her tattoo business, and that would be that. She shoved away the vaguely disappointed feeling. *It's a good thing, really.*

The eggs finished boiling just as he strode back into the kitchen. With his wet blond hair slicked back and the scent of body wash reminiscent of sandalwood wafting off him, she almost burned her hands with the hot water.

"Whoa. Here, let me help you with that."

"That's okay. I got it." She ran cold water over the eggs and expertly cracked the shells, peeling them with deft strokes. "Hand me that plate there, would you?"

He held it out and she added the egg to the bacon already piled on it. He raised an eyebrow. "Those don't look poached."

She snorted. "Just wait. I'll show you."

She finished preparing his breakfast then took all the food to the table. He helped, still wearing a dubious expression.

"Let me get the coffee and we'll eat."

"You didn't have to wait for me, you know."

"I didn't. You came back from your run just as I finished preparing my own breakfast." She returned to the table with two mugs of coffee. "It seemed only polite to wait for you."

He smiled as she sat and she pointed to the eggs. "If you cut them with your fork, they're just like poached, just less messy."

"Wow." He cut one and put it in his mouth.

She tried not to watch him eat, but she couldn't take her eyes off him. *What's wrong with me?* She liked him and she liked looking at him. *He's sexy.* But she also liked having his company at her table. *Weird.* She'd been alone a long time and it had never bothered her. With Greg in her kitchen, it felt like home for the first time ever.

"Good, huh?"

"Yeah, really good."

"Good." She grinned as he chuckled. "So how is your arm feeling this morning? Is it any better?"

"Yeah, it is, thanks." He sat back long enough to drink some coffee. "A lot better. It doesn't hurt as much today."

"That's very good to hear. Try not to overdo it today and we can do some more energy manipulation this evening." She stopped and grimaced. "If you want."

"Yeah, that would be great. It really helped. And I won't be moving a house full of furniture and boxes." He grinned. "What are your plans for today?"

She snorted. "Something really exciting. Ready?" He nodded. "Laundry, wash my car, and check on the shop. I usually get my equipment and ink orders ready on Sundays so I'm ready to go Monday morning."

He frowned as he chewed on some fruit. "Is your shop ever closed?"

"Yeah, Mondays and Tuesdays. I can still get business done if need-be, but I don't miss out on the weekend customers." She sat back with her coffee cradled in her hands. "I find most folks like to get tattoos when they have time to drink, but don't have time to regret them."

Greg laughed. "Monday comes pretty fast after getting inked, doesn't it?"

She grinned. "Yep."

"Are you working today?"

"No, I take Sundays for myself, but the shop is still open so I like to check on it."

He scraped the last of the yolk off his plate with his

toast. "If you don't mind the company, I need to go into town to get a few toiletries. You could do what you need at the shop and I can do my shopping."

"I don't mind the company."

On the contrary, she'd been trying to figure out a way to spend the day with him without appearing to be desperate for his company or clingy. She didn't know why she wanted to be with him or find out more about him. *He's just a short term guest.* But something about sharing her energy with him last night made her want more time with him today.

"Great. When do you want to go?"

"We can go after I clean up breakfast." She rose and gathered her plate.

"I'll help." He snagged his plate and stacked it with the empty serving plates.

"Thanks."

They cleaned up in companionable silence before he headed back to his room for his shoes. She prepared to head to the shop, but her mind kept straying to how comfortable she felt with Greg. She didn't understand it and it scared her a little. She didn't want to get attached to him, especially because of his profession as a SEAL. While she hadn't considered having a relationship with anyone for a long time, SEALs had never been on her list of possible partners. Their jobs were so dangerous, they often didn't come home and they couldn't talk about what they experienced even if they did.

She'd seen how her parents lived and vowed she'd have a partner who talked to her instead of hiding anything, insignificant or otherwise, from her. She wanted someone who shared and was himself no matter the situation. SEALs excelled at being everything except forthcoming. *Maybe that's why his first marriage failed.*

Zamora shook her head. She needed a partner who'd talk to her. She couldn't help whom she loved, but while love was important, so was communication.

****

Greg offered to drive them into town since his FJ Cruiser sat in the driveway blocking her car. Zamora didn't argue and climbed into the vehicle as if she'd done it hundreds of times. The familiarity of having her in the vehicle with him struck him as odd, but he couldn't argue it existed. *What is up with that?* He'd been separated from MaryAnn for fifteen months, living more like a bachelor than anything. He hadn't bothered to move out of their house until the divorce came through because he was rarely home anyway.

But one night with Zamora—well, two if he counted sleeping on her futon—and he'd settled into a comfortable dance as if they'd gone out for months. He shook his head in disbelief.

"What?"

"Sorry?"

"You shook your head and snorted. What's that about?" Zamora crossed her arms over her chest and pushed up her breasts. His body took note, but he willed his cock to stay put.

"I was just thinking of how good I slept last night at your place. Kind of blown away by that." He shrugged, hoping she wouldn't press him for more information. "I don't sleep well in new places. It's a product of being sent to less-than-safe locales. But I slept really well at your house. I must feel pretty safe there."

Zamora raised her eyebrows. "Really? I'm kinda flattered to hear that. I like knowing my home makes you feel safe and secure. That's quite a compliment."

"Yeah, I do. Your house is…" He struggled to find the right words to explain. "Comfortable."

"I'm going to take that in the literal sense, as providing

comfort, and leave it at that."

He nodded and pulled into a parking spot at the shopping center down the way from her tattoo parlor. He didn't know why he should be so comfortable with Zamora or her home, but he didn't want to ruin it with inappropriate affection. He wanted to get it right with her.

Wait, what? Get what right? They weren't dating or involved.

Greg mentally smacked his head and locked the vehicle as they got out. *Keep your focus on the end goal.* Which was…what? Moving on with his life and returning to the Teams when he'd healed. He'd accepted her hospitality for a short time, a temporary fix until he got a place on base.

"So I'm going to get my shopping done and I'll meet you back at Think Ink."

She hoisted her bag onto her shoulder and stuffed her hands in her Capri pockets. "All right. Sounds good. Thanks for the ride down here."

"Not a problem. See you soon."

He didn't mean to stand there and watch her ass as she sauntered away, but the woman's physique captivated him in ways no one else had. She had curves, beautiful ones that made his mouth water, and yet he liked her personality, the smart, no-nonsense person who lived in her hot body.

Get a move on, Killian. He shook his head and forced himself to head toward the stores. The day had warmed up and the clouds cleared from the sky. He was glad he'd left his sweatshirt at the house as the sun beat down on his shoulders. It would be a warm one despite it only being the beginning of May.

Greg jerked his awareness toward what he needed to be doing, but it kept sliding back to Zamora and how at ease he felt around her. He'd never been comfortable around women to start, though he had a reputation of being a ladies' man. *Yeah, when Retro's bad boy stepped out of the way.* It always took Greg a while to get to know women. Oh, he'd slept with them, sure, but know them? Not so much.

But he'd spent two nights in Zamora's company and he wanted to know more about her. He wanted to know what made her smile rather than keep chasing all the Navy Bunnies who trolled for SEALs at the bars. Zamora didn't need a man to take care of her, and it made her fucking sexy. His ex-wife always needed him, but not like a self-sufficient person. More like a stop-gap in her own insecurities.

To be honest, he'd picked MaryAnn for her body and the interest she'd shown in him. He'd grown to like her, but he had his job as a SEAL, and he'd thought she understood what that meant. He suspected Zamora knew and he'd have a hard time convincing her to be with him.

But that doesn't matter because I'm just staying at her place for a short time. He ignored the niggle of sorrow at the idea of moving out of her space.

CHAPTER EIGHT

Zamora waved at the woman manning the front counter as she entered the front doors of her tattoo shop. "Hey, Brianna. How's it going today?"

"Good, slow, but good. How about you?" The woman with multicolored hair winked. "How's it going with your hot new guy?"

Zamora blinked. "What hot new guy?"

"The one who stopped here yesterday to pick up the key to your place. You know, tall, blond, and built?"

"Oh!" Zamora laughed. "He's not mine, he's just staying at my place for a few days until he gets his own."

"Really? You're not playing hide the submarine with the Navy guy? What's wrong with you?"

What's wrong with me, indeed? "Has anyone ever told you those euphemisms are really disgusting? No, I'm not having sex with him."

"Oh, why not?" Brianna shook her head. "I'd have had him stripped down and swabbing my decks the moment I got him home."

Zamora sighed. "Yes, well, as much as my decks need swabbing, that's not why I offered him a room for the weekend."

"Too bad. If you're not doing him, would you mind if I took him for a ride?" Brianna grinned. "He's hot and sexy, and any woman would cream her panties just looking at him."

She's not wrong.

"I can't make sexual decisions for him, so you'll have to ask him. We're not seeing each other, so it's not really my call." She gave her receptionist a one-shouldered shrug, trying to ignore the irrational fear that Greg might be interested in the eclectic beauty. "I'm gonna go finish up the orders for the week and then I'm outta here to do chores at home."

"With the hot Navy guy."

Zamora rolled her eyes. "Right. With the hot Navy guy."

Brianna wasn't wrong. Greg was sexy and hot, but she liked other things about him. Like their shared coffee snobbery and his willingness to admit his weakness in front of her. It seemed like an odd thing to value, but she suspected it had been difficult for him to show his frailty. SEALs were the toughest of the tough, and any weakness could get them killed. But he'd trusted her with his vulnerability and she treasured the gift it was.

Zamora shook her head and sat down at her desk in the office. *Just get your stuff done and you can head home to do your chores.* At least Greg would be there to provide a nice view while doing her work. She groaned and rubbed her face with her hands. *Seriously, get to work.*

She checked her orders and found them finished. *What the?* Then she remembered she'd done them on Friday before Greg wandered into her shop. It'd been a slow day and she'd taken advantage of the empty time. She checked her work email, made some corrections to the orders, and answered what she needed to before Toby stuck his head in the door to the office.

"Hey, Zamora. Can I come in?"

"Yeah, sure. I'm pretty much done here anyway. How are you?"

Toby closed the door behind him before answering. "I'm fine. How's it going with the petty officer?"

Zamora paused and scanned Toby's body language. "Fine. Why?"

"You didn't have sex with him, did you?"

"Oh, for the love of Dr. Who, what's up with you and Brianna? The petty officer is fine, healthy, and no, I didn't have sex with him."

Toby sighed. "Good."

She narrowed her eyes. "Why good?"

"Because he's a SEAL, a love 'em and leave 'em kind of guy." Toby shrugged. "I just don't want you to get hurt."

"Stop." She held up a hand and he gaped at her. "I appreciate your concern, but you're not my father or my older brother, and I can take care of myself. Your concern won't keep me from getting hurt, and I can make my own decisions about men and love. I don't warn you off your chosen partners, I don't need your warnings in mine."

"But—"

"Besides." She shook her head in her own warning. "He and I don't have that kind of relationship. We're friendly roommates. That's it."

"You sure?"

"What the hell kind of question is that? Of course I'm sure. It's my relationship." Zamora shook her head and gathered up the papers on her desk to put them in her files. "Look, Toby, I appreciate your concerns, but I don't need anyone to mother-hen me. I can take care of myself and if I choose to have a one-night-stand with the petty officer, I will without shame or remorse. We're both adults and can make our own decisions."

"I know." Toby sighed and rubbed his chin with one hand. "I just don't want him to treat you like Stan did. You deserve better."

"Damn right, I do. But I've learned a lot since Stan and know myself pretty well." She took a deep breath. "I still have a good feeling about the SEAL, Toby."

He groaned. "Lord help me, you're thinking of sleeping with him, aren't you?"

"Yeah, maybe. But he's more than what he seems. And I like him."

"That's just your libido talking, honey."

"No, it's not. Stop being a dick." She shot him a glare. "I'm not just talking about his body. Yes, he's pretty, but there's more to him than that." She sighed. "He let me do energy manipulation on him."

"Oh, shit." Toby sat down in the chair across the desk from her. "Did you get a good look at his heart?" He knew about her color vision when working with energy.

"Yeah. Yellow, damaged, but functioning."

"You know if you help him heal it won't make him love you, right?"

She shot him a flat look. "I'm not stupid, Toby. I'm not doing this to make him love me. I'm not as desperate as you."

"Ouch!" He pressed a hand over his chest as he grimaced. "That's low."

"But true."

"Damn, woman, you got a sharp tongue on you." He rolled his eyes. "Are you really going to try to help him with that injury?"

"Yeah, of course. I don't like leaving energy work half-done."

"Even if it means his healed heart isn't interested in you?"

The idea was repugnant, but she reminded herself she wasn't doing the energy work for such a reward. Greg needed healing and she could give it to him. She intended to help a fellow human being, not get a lover out of the deal. *And I can always just have physical love with him and let our hearts sort out the rest.*

"Even if it means he isn't interested in something more than friendship."

Toby shook his head. "That's crazy, you know. Why expend that kind of effort for no reason?"

"There's a reason. No one should hurt like that."

"But you don't know if he'll give any of that effort back to you." He threw his hands out in disbelief. "Why do so much for so little?"

Why, indeed?

"Because I have a feeling about him."

Toby scowled, but she shook her head. "I know you don't like to hear that, but even if we end up only as friends, it's worth it to me. I can't explain it to you, and honestly, I shouldn't have to. Just try to have a little faith in me."

"It's not with you I'm having a crisis of faith, Zamora. It's him." He sighed and dropped his shoulders. "Okay, I'll give him the benefit of the doubt and hope you're right. Just promise me if he ever starts giving you orders like your ex, you'll cut him loose and send him back to the Navy for better conditioning."

She laughed. "I'm not sure the Navy will help at this point, but it's a deal."

Toby nodded, but they were interrupted by a knock at the office door. They looked up as Brianna stuck her head in.

"Sorry to interrupt your lovers' quarrel, but Tall, Blond, and Built is here to see you, Zamora."

Toby shot Zamora a pointed look, but he rose from the chair with a sigh. "I'll leave you to it, then. I got an appointment in ten minutes anyway. Just do me a favor, Zamora."

She raised an eyebrow. "What's that?"

"Watch your back around him."

She snorted as she got up. "You know that's physically

impossible, right? And it's not my back I have to worry about with him."

"You know what I mean. Just be careful."

"Hey, I'm a big girl, Toby. I'm not afraid of being hurt."

He shook his head, his eyes sad. "You should be." But he ducked out, effectively ending the conversation.

Zamora turned off the lights and closed the office door, trying not to give into the misgivings from Toby. *Why is he so negative about this guy?* She knew what she was doing with Greg, even if they didn't end up as more than friends. At least that was what she told herself as she walked out to meet him.

****

Greg did his best to ignore the looks the turquoise-haired woman kept throwing him, but each time he met her eyes, she'd wink and lick her lips. *The message can't get clearer than that.* To be honest, he couldn't remember why he didn't take her up on the invitation. It had been a week since he'd last had sex, and she was both pretty and willing, but his cock didn't even twitch.

At least until Zamora came to the front of the shop.

"All done shopping?" She gave him a welcoming smile and his whole world looked better.

"Yeah, I got what I needed. You ready to go or do you need more time?" His phone vibrated in his pocket and he fished it out with concern. Were they going wheels up? *Not that I will this time.* The doc still hadn't cleared him for active duty.

"No, I'm pretty much done here. Bad news?"

Greg smoothed the frown and shook his head as he stuffed his phone back into his pocket. "Nah, just a reminder. Got a meeting tomorrow." He shrugged. "So if you're ready, we can go."

"Yeah, we're good. Have a good night, you guys, and I'll see you on Wednesday." Zamora waved as he escorted her out the door to the street. The others waved.

The warmth of the sun heated his shoulders again, but not as much as the stare from the woman in Zamora's shop. *Damn, she has laser vision or something.* He'd gotten her message loud and clear, but she wasn't his type. *Which is what, exactly?* He didn't know anymore. He'd always thought his type consisted of women who looked like MaryAnn, perfectly coiffed and slender with big boobs. But while Zamora had large breasts, she didn't share MaryAnn's need to do her hair and makeup before stepping out of the bedroom, nor the adherence to the perfect outfit. Zamora brushed her hair, threw on some comfortable, practical clothes, and headed out. The SEAL in him appreciated that more than he could articulate.

"So I thought we'd stop at the Navy Bean to get some coffee before we headed back to your place. I didn't get enough this morning."

Zamora shot him a smile. "That sounds great. Are you sure you're okay?"

He raised his eyebrows. "Yeah, why?"

She grimaced. "I don't mean to pry. You just had a big frown as you looked at your phone and I thought maybe something had happened."

"Oh, no. I was worried the squad would be sent out, but it's just about a team meeting. No biggie."

"Oh, right. Sent out for "training," right?" She swallowed hard and looked away, her gaze trailing across the cars and shops across the road.

"Right." He couldn't say more so he didn't, but he wondered what caused the tension across her shoulders. He tried to think of something to ease it. "It's hard not being with them. We've been a team for so long, being on the injured list is frustrating. But hanging out with you makes it easier."

He hadn't meant to say that aloud, but the smile she turned on him made it worth it.

"Thanks, Greg."

He held the door to the Navy Bean open and followed her inside. Soft music played in the background and the scent of ground coffee filled the air. They stood in line behind some giggling college kids and a woman in a business suit. A few people raised their eyebrows as they passed Zamora, taking in her big breasts and her tats, but she seemed oblivious to it. Or at least immune. He shifted his body closer to hers without actually touching her. He wanted to and had to fight the urge to gather her against his side, but he didn't think she'd put up with it.

"What else do you need to do today? Anything?" She returned her gaze to him after checking out the coffee selections.

"Nope. Just needed to get a few things at the store and that was it. How about you?"

"Yeah, I need to do some laundry and wash my car before the sea salt messes up the paint. But other than that, nothing."

"Sounds like an easy afternoon."

"Well, I'm no SEAL, but sometimes the laundry feels like an exercise in Hell Week." She grinned and he couldn't hold back his bark of laughter.

When they reached the counter she ordered a caramel macchiato and he ordered a straight black coffee, both to go. He still laughed at her comparison of laundry to Hell Week and insisted on paying for the coffee.

"I promise to help you with both the car and the laundry." He handed over the money to the barista as Zamora snorted.

"You want to help with my laundry?"

"Sure. Everyone needs a buddy during Hell Week. I can't leave you hanging."

She laughed. "You just want to get a look at my

drawers."

He winked. "Well, there is that."

The barista smiled coyly and winked at him as she handed him the cups of hot liquid, but he only nodded and gestured for Zamora to precede him. It was too nice to sit in the air conditioned coffee shop, but they needed cream. Again, he caught a few looks shot in her direction, but she didn't seem to notice as she led him over to the counter with the cream.

"You know, I've never pictured guys like you being domestic. No one ever thinks of SEALs as the kind of people who do laundry, clean the bathroom, or do the dishes." She shook her head. "I guess it's the mythos of the profession. I mean, you guys gotta eat and wear clean clothes every now and again, right?"

He snorted as he added cream to his coffee. "Most of the time doing laundry seems like a luxury. You don't get a lot of chance to be clean and dry when out in the field."

"Ugh, yeah, I guess so." She shook her head as they headed outside. "I don't mind being wet, and I can handle being cold, but I really don't like to be wet and cold."

His mind drifted to other places when she said the word 'wet', but he mentally snapped his attention back to the conversation in front of him. They sat down at the last unoccupied table in the little fenced area beside the street and he told his cock to behave. Now wasn't the best time for a hard-on, especially since he hadn't made his move on Zamora yet.

Which meant he planned to do so. The idea surprised him and he covered his uncertainty by taking a sip of his coffee. Why the hell was he considering asking her out? He'd just gotten through a divorce, for God's sake. How the hell did he think he was ready?

But if he was brutally honest, he'd been moving on from MaryAnn for the last year. It'd been eighteen months since he'd found out about her infidelity, and he'd lost his interest in making it work with her six months after that. When he met Zamora at the hospital, he'd looked forward to her visits and her wagon full of treats. Now he had her in front of him and he wanted to see if there was more than just friendly cordiality.

"You know what I mean?" Zamora waited patiently for him to respond and Greg quickly reviewed the conversation before he'd started woolgathering.

"I've never been a fan of wet and cold either, but at some point in the field you kinda forget what you're feeling in favor of survival, and the debate about wet or cold loses focus."

"Yeah, I guess. I think I'll leave it to you experts." She stood and he raised his eyebrows. "I'm going to use the bathroom."

"All right. I'll guard the coffee."

She grinned and it warmed his whole being. *Damn, I gotta ask this woman on a real date soon.* He sat back and sipped his coffee, enjoying the warm weather and salty breeze. He liked Zamora, he just had to figure out a way to ask her out without spooking her. She didn't strike him as a woman who accepted everyone's suit.

"Excuse me, young man, might I offer you some advice?"

The question startled Greg. He focused his attention on the silver-haired woman who'd approached his table, smiling sweetly at him.

"About what, ma'am?"

"About your…friend." The last word sat laced with upper-class disdain. "You look like a nice, clean-cut boy."

He hadn't been a boy for a good ten years or more, but he dropped his chin and tilted his head. *Where the hell is she going with this?*

The old woman grimaced. "Girls like that, all painted up like a comic book, aren't the long-term, good-relationship types. They have loose morals and no sense of what's appropriate. You'd do well to let her go and find someone more suitable."

Greg blinked as he took in the woman's words. *Is she shitting me?* He mulled them over while his anger simmered at her audacity, but he let his gaze slide away from her for a few moments while he gathered his thoughts.

"Well, ma'am, I firmly believe in never judging a book by its cover." He shifted his gaze back to her with a noncommittal smile. "For example, looking at you I'd never have guessed you're a judgmental, disdainful and bitter woman hell-bent on ruining a stranger's day because they've chosen a path you wouldn't choose for yourself. And you couch it so beautifully in a kindly façade of well-meaning advice and instruction." He gathered up the napkins and coffee cups as he prepared to leave. "I believe in taking folks on a case-by-case basis and dealing with the real person, not just the appearance. I would've thought you were a kind soul, but your appearance is deceiving. You have a good day now." His smile turned icy and he strode toward the door just as Zamora came out. His anger beat a tattoo inside his chest so loud he swore the whole street vibrated.

"Whoa, what's going on, Greg?" Zamora took the coffee cup he offered and his hand as he practically dragged her away from the coffee shop. "You look ready to storm a beachhead or take down a terrorist cell."

He had to tamp down on his anger before he snarled at anyone, but the few people sharing the sidewalk with them hastily got out of his way. Zamora strode along, her long legs keeping stride with him, but she shot him concerned looks until they reached the overlook facing the base. He leaned on the railing as Zamora settled beside him.

"An old lady came up to me at the coffee shop to spent some effort on convincing me to cut you loose because of your 'questionable moral character.'" He stared out at the waves to keep from making any sudden moves that could hurt her. *Or me with my fucked up arm.*

"What?" She raised her eyebrows.

"Yeah. Apparently she thinks a clean-cut guy like me shouldn't be with a woman as inked up as you." He ground his teeth. "She has no idea the person you are. Hell, she can't tell what I'm like just from looking at me. Clean-cut my ass."

Zamora grunted and bumped his shoulder with hers. "Yeah, there are a lot of people like that. They make judgments on what they see and can't quite keep it to themselves. It's the stigma of ink."

"I wanted to pummel her into the asphalt."

She nodded and sipped her coffee, letting her gaze settle on the waves. "Don't let it get to you too much."

"Why?" He shot her a look of incredulity.

"Because her opinion doesn't matter to me. She can't hurt me because I don't care what she thinks." She turned to him with a warm smile. "And I don't need rescuing."

He snorted and grimaced. "Not even a little?"

"Well, maybe a little every now and again. But not from someone like that." She tilted her head and squeezed his arm. "The reason it doesn't bother me is I don't think she's right and I don't value her opinion. The only person whose opinion I value is my own, and maybe my friends'."

"Do I count as one of those friends?" He held his breath. For some reason he wanted to be one of her friends so much his heart pounded in anxiousness.

Zamora settled her gaze on him, her expression thoughtful. She didn't say anything for a long time and his anxiousness increased with each heartbeat. He'd never been one to worry if someone valued him or his opinion until now. He wanted Zamora to consider his thoughts worth hearing more than he'd wanted anything in a long time.

"Yeah, I'd say you're getting there." She squeezed his arm again. "Come on. Let's go back to my house and enjoy our coffee away from others' opinions."

Okay, it wasn't the answer he'd hoped for, but he could work with it.

"Sounds like a plan."

They headed back to his Cruiser and climbed in without much conversation. Greg kept throwing glances her way, but she kept whatever she thought to herself. He started the vehicle when his phone chirped with another text message and unease hit him again. *Now are we going wheels up?* He pulled the phone out with an apologetic look at Zamora before checking the message.

This is a reminder of your 8 am appointment with Dr. Meecham on Monday at the Coronado Medical Center.

Greg blinked. He'd totally forgotten the appointment what with his divorce hearing and the resulting alcoholic binge. His gut clenched. He'd find out if he was cleared to return to duty or permanently beached. *God, please don't say I'm done.* He needed the Teams, and his squad. They were his friends, his backup, and his life. What would he do if he couldn't be a SEAL? Who would he be, really?

"Hey, are you okay, Greg? You look like you've seen a ghost." Zamora laid a hand on his shoulder. "What's wrong?"

"Nothing." He cleared his throat and dredged up a smile. "Just a reminder for an appointment tomorrow I'd forgotten. With the doc."

She raised her chin in a slow nod. "Do you want me to go with you?"

He blinked. "Go with me? To the doctor's appointment?"

"Yeah. Sometimes it's good to have a friend there when you get good or bad news." She squeezed his shoulder. "I don't mind and tomorrow is a day off, technically. I have the time to go with you."

Greg stared at her for several seconds, surprise pinging through him. *She'll go with me.* Even MaryAnn as his wife had never made time to go with him to any appointments.

Of course, he'd never been this badly injured, but she'd always had a spa day or hair appointment and couldn't get away. *Or she was fucking Mr. CRTAGNT.* The license tag still pissed Greg off.

"Earth to Greg, come in, please." Zamora waved a hand in front of his face and he blinked back to reality. "Do you want me to go with you?"

"Yeah." He heard his voice respond with the affirmative before his mind had caught up with it. "Yeah, I'd like that. It's always good to have someone at your back. Thanks."

"You're welcome."

The smile she shot him eased some of his anxiety and he shoved his phone back into his pocket. Just her willingness to go with him made him feel better as he started the vehicle and set it in gear.

By the time they reached her house, his good humor had returned and he parked in front of so she could move her car into the driveway.

"I'm gonna start some laundry before I move the car. Do you have anything that needs washed?" Zamora slipped out of the cruiser and headed for the house.

"Yeah, if you can handle skivvies and stuff like that."

She snorted as she unlocked her door. "Body fluids on clothing never squicked me out. I run a tattoo parlor, remember?"

He laughed. "Yeah, okay. Let me dig through my duffel."

It didn't take them long to get the laundry started and Zamora showed him how she liked her unmentionables to be cleaned. He'd never learned with his ex-wife. Zamora didn't flinch, just tossed her panties and bras in a mesh bag and threw it in the washer with his shorts. She didn't seem embarrassed by anything and he found the attitude refreshing.

She changed into shorts and a tank top, and he had to

think of running down a sand dune carrying a sixty pound pack to keep his attention from zeroing in on her large breasts. Damn, she looked sexy in anything she put on. *It could be her huge tits, jackass.*

He had to admit her breasts had definitely caught his eyes first, but he liked her and her forthright perspective on things. And he liked hanging around with her. They didn't have to be doing anything special for him to enjoy himself.

"Here, fill this bucket with warm, soapy water. I'm gonna move my car."

He did as she asked, but not before watching her saunter away in her cutoffs. Damn, she had a nice ass, all round and full. He loved women with curves and confidence. He filled the bucket and headed for the driveway. The sun kept the air warm, but the breeze made it comfortable as he set the bucket down beside her little pale green Chevy Cruz. Zamora dragged the hose around from the back of the house and winked at him before she sprayed the car.

"Hey!" He jumped out of the way as the water hit his chest.

"Oh, I'm sorry, did I get you?" She didn't look sorry at all as she grinned and aimed the hose away from him.

"Yeah, uh-huh. Do that again and I'll come over there and disarm you." He shot her a dark look, but amusement rumbled in his chest.

"Sure you will."

But she aimed the water away from him until she'd wetted down the entire vehicle. When she finished, she tossed him a rag and they went to work scrubbing the car. He tried to keep his focus on the dirty panels, but the flash and bounce of her breasts repeatedly caught his eyes. His cock grew in appreciation inside his shorts and he forced himself to crouch as he scrubbed the wheels. Anything to keep control over his errant anatomy.

"I think it's clean now. You might try the other three."

Greg glanced up at Zamora standing beside him, surveying his work with a smirk. She held the hose at the ready, her breasts straining against the wet fabric of her tank top.

"Uh, yeah, I'll move to the next one."

She nodded and waited until he took the bucket and rag to the next wheel before spraying the one he'd scrubbed. He tried to control his mind, but it kept putting up images of her nipples poking through the wet material and his mouth watered with the urge to taste them. *Focus, jackass.*

He would've been fine had she not spritzed him with the hose.

"Hey!" He lurched to his feet, shaking off the excess water. "What was that for?"

"I was just making sure you hadn't fallen asleep over there. You were concentrating far too hard on that wheel." She grinned at him and waved the nozzle in a hypnotic dance.

He tilted his head and let a smirk curl his lips. "It was either that or stare, abashed, at the wet tank top over your breasts. I thought I'd have less of a chance of getting slapped if I stared at the wheel." He nodded to the hose in her hand. "Guess not."

She blinked. "I don't know what's more surprising. A SEAL using the word 'abashed' or admitting to me he wants to stare at my boobs."

"Oh, I want to do more than stare, Zamora, but I'm trying to be a gentleman." He stalked toward her, backing her against the wet car before grabbing the hose.

"Oh yeah? A gentleman?"

"I said I was *trying* to be one, not that I was one." He disarmed her and pressed his body up against hers, the water from her shirt soaking his chest.

"Oh, I see. And what are you going to do about it?" She tilted her head to look up at him, her smirk still curling her lips.

Greg didn't say a word, just tilted his head and leaned forward until he brushed his lips against hers. The sound she made resembled a whimper before she opened her mouth and thrust her tongue between his lips. He didn't stop to think before he dropped the hose and grasped her head in his hands, tangling his tongue with hers.

His cock surged in his shorts, pleasure and arousal mixing in a heady brew when Zamora took his kiss and gave back as much as she got. She wrapped one hand around his waist, holding him tight, while the other grabbed his ass and squeezed.

Aw fuck yeah. He wanted her to squeeze a lot more than his ass, and if he had any say in the matter, it'd happen soon.

CHAPTER NINE

Zamora hadn't intended to flirt so much with Greg that he'd come on to her, but now that he had, she wouldn't let the opportunity go by. Her logical mind screamed a warning about his chosen profession and his bad reputation with relationships, but her attraction stuffed a rag in its mouth and covered it with duct tape. She'd wanted Greg since she'd seen him lying asleep in the hospital bed and now he showed her his own interest.

Is that a weapon in your shorts or are you just happy to kiss me?

His cock pressed against her as hard as his chest and she wiggled her hips to take full advantage of it. He moaned and deepened the kiss, sending her arousal higher than ever. She dropped her hands to his waist and pulled up his t-shirt to run her hands over his back. Most of the skin stretched smoothly over his muscles, but every now and again she found scar tissue from battle wounds.

He growled and released her from the kiss, burying his face between her neck and shoulder as he peppered her with nipping kisses. "You smell so damn good."

She whimpered and pushed him back until she met his gaze. "That's the soap for the car."

He gave her a lazy grin. "You got it all the way up on your shoulders?"

"Uh…"

He dipped his head again to lick her neck. "'Cause all I taste here is your soft skin."

He could taste all day long if he wanted to. *No, no, no. I want him to myself.* She pushed him back again and shook her head. He raised his eyebrows in question.

"If we're going to do this, and I definitely want to, we have to do it inside because I'm not going to share you with my neighbors."

His eyes crinkled when he grinned. "Well, when you put it that way, I guess we'll just have to take this indoors." But he hesitated with his hands on her hips and his cock pressed against her belly. "Are you sure you're okay with this?"

She frowned. "Aren't you?"

"Yeah. It's just…" He paused, uncharacteristically cautious. "I like you and I don't want to screw up a good friendship."

Excitement bounced around inside her chest. *He wants to be friends!* The little girl in pigtails inside her twirled around and kicked up her heels. She resisted the urge to fist-pump and forced her logical mind to take the lead.

"You just want to be friends or friends-with-benefits?"

"Oh, I'm definitely a friends-with-benefits kind of guy, but I do really want to keep our friendship. I don't have a lot of friends outside the Teams." He had the grace to wear chagrin. "There isn't a lot of time to meet people."

She nodded, honored he wanted more than just sex with her. "You'll always have my friendship, Greg." She leaned forward and kissed him softly on the lips.

It was his turn to whimper and he opened his mouth to taste her tongue.

She jerked back as her pussy spasmed. "Okay, in the house. Now."

He laughed and took her hand, pulling her toward the door. She paused long enough to turn off the water to the hose before following him inside. He locked the door behind them and marched down the hallway to her bedroom.

"Let's get you out of those wet clothes before you get chilled."

She laughed. "No chance of that happening. I have a hot guy to fuck."

"Damn, woman. You kiss your mother with that mouth?"

"Nope, not in years. But I'm hoping to kiss your cock with it."

"Holy shit." He growled and dragged her into her room, feral arousal lighting his eyes. "I'll let you do that, inkheart, if you let me kiss your pussy."

She grabbed his cock through his shorts and grinned. "I want you to do more than kiss it, Greg."

"Oh, fuck yeah. I'm planning to lick, suck, and fuck it too."

"Now who's the one with a dirty mouth?" She winked and pulled her tank top over her head. The wet fabric snagged on her breasts, making them bounce when it finally came free. His eyes seemed to bounce with them and he pushed her to the bed.

"Hot damn, your breasts are beautiful."

She glanced down at her chest encased in plain white cotton. "In a plain white bra?"

"The bra is just window dressing, inkheart. I've been dreaming of your breasts since I met you in the hospital." He licked his lips as he peeled the wet material off one full mound. "Oh, God, I've wanted to taste these forever." He sealed his mouth over one of her chilled nipples and her eyes rolled back in her head.

"Oh, yeah, that feels so good." She grabbed his head and dug her fingers into his short hair to hold him there as she sat on the bed. "Yeah, suck on my tits. I love your mouth there."

He growled and switched from one nipple to the other. Her nipples weren't the most sensitive, but the heat of his mouth on her skin turned her on. He massaged the neglected breast while he feasted on her nipple, and she reveled in his touch.

He hummed below his breath as he slid from the tight little peak to the rounded underside of her breast. Hot, slick pleasure curled through her chest and zinged between her legs, making her pussy clench. She whimpered and writhed under his ministrations as he sank lower on her body.

"Let's get you out of those wet shorts." Greg gave her a hot look as he peeled the wet denim off her hips and down her legs. "Oh, sweet jesus, you're not wearing underwear."

Zamora chuckled. "Not while washing the car. I hate when my ass gets soaked and it just sits there."

"And that doesn't happen with your wet shorts?" He tossed the soaked cloth away and knelt between her legs.

"The denim doesn't cling like the cotton. I hate them riding up."

"We can't have that." He dipped his head between her legs and her world went white with ticklish pleasure.

"Oh my God."

He swiped his tongue through her folds and flicked her clit with the tip, sending electricity throughout her body. She moaned and writhed, grasping his head with her hands. He rumbled his own groan against her flesh, making her gasp at the vibrations.

He licked and suckled with abandon, as if he couldn't get enough of her. His hands slid over her hips, tracing the lines of her tattoos. The hibiscus flower had never felt so luxurious as it did under his fingers. When he peeled her nether lips apart she realized she wouldn't be holding out for long.

"Come for me, inkheart. Don't hold back." He dropped his head and suckled hard on her clit.

Her orgasm exploded out of nowhere, surging through her and flinging her mind out into the starry cosmos. She flew with it, crying out her joy and pleasure. Greg hummed against her flesh, drinking down her release with approval and relish.

At last she settled back onto the bed and opened her eyes to stare down her body at him. He shot her a smile, something reminiscent of the cat with the canary, and licked his lips.

"You have the sweetest pussy I've ever tasted." He rose and crawled up her body. "And you're even more beautiful when you come, Zamora."

"Come on, really? I'm sure you've said that to every woman you made love with."

For a moment, hurt filled his expression and she regretted her words immediately. But a smug smile curled his lips, burying the hurt.

"No, not in a long time." He settled his body over hers, his cock still swathed in his shorts. "To be brutally honest, I haven't noticed if the other women were beautiful when they came, although I did make sure they came. But they weren't important to me."

"And I am?"

"Yeah, you are. I wasn't kidding when I wanted to make sure our friendship stayed intact. And you're beautiful, Zamora. So beautiful you make my chest ache."

She blinked. "You're really quite a romantic poet when you care to be, aren't you?"

He shrugged, rather abashed. "I don't know. My ex never thought so, but she never wanted to hear it, either."

To her surprise, he ducked his head and pressed his face between her breasts, hiding his discomfort.

"Hey, look at me, please." Zamora urged him to meet her eyes. "Thank you for the lovely orgasm and the compliments. I've never been told I'm beautiful when I come, and after seeing porns and other sex videos, I think everyone looks like they're in severe pain. But if you think I'm beautiful, thank you very much."

He smiled and her heart fluttered with joy. She would've sworn she'd given him a priceless gift.

"But I want to see you naked and hard, because I think that's beautiful. So, strip, SEAL, and show me the goods."

Greg laughed and stood, yanking his t-shirt over his head. Her breath caught. She knew SEALs kept in great shape out of necessity, but the washboard abs covered in soft golden hair took her breath away. More scars marred his skin, but they only made him more beautiful to her. She preferred men with experience, old enough to know what they were doing, and Greg had plenty. He unsnapped his shorts and slid the cotton along with his briefs off his hips.

His cock rose with a slight curl toward his navel from a nest of golden curls a shade darker than the hair on his chest. Her mouth watered with the idea of getting his hot flesh into her mouth, but her pussy ached to feel the hard length inside. She licked her lips.

"Like what you see?" He grasped his shaft and stroked up and down, his gaze on her.

"Oh yeah. You're sexy just standing there, stroking your cock." She grinned as his eyes flared with lust. "But while I like looking, I'd really like to feel it."

"So you want this cock?"

"Yes, sir." She winked at him. "Permission to come aboard?"

"Oh, so you want to ride?" He crawled onto the bed beside her and rubbed his cock against her hip. "I think that can be arranged." He rolled onto his back and reached for her. "Permission granted."

"You're so pretty, Greg." She scooted closer to him and ran her hand over his chest and belly, enjoying her hands bumping over the hard muscles. "I could look at you naked forever."

"As much as I appreciate your surveillance, inkheart, I'd much prefer your pussy wrapped around my cock."

"Me, too. But you need a condom first." She rolled off the bed and padded to the bathroom where she kept her stash. It had been months since her last one-night-stand, but she always had condoms on hand. *A woman can't be too careful, and can't depend on him to carry protection.* She wasn't going to give up sex just because he couldn't remember his cock-cover.

She sauntered back to the bed, enjoying the sight of him lying there with his cock flexing with insistent arousal. *Now if I could just keep him in that bed from now on.* Yeah, well, the likelihood of that happening was slim. As a SEAL, he'd rarely be around and he'd never be able to talk to her about it. Sorrow threatened to kill her sexual buzz, but when her gaze rested on his, his sexy smile set her ablaze again.

"You have a lovely curve to your cock." She settled beside him on the bed and ran her fingers of one hand over his abs while she held up the condom package with the other. "And it looks tasty. Still want me to kiss it?"

"At some point, sure, but right now I want to feel you riding me and see those beautiful breasts bouncing on your chest." He licked his lips and her pussy spasmed with erotic pleasure. "So give me that condom and let me pleasure you."

He reached for it, but she pulled it out of reach. "Oh, hell, no. I'm gonna roll this baby on and enjoy every moment of it." She tore open the package and grasped his cock with a grin. "But first I get to taste."

She lowered her head and licked the tip of his cock, savoring the tart flavor of his precum. He moaned and it only encouraged her to take more of his straining erection into her mouth, but she didn't stay long. She rolled the condom down his shaft and tugged the tip before stroking his balls with her fingers.

"Oh, my God, Zamora. Fuckin' ride me, inkheart." He pulled on her shoulders, urging her up his body. "Take my cock into your sweet pussy and ride me hard. I want to see you pleasure yourself on me."

His voice sounded as if he chewed on gravel and his hands steadied her hips as she straddled him.

"You want me to fuck you, Greg?" She grasped his cock and pointed it toward her dripping pussy.

"Yes, ma'am."

"Well, all right, then." And she sank down on his thick shaft.

"Oh, shit." He threw his head back and swallowed hard, but he never dropped her gaze. "You're so fuckin' tight, inkheart. And so damn sexy."

She had no idea if he was normally a talker, but she loved the sound of his rough voice and the dirty things he said as much as she loved the slick, hot pressure of his cock within her. She loved the way his nipples hardened into taut little peaks and how his pectorals bunched as he rocked his hips. He was the most beautiful man she'd ever seen and she had him all to herself.

I want to keep him.

The irrational thought made her gasp. Fortunately he pulled his cock out and thrust back in hard enough to distract her from her surprise. Exquisite pleasure shivered through her and she clenched her pussy around his hard intrusion.

"Oh, God, Greg. That feels so damn good." Zamora let the pleasure of his body under hers push away the unnerving thoughts. *Don't think, just feel.* She tightened her inner muscles around him and his moan lit her fires more.

"Oh yeah, you're so beautiful, Zamora." He stared at her tits, his lips pulled back from his teeth in an intense grimace.

"I know you think so." She ground her hips down until

his balls rested against her ass. "It's the boobs. Everyone loves them. They're kinda eye-catching."

He stopped moving and tightened his grip on her hips, his expression becoming serious. "That's not what I meant."

She blinked. "It's not? Are you sure, because these things are right here, in your face."

She'd meant it to lighten his intensity, but he didn't smile.

"It's not about your breasts, or your pussy, or that you're sitting on my cock." He cupped one of her cheeks and rubbed his thumb over it. "You're beautiful. Period. I noticed it when you came to the hospital each week. And it wasn't just how you looked." He snorted. "I might be a dumb guy, and a SEAL, but I could see how you treated everyone in the room. Hell, even that obnoxious seaman who lost his arm to an ignored infection was sweet on you. You were kind to all of us, and God knows, military guys are shit to everyone when injured."

His words warmed her heart, but she shrugged them away. "Everyone's nice to the woman with big tits who brings treats. There's a reason for the phrase about the way to a man's heart is through his stomach."

"Heh, I can't argue with that. But the food wasn't what I noticed about you." He met her gaze as serious as she'd ever seen him. "Your beauty, to me, isn't just the body you wear or the ink scrolling your skin. It's you, Zamora. I like you." He cracked a smile, his lids dropping over his eyes in a sexy smirk. "I wasn't kidding when I told you that before. And now, when your hot pussy is wrapped around my cock and your beautiful breasts are pressed against my chest, I get to appreciate your physical beauty along with the person inside."

"Pretty words, Petty Officer—"

"Not just words, Zamora." He rocked his hips slowly, his gaze heating. "I've never met anyone like you. So strong, sexy, smart. There are a lot of women who come to the bars trolling for the SEALs, and they come in all shapes and sizes." He dropped his hands to caress her breasts, thumbing her nipples. "But you didn't meet me at a bar and you didn't come on to me. You just treated me like a person, regardless of my skills, or lack thereof now that my arm's fucked up. You have no idea how refreshing it is to know someone likes me as me. It's not what I do or can do or even how much money I make."

Zamora allowed him to set the pace as she listened to what he said. *He isn't treated like a person? Has he seen my tattoos?* But she understood what he meant as he rocked her slowly, building up her arousal again despite their discussion. She wanted to believe he wanted her for more than the sexual pleasures she could give him or the size of her boobs, but that's all people seemed to notice about her. Between being obviously female and the ink, she was often regarded as a fuckable art piece.

"Do you remember the line from that sci-fi movie about the blue aliens, when she rescues him from his dream-coffin?" Greg brought her back to the present with a harder thrust. "When he could breathe, he looked up at her and said 'I see you.' Damn, it chokes me up every time I think of it. But that's what it felt like when you came to the hospital each week. You saw me. Not the SEAL, not the pathetic injured body, hell, not even the weak, whiney loser whose wife cheated on him. You just saw me, and that meant more to me than any food or big boobs ever could."

Her heart melted as her pussy heated up and she met his gaze with her own pleasure. The romantic in her pushed ahead of the arousal, and she tried to give him a warm smile. "I see you, Greg."

Intense heat flared in his gaze, and he rocked his hips again, sending pleasure spiraling through her. She ground her pussy down on his cock and rode him, enjoying his grunts and moans as she clenched her inner muscles on him. She wanted him to know she did indeed see him, the man. She didn't know the SEAL or the man he'd been before his injury, but she knew the man she'd met in the hospital and the one at her tattoo parlor, the one hurting emotionally as well as physically.

"And I'm going to make love with you. Right here, right now." She rocked harder on him, holding his gaze as her arousal flared in her pussy. "I'm going to fuck you hard enough both of us come and see stars."

"Damn, I love your dirty mouth."

She laughed. "Just wait until I get it around your cock." And she squeezed her inner muscles.

He groaned and thrust. "I think I can imagine."

"So let me improve on your imagination." She pressed her hands into the pillows beside his head and arched her back, grinding her hips down on his.

"Fuck me hard, Zamora."

She didn't need any other encouragement. She rode him, watching his expression to see how he reacted to her ministrations. Despite her intention to learn how he liked his pleasure, her own arousal kept distracting her. Her orgasm started before she was ready, but she needed him to come with her. She wanted to take pleasure with him rather than alone. He'd already pleasured her once. She'd be damned if she took without giving this time.

"Oh, God, Greg, I'm gonna come. Oh, oh, yeah. Come with me."

"Fuck yeah, Zamora. Ride me hard with your sweet pussy. Oh yeaaahhhhhh..."

His cock hardened to silken steel and he roared as he pumped into her. She threw her head back and rode the wave of bliss shooting through her. Greg's pleasure ramped up her own and made the orgasm complete. She'd had empty orgasms, physical pleasure without the emotional connection. But this felt more than just the sating of appetites. She *wanted* him to take pleasure, she wanted to give it to him, more than she wanted her own. That he found his release in her made her own complete.

I want to keep him.

She did, but she suspected she couldn't.

CHAPTER TEN

Greg scrubbed his face with his hands as his phone chirped with his alarm. He sat up and let the wakefulness come into being. His mind reviewed the day before and a satisfied smile curled his lips. *Holy shit, I'm fuckin' lucky.* Lucky was an understatement. He'd had the opportunity to spend the day and make love with Zamora, and he didn't regret a damn thing. His one-night-stands with other women had left a queasy feeling in his gut, but he wasn't planning on only having one night with Zamora.

They'd managed to finish washing her car and spent the evening doing domestic chores, but it resonated with him in a way life hadn't in months. Zamora was real, forthright, and down-to-earth. They made dinner together and ended up sitting on her deck to watch the sunset over the base to the west. He couldn't remember having a better night in a long time.

But real life intruded on his relaxing domestic weekend and now he had to face whatever came at him. *Yeah, doc's appointment and a team meeting.* The good news was Zamora had promised to go with him to see the doc. So he'd get a little extra time with her before it all ended.

He didn't want it to end. He wanted more time with her. He could probably get away with staying an extra night at her place, but he'd have to move on Tuesday.

I don't wanna. He shoved the whiney voice back into the darkness and dragged himself into the shower. His arm ached and he realized they'd forgotten to do more energy work on it the night before. *Damn.* He wanted her hands on him more. Of course, she'd had her hands on other parts of him earlier.

His cock rose, but he told it to behave and got out of the shower to dress in his utilities. He had to be in the right frame of mind when he saw the doc this morning. His gut clenched with unease, but he pushed it away. *No use borrowing trouble.* As a SEAL, he got plenty without trying. Hell, they usually went looking for trouble just to see if they could avoid it later on. He snorted ruefully.

He packed up most of his stuff in case he had to leave quickly after the meetings today, but he hoped he'd get more time with Zamora. The worry made his arm ache and he rubbed it. The arm hurt, but his first two fingers on his right hand remained numb. They were better since Zamora worked on his biceps, but nothing like before the injury.

He was still rubbing his arm when he strode into her kitchen, but he forgot everything at the sight of her. Zamora sat in one of her kitchen chairs with a mug of coffee steaming in front of her as she stared out the windows at the ocean. Her expressive face remained still and serene as she leaned on her elbow with one hand wrapped around her mug. His cock hardened while his heart softened at her quiet beauty, and the urge to spend more time with her rose in her chest.

"Morning."

The smile she gave him as she turned her head flattened him. *I want to see that every morning.*

"Morning. There's coffee and some eggs and sausages on a plate in the microwave."

He raised his eyebrows as he grabbed a mug for his own black libation. "You microwave eggs and sausages?"

"No, silly. I put them in there to keep them warm." She shook her head. "Eggs explode in the microwave. Didn't you try that experiment when you were a kid?"

Greg laughed. "Yeah, I guess I did. It was a helluva mess to clean up." He poured some coffee and retrieved the plate from the microwave. "Thanks for breakfast."

"You're welcome. Are you still okay with me going to the doctor with you?" She sipped her own coffee.

"Yeah, why?"

She shrugged. "Well, some folks don't like others to know what's wrong, and I didn't want to pry or step on your toes this early in our friendship."

The word friendship caught him off-guard. He wanted so much more with Zamora, but he didn't want to push her too fast. *Hell, I'm not sure I'm really at a place where I can be in a relationship.* But he definitely wanted more.

"Nah, I did that for long enough, though not necessarily by choice. My ex didn't always want to know." He shrugged and sat down to eat.

Zamora stared at him, her eyes wide. "She didn't want to know when you were sick or injured?"

He shook his head and shoveled eggs into his mouth. He didn't want to talk about MaryAnn. She existed only in his past at this point and he didn't have time for it.

"That's crazy." Zamora shook her head. "I'd want to know you're going to be okay, and be there if things aren't. So I'm happy to go with you today."

Her statements warmed his chest. "Thanks. I appreciate it. Just let me finish my coffee and we can go."

"I'll follow you there since I have to do a few things in town. Did you want to leave the key here or will you need to come back for your stuff?"

The moment of truth had arrived and he had no idea what to say. His profession demanded he make quick decisions, but this had repercussions for the long term. Personal repercussions rather than professional.

"Would you mind if I stayed one more night?" He gripped his coffee cup tight to keep his hand from shaking. He hadn't been so nervous since he applied to get into the SEALs. "I don't know how long it'll take for base housing to get on the ball and it's always good to have a backup plan."

She smiled. "Sure. Not a problem. You can stay as long as you need to, Greg. I don't mind having you here."

His tension melted away so fast it felt suspiciously like relief. "Thank you. I'd like to stay. You're place is really comfortable."

"Thanks." She glanced down at a pocket watch she withdrew from her jeans pocket. "Oh boy, we better go. Your appointment's at eight, right?"

"Yeah." He stuffed the last of the eggs into his mouth, picked up the sausage in his fingers, and took his plate to the sink. "I'm ready to go."

She laughed. "I didn't mean you had to go wheels-up this instant, but with traffic at this time of morning, getting the medical center on time can be tough."

He grinned as he swallowed. "Where do you know the term 'wheels-up'?"

She shrugged as she brought her mug to the sink. "I live in Coronado. I've heard the term from enough of the Navy guys who come to my shop. I suspect it means getting the hell outta Dodge or some such cultural reference."

"Cultural reference?"

"Yeah, you know, like 'scratching gravel', 'making tracks', 'hauling ass'. That sort of thing."

"Scratching gravel?" He shook his head. "That's one I haven't heard."

Zamora nodded with a smile as she grabbed her backpack and keys. "My grandmother used to say it when she'd urge us to get going. She grew up on a farm with a long gravel driveway. Some of the idioms stayed after she got married."

Greg grabbed his cap as she ushered him out the door and locked it behind her. "So I'll follow you to the medical center. No point in me getting there first."

"Right. See you there."

He headed for his FJ Cruiser and started the engine, but waited for her to get into her car before he moved. The morning sunlight gleamed on the car's hood and he enjoyed the sight of a pretty woman in a pretty car. *And washing it was so much fun.*

The drive to the doc's office didn't take long despite the morning commuters, and there were enough of them to keep his focus on the road rather than thoughts of Zamora in her denim capris and v-necked t-shirt. Today it had read, "To love is to recognize yourself in another. Eckhart Tolle". Given her ink and the old woman's reaction to it the day before, he thought it rather apropos.

They parked their vehicles and headed in to Dr. Meecham's office. They didn't have to wait long, a rarity Zamora remarked upon as he rose to go into the exam rooms. She didn't get up with him.

"Aren't you coming?"

She tilted her head. "I don't think I can, legally. I'm not your wife or your next of kin. But I'll be here when you come out. I won't leave until you do."

For some reason he didn't like the idea of facing the doctor alone, although he liked Dr. Meecham herself. But he had to concede to Zamora's reasoning. She'd just met him a few days earlier, but he wanted her with him.

"Hey, it'll be okay. I'll be here. No worries." She squeezed his good arm. "Go on, now."

He nodded and headed into the hallway with the exam rooms. It always smelled like disinfectant and carpet cleaner to him, but the office had soothing cream-colored walls and landscape art depicting beautiful vistas of both mountainous and tropical terrains.

Greg sat on the exam bed in the center of the little room while the nurse took his vitals and asked him a few informational questions. He answered automatically while he wondered what the doc would have to say. Would she clear him to go back to his squad?

He didn't have to wonder long before Dr. Meecham came in and smiled at him.

"Good morning, Petty Officer Killian. So good to see you. How are you feeling?"

"Good, ma'am, thanks for asking." He smiled past his nervousness.

"Good to hear. Let's get down to brass tacks because I suspect you don't really care for pleasantries. You want to know if you can get back to your squad, right?"

He appreciated her directness. "Yes, ma'am."

She nodded and her expression turned professional. Greg ignored the unease in his gut and waited to hear what she had to say as she stood.

"Let's take a look at your arm. Any soreness or inflammation since your last visit?"

He took off his shirt and set it to the side as she examined the scars on his arm.

"No, ma'am, not beyond the usual ache."

She grunted and squeezed his muscles gently. Twinges of pain greeted him, but they were manageable and he didn't flinch. She poked and prodded a little more before nodding with apparent satisfaction.

"It looks good and is healing well. How is the grip in your right hand?" She fixed him with a sharp look, her eyes assessing him.

He wanted to tell her it was fine, he didn't have any problems, but the words wouldn't come. She reminded him of his grandmother when she'd caught him with his hand in the cookie tin.

"My grip is pretty good, but my index and middle fingers are numb most of the time. So I can hold things tightly, but can't feel them."

"Hmm." She frowned and massaged his arm again, watching the muscles and fingers move as she manipulated the tendons. "Let me try a few things to test your reflexes."

She brought out a little reflex hammer and thumped his elbow, testing his movements. She rubbed her thumbs in his forearm to manipulate the fingers of his hand. They moved, but he couldn't feel the first two digits. Using a sharp implement, he poked his two fingers gently, watching his face for reaction, but he felt nothing.

The doc administered a few more exercises testing his strength and his responses, but the longer she said nothing, the quicker his gut sank. Something was wrong and it didn't bode well for him getting back to active duty.

"Have you been going to the physical therapist appointments?" Meecham sat down and wrote some of her notes.

"Yes, ma'am. My last appointment was on Thursday last week."

"Did you tell your therapist about the numbness?"

He glanced away, gathering his thoughts. "No, ma'am."

"Why not?" She stopped writing and met his gaze.

"I thought it would go away." He knew it was a lame answer, but it was truth.

She sighed and nodded. "I can understand that, Petty Officer. And it still might. There was a lot of damage done to your arm and it caused breaks in your nerves. We repaired what we could, but I'd hoped time would provide the healing you'd need to use your arm at a combat level."

"What are you saying, doc?"

"I'm saying your arm still needs recuperation and healing. While it does function and you have use of all your fingers, the damage was extensive enough that the nerves haven't healed as much as I'd hoped."

"Will they ever?" Greg's heart landed somewhere in his boots. *Oh sweet Jesus, I'm out of the squad, off the Teams.*

"I'm not one to say 'never', Petty Officer. Nerves are funny, and they do things no one ever expected or hoped. Yes, your nerves could heal completely with more time. It's not outside the realm of possibility." She gave him a lopsided smile. "But, that said, they aren't there now, and we don't know if they'll come back to where you need them to be." She took a deep breath, her expression filling with compassion. "I know you don't want to hear this. You've come a long way and your recovery is remarkable. But it hasn't come far enough to clear you for active SEAL duty. I'm very sorry, Petty Officer."

Greg clenched his jaw tight to keep the agony and disappointment from escaping in a moan, but it was a close thing. He felt like he'd run into a dragon's cave and killed the dragon only to find someone else had beaten him to the hoard of gold.

He had to clear his throat before he could ask any questions.

"Do you think, with proper workouts and manipulation, I'll ever get feeling back in my fingers?"

She took a long time to answer and he needed every bit of his SEAL training to wait for her. He wanted to scream and rant and hit something, but it wouldn't do any good, and it wouldn't give him the answers he sought.

"That's a tough question to answer." Meecham held up her hand to stall his anger. "I'm not trying to be vague or annoying." She gave him a brief smile before she sobered. "I don't want to tell you one thing and set your hopes too high, but I don't want to kill your drive to succeed, either. I will say this. I've seen nerves heal and regenerate with proper rest, exercise, and manipulation. There's no guarantee it'll work with you, and there's no specific time duration. It could take a week, or it could take decades. There's just no way of knowing. But it's not impossible."

"'When you've eliminated the impossible, whatever remains, however improbable, must be the truth.'" Greg shrugged with a grimace. "So you're saying I could get full mobility and sensation back in my hand, but you don't know when."

"Yes, when or if ever."

He swallowed hard and willed the welling emotion to settle as he met her gaze.

"I'm not going to bullshit you, Petty Officer. There's always a chance you'll get full mobility and sensation back, but it's not guaranteed."

He didn't flinch. "I'm out of the Teams, though, aren't I?"

Meecham squared her shoulders and nodded. "Yes, sir, that's going to be in my report. I'm really very sorry."

"I know, Doc. Thanks."

She nodded again, her professional mask falling over the look of sorrow. "I recommend continuing with the physical therapist. They'll be able to give you a better idea of how much strength training you can do with it to get it back up to speed."

He wanted to ask what kind of speed she meant now that he was no longer an active SEAL, but he nodded anyway.

"Do you think Reiki and energy manipulation will help with the nerves?" He didn't know why he asked. He already felt less than dirt with his inability to heal fast enough. Asking a medical doctor about alternative medicine seemed as stupid as running into a dug-in nest of terrorists.

Meecham raised her eyebrows. "Yes, actually, I do. Do you have a good Reiki practitioner?"

"Yeah, I have a friend who does it, but I'd never heard of it until she mentioned it. Do you really think it works?"

"I know it works. I've seen the results, and used in conjunction with traditional medicine and physical therapy, it works wonders." She gave him a real smile. "Have you found it beneficial?"

"Yeah, a little." He shrugged as she finished writing her notes. "I've only done it once, but my arm felt better afterward."

"Good. I think you should definitely continue that." She closed his file and stood, holding out her hand to him. "I want you to make a follow-up appointment with me in a couple of weeks so we can see where you are with your recovery. Take care of yourself, Petty Officer."

"Thank you, Dr. Meecham."

He followed her out of the room and back down the hallway to the waiting room, his thoughts turning darker as he closed on the door. He paused long enough to schedule the follow-up, but he barely registered when the woman handed him the schedule card. What would he do now? The SEALs had been his dream and he'd lived it for the last six years, but he'd stupidly never made plans for after. *That's because I didn't think I'd live to see retirement.*

Taking a deep breath, he pushed out into the waiting room and scanned the area for Zamora. True to her word, she sat separate from everyone else, her attention on her phone. Relief cascaded through him. He hadn't really doubted she'd wait, but to have her there when he'd been dealt a rough hand made some of the pain fade.

His approach made her look up and she smiled at him, her eyebrows up in question. He shook his head and she nodded, rising. He took her arm and led her out of the office to the elevators. They didn't say anything until they reached the parking lot. The warm sunshine heated his shoulders as he threw his cap on his head, but the ache in his chest just kept building. When they reached the cars, he swung Zamora around and wrapped his arms around her, hugging her tight. A shuddering sob left his chest and tears started from his eyes as she closed her own arms around his waist.

"I've got you. I'm here." She just held him, resting her head against his chest as he wept on her shoulder.

He'd never been so emotional, but Zamora gave him a safe place to let go without judgment or censure. She didn't ask what was wrong, she merely held him while he cried, murmuring soothing nonsense. Eventually his sobs slowed down and he stood breathing in her scent. He didn't want to let her go, but time marched on and he had a team meeting to attend.

"Feeling better?" Zamora released him as he stood back.

He shook his head with a rueful smile. "No, but I'll be able to face the rest of the day."

She nodded. "I hear you. Do you want to talk about it?"

"Thanks, but I gotta get to my meeting on base. But we'll talk tonight after you're home. What time do you think you'll be done for the day?"

She shrugged as he escorted her to her car. "I usually work most of the day just in case the deliveries come late. I'll probably stay until about five."

"Sounds good. How about I meet you at your place around five thirty?"

"Yeah, that'll work. Anything you'd like for dinner?"

The conversation had become so familiar he simply gaped at her for a moment. And even more strange, he wanted more such conversations with her, discussing dinner and groceries and errands. *What's wrong with me?*

"How 'bout you let me cook tonight? I make a mean burger with all the fixin's. I'll even throw in some root beer."

"Really?" She smirked at him. "You want the run of the kitchen?"

"Yeah, I can pick up ground beef on my way home."

The word 'home' fit her house more than it had ever fit his, but it still seemed weird to use it for her place. *Even if I want it to be home.* He shut that idea off as he waited for her response.

"Would you mind picking up ground turkey instead?" She grimaced and shrugged apologetically. "Beef makes my stomach rebel. It isn't pretty."

He frowned. "I don't know how to season ground turkey."

"That's okay, I can help you. We can make the burgers together."

That idea warmed him from the inside out. *Maybe I can convince her to cook naked tonight.* He mentally smacked himself as he nodded.

"That would be great. So I'll see you around seventeen thirty?"

Her brows bunched as she translated his words. "Oh, yes. Yeah, I'll see you then."

"Thanks for coming with me to the doc's today, Zamora." He meant it. Without her, he wouldn't have made it through the morning.

"You're welcome. I'm glad I could be here." Her smile warmed. "So I'll see you this evening."

"Yeah."

She patted his chest and got into her car. He stood back to let her go, watching as she drove back toward town and her tattoo shop. He was damn lucky she'd come to the hospital while he recovered. And even luckier she'd taken pity on him when he staggered into her shop on Friday.

He just hoped her kindness and support continued. He had a feeling after today, he'd need it.

CHAPTER ELEVEN

Zamora stopped by the local market to pick up a sandwich for the day before she headed to her shop to clean and do payroll. She'd gotten the orders done on Sunday and now only waited on deliveries. In the meantime, the floors needed to be mopped, the windows, mirrors and bathroom needed cleaning, and the employee paperwork needed to be done. *Thank God tax season is over.*

She parked behind her shop and entered through the back, her mind switching from the dreary chores to the morning she'd had with Greg. He'd found out something difficult from the doctor she knew, but she suspected he needed time to process it before he told her. Not that he was required to tell her, but she hoped he would. Whatever he'd learned had hurt bad enough to make a SEAL cry. He'd been heartbroken, of that she was sure.

And he'd hugged me like his life depended on it.

She let herself into her office, shaking her head. Despite his unhappiness, she'd enjoyed holding him when he needed support. She liked being there for him. *You need to stop those thoughts right now.* No good could come from them. They were friends-with-benefits, and they were damn good benefits if last night had been any indication. But still, that's all they'd agreed to. Neither of them were looking for anything else.

She reminded herself he'd just gone through a divorce as she sat down at her desk and booted up the computer. *Emotionally unavailable, remember?* It didn't seem to have any effect on her heart. The traitorous organ only wanted more of his attention and company. *Ugh, I'm hopeless.*

Zamora threw herself into payroll, reconciling hours worked with wage rates and taxes. She let the computer chew over the numbers and forced herself to go clean the bathroom. She required the employees to clean it each night, but made sure she performed a more thorough cleaning each week to get whatever they missed. And sometimes that equated to a lot.

She finished the bathroom and checked the computer to scan her emails for any delivery confirmation or questions. Nothing jumped out at her, so she returned to the main room and ran some water to mop the floors.

She'd just filled the bucket when someone knocked on the door. She strode to the front to let in her ink delivery. Melvin, the driver for Inkworx, greeted her with his lopsided smile and wheeled in the crates filled with a rainbow of India ink. He rarely spoke aloud because of his deafness, but she'd taken a class on American Sign Language just to communicate with him when he came by. She didn't have the skill he did, but she could sign enough to have stilted conversations.

"You seem distracted, Z," he signed. "Everything okay?"

She smiled, shrugged, and nodded.

Melvin dropped his chin, and shot her a dubious look from under lowered brows.

She laughed. "Have lot on my head. Made new friend. Needs help."

His brows rose. "What kind of help? Not financial, right?"

She shook her head. "Not like that. Life help. Place to sleep, friendship, understanding."

"What kind of understanding?" Melvin signed air quotes around the last word.

She frowned, trying to remember how to put it in ASL. "He's injured. Needs healing and friendship. Just got divorced." She shrugged again. "Giving him a place to stay."

Melvin blew out a breath and fixed her with a stern gaze. "Don't let him use you, Z. And don't be his rebound. Not worth your heart."

She nodded. "Not like that. Just friends."

He snorted, but didn't call her bluff. "Okay. Just be sure. I'll see you next week, yeah?"

"Yeah, see you."

Melvin left with a wave and Zamora went back to her mop and her thoughts. Sure, she and Greg were friends-with-benefits, but something had shifted this morning at the doctor's office. He'd trusted her with his vulnerability and anguish. She didn't know exactly what was wrong, but it warmed her heart to know he'd turned to her for solace.

Still, that doesn't really mean anything other than friendship.

It didn't and she didn't know him well enough to be sure it did, but it felt different than when he stumbled into her shop on Friday night. She shoved the mop into the water, squeezed out the extra, and plopped it on the floor to scrub. The repetitive motion of mopping the floor let her thoughts drift.

Did she want more than friends-with-benefits from Greg?

The question banged around the inside of her skull without a clear answer as she finished up the floor of her shop. She emptied the dirty water down the utility sink and refilled the bucket, thinking. *He's a SEAL and he's not going to stay longer than tonight.*

The idea that he'd move onto base made her sad, but she didn't have any reason to convince him to stay. And she shouldn't want him to stay. She lived alone and that was the way she liked it.

Didn't she?

Her thoughts were interrupted when someone knocked on the glass doors of her shop again. She looked up from dropping the bucket in surprise and grimaced as soapy water sloshed over the side, soaking her feet. Her heart galloped in her chest as she took a deep breath to calm down. Who the hell was knocking on her shop door when the sign read CLOSED?

She set the mop to the side and peered through the glass. A man dressed in khaki shorts, boat shoes, a pastel blue Izod collared shirt, and an honest-to-god white cable-knit sweater tied around his shoulders stood looking in with his hands against the window. *Good God, who let him out of the 1980s?*

As she approached the door, he stood back and smiled. The sunlight burnished his slickly styled light brown hair and his confident grin, and Zamora's steps faltered.

What the fuck is he doing here? She almost didn't open the door, but he'd seen her and she had enough manners to be civil. Taking a deep breath, she unlocked the and pushed it open just wide enough to speak.

"Yes?"

"May I come in?" He looked so sure of himself. Stan Lords always had been, right up till the moment she handed him back his gaudy ring and walked away.

"We're closed. Come back Wednesday during business hours." She stepped back to shut the door, but he caught it with one perfectly manicured hand.

"Don't you recognize me, Zamora?" His smile hadn't slipped despite her chilly reception.

She wanted to say no, but six years wasn't long enough to forget the smug bastard. She shrugged. "You haven't changed much, Stan. What do you want?"

"I want to talk to you. It's been a long time."

Not long enough. "It has, which makes me wonder why you're here. I thought I made it pretty clear I wasn't going to live on your terms."

"Aw, that was then. I figured you just needed time away to find yourself or some such excuse." His smile turned determined. "But now you've had your fun and I thought we could give it another try."

Zamora gaped at him, swallowing against the bile threatening to come up. He thought she'd just needed time? She couldn't quite fathom such complete lack of understanding. As if starting a business and making it successful all on her own was simple 'fun'. She'd worked her ass off and now collected the dividends on her hard work. And that didn't even begin to cover the real reason she'd left.

"No." She shot a look at her clock. Thank goodness it read close to four thirty. She could get out of here as soon as she finished mopping. "Look, I need to finish my chores and head out." She closed her lips around the traditional 'but thanks for stopping by' comment. She wasn't grateful for his presence.

He glanced behind her at the clock. "Is running out a thing with you?"

"No, I just have a life and work for a living." She pushed on the door. "Take care, Stan."

"You don't have to, you know."

Zamora raised her eyebrows. "I don't have to what?"

"Work for a living." Stan widened his smile.

"How do you figure?"

"You can always marry me. I'll take care of you and you'll never have to work again."

Zamora didn't know whether to laugh or scowl. *Marry him and be his little Stepford wife? Fuck that shit.*

"I think I'd rather work for a living. If you want a

tattoo, you're welcome to come back when we're open. Until then, take care and leave me alone." She closed the door and locked it, turning her back on him as she strode to the mop and bucket. To hell with it. She'd finish the mopping tomorrow. There was no way on God's green earth she'd stay there while he stood outside banging and cajoling her to open the door of her shop again.

Holy hell, he wanted her to throw away all her efforts and independence to become his little wifey? To wait on him hand and foot and look like a perfect little doll in his mausoleum of a house? Again, fuck that shit. She'd left that six years earlier when she told her parents what he'd done. She got her MBA and started her own business.

She dumped the water down the sink and stored the mop more roughly than necessary with her returned anger. Her father had smiled and essentially patted her on the head, saying that business was a man's endeavor. Her mother had been horrified at her lack of fashion sense or the disregard of their need to look better than their neighbors. When she'd insisted she wanted to something other than being Stan's trophy wife, especially after his behavior, they'd put their foot down. Either marry Stan or be cut out of the will.

She'd left the next day with only the clothes she'd bought for the various school trips she'd taken to places like Bali, Egypt, and Australia. Her grandparents' inheritance had been a godsend for starting her business, but she'd still depended on the kindness of her friends to give her a place to stay while she was starting out. She'd gotten her first tattoo that week so her parents wouldn't want her to come back. To them, only convicts and whores wore tattoos, a blessing because she wanted it clear that she meant to keep her independence.

Deep breaths, Z. She turned off all the lights in the shop and checked the front doors again. Stan had gone, but she worried he might be hanging around the back entrance.

She hadn't seen him for years, but something about his demeanor set off warning bells in the back of her head. She had no idea why he showed up now, but she wasn't interested in his reasons. She'd earned her independence and she'd be damned before she let it go.

Zamora closed down her computer and locked the office before she headed for the back door. Taking a deep breath, she pushed the door open and scanned the parking lot, her keys gripped in her fist. No one waited on her and she breathed a sigh of relief as she ducked through. She quickly locked it before she trotted to her car and got in. Her heart thundered in her chest and she took a few deep breaths to calm down.

Why the hell am I so freaked out? She had no answer as she started the engine and backed out of the parking space. Stan couldn't make her do anything, and he couldn't take away her livelihood. She had no connections to her erstwhile family or their fortune. She was safe.

If I'm so safe, why do I feel like I need to watch my step?

CHAPTER TWELVE

Greg settled into his seat in the meeting room on base and tried to rein in his emotions. The news from Dr. Meecham still burned, worse than the knowledge of MaryAnn's infidelity. He wouldn't be an active SEAL after the doc sent her report to his CO. The only bright spot in the morning had been Zamora's acceptance and comfort without explanation. She'd let him mourn the loss of his dream career, holding him and offering her compassion.

Now he had to face the Squad when the news came through. He didn't want to see their pity, but he'd been through worse situations. *The only easy day was yesterday.* To be honest, yesterday had been damn easy and fantastic. Being with Zamora reminded him of all the good he could have when he was home. And he'd be home a lot more now. *What the hell am I gonna do?* He'd never taken the time to consider what he'd do after he retired from active duty. Now it loomed ahead of him like a tsunami wave, ready to crash over his life, like it or not.

"Hey, Bam-Bam, good to see you. How's it going?" Petty Officer Third Class "Deli" Rubenovich settled into a seat beside him, his New Jersey accent flavoring his words.

Greg shrugged. "I'm upright, awake, and fed. That

seems like the best I can say."

Deli nodded and handed him a to-go cup from the Navy Bean coffee shop. "I brought you this. I figured it's the least I could do since I couldn't help you move your shit this weekend. All cleared out and stowed?"

"Yeah. Bronco and Lindsey helped me get it into the storage space." Greg nodded as the rest of the squad came in.

"Hey, Bam-Bam." Lieutenant Jim "Retro" Waters waved as he and Chief Warrant Officer Todd "Magic" Hunter sat down in the chairs beside Greg. "Damn, man, you look friggin' relaxed. You have a good weekend, pretty-boy?"

Greg mustered up a grin. After Retro moved in with Chris and Todd Hunter, he'd been off the singles market, leaving the ladies to go after Greg. But after meeting Zamora and spending the weekend with her, Greg wasn't interested in the singles life anymore. *Odd, since we aren't an item.* But he wanted to be.

He shot Retro a smirk. "Probably easier than yours. Divorce finalized, shit moved, and a day off. Not bad considering I can't lift much."

Retro sobered. "Sorry to hear about the divorce."

Greg shrugged. "Don't be. It's done and I'm free of the lies. Better in the long run." He ignored the needle of pain in his heart.

"How's the arm? Getting better?" Magic had worked on it just after the bullets had ripped through his muscles.

Greg grimaced. "Still working on strength and endurance, but I can use my hand with full mobility." He left out the numbness.

"Mornin', Bam-Bam. Blow any shit up lately?" Rimshot settled into a chair behind him, thumping his shoulder with one fist.

"Nah, not this weekend." Greg snorted. "Why, you got something needs expansion?"

"Heh, always. So you left the house intact?" Rimshot sipped his own coffee as he leaned back.

"Except for my shit, yeah. It's still standing. Are you planning on dropping by?"

"Hell no. Jaime's got a nicer place. A little smaller than your house, but warmer in some ways."

Yeah, Zamora had a nicer place for the same reasons. It was a home rather than a domicile or shelter.

"Not my house. Not anymore. Gave it to MaryAnn to make this easier. I barely lived there anyway." Greg sipped his coffee to keep from spitting out his anger. *Let it go. Not worth the energy.*

"Did you get a place on base?" Deli leaned forward on his elbows.

Before Greg could answer, four more men entered the room and everyone silenced. The first was Lieutenant Commander Thom "Whistler" Whittleton, their CO, his hair showing silver despite the high and tight cut he kept it in. While he'd been a badass SEAL in his own time, he came from a family of Marines, and the body maintenance carried over.

The other three men carried themselves like SEALs with the easy, graceful movements and watchful attention of professional military. The first man stood tall, close to six and a half feet if Greg had to guess, and had the shoulders to match. He scanned the assembled men in the room with an expression reminiscent of the Mona Lisa painting by DaVinci. The almost-smile effectively hid everything.

The second man moved like a cowboy, all loose, ambling motion and an 'aw-shucks' easiness, but Greg suspected it hid a sharp mind and intense scrutiny. Greg shoved his thoughts and feelings behind a wall of impassivity to keep this stranger from learning his secrets.

His mind almost skipped over the third man. He stood average height, average build, and average brown eyes. The only thing remarkable about him was his steel gray hair left long enough to reach his ears. The nametag on his chest read "Szellem" and he stood at parade rest as Whittleton called the room to order.

"Good morning, gentlemen. Thank you for being so prompt." Whittleton scanned the room with his sharp gaze. "We have a situation developing in Peru that needs our attention, but first, let me introduce some new players to our game. Petty Officer First Class Martin Skelling is a master interrogator and spotter, and will be joining Bravo Squad permanently, working with Chief Petty Officer Stanton."

The tall man raised a hand in a wave, his expression never changing.

"Master Chief Petty Officer Gabe Szellem has skills in infiltration and extraction as well as a specialty in cyber terrorism. He'll be working with Rubenovich to get our squad up to speed on cyber tracking and infiltration." The average man with gray hair raised his hand and nodded.

"Gentlemen, if you'd take a seat, we'll get the rest of the meeting going."

Skelling and Szellem found chairs and sat down, and Greg's focus returned to the third man waiting beside Whittleton.

"This is Senior Chief Petty Officer Cyrus Finch, on loan to us from Echo Squad to brief us on the situation in Peru. I'm going to hand him the reins as he can tell us better about the developments and what we're likely to be facing in the coming weeks."

The cowboy stepped forward and fixed the room with his faded blue gaze. "It's nice to meet you, boys. I've been working on the Peru mess since I PCS'd here last year, and it's getting worse. I won't bullshit you. It wasn't nice to begin with, but things are heating up."

He clicked on the computer in front of him, the powerpoint presentation starting with a map. "The

Tayabamba District of the eastern Andes Mountain range in Peru is known for their coffee plantations, particularly those subsidized by the Peruvian government. Recently, intel started filtering through the CIA about hostile takeovers of the coffee plantations by an unknown group of renegades fighting the government's hold on the indigenous peoples."

Finch changed the slide to the devastation left in the wake of an attack. Buildings burned in a village and bodies lay around in disarray. "While we normally don't get involved with domestic strife, it showed up on our radar because certain names were mentioned in the communiqués going out from the raiders. Casita de la Sabiduria, the cartel y'all tangled with a few months back."

Greg blinked and shot a look at Rimshot. Stanton swore.

"Yeah, apparently when y'all took out Mercedes Hermanas de Olvidado, someone picked up the mantle and changed their focus." Finch nodded. "At first we didn't have any idea why they were moving into Peru and attacking the coffee plantations. I mean, they couldn't get good coffee in Columbia?" Snorts around the room mirrored his dry smirk. "But more intel came out that the CIA had lost a drone in the region and our friendly neighborhood cartel would really like to recover it, not only for the pretty pictures the CIA took of their compounds, but also the strategic locations of all their competition."

"Are we looking at high tech hardware and data recovery, sir?" Deli typed some notes into his tablet.

"Yeah, but here's the thing. We gotta go in quiet, like ghosts, because we don't want anyone to know we're there. Not the indigenous people, not the Peruvians, and not the cartel. Everyone would love to get their hands on that drone."

Greg snorted. *Talk about a big time payday.*

"Do we have eyes or coordinates on the downed

drone?" Retro pointed at the map.

Finch shook his head. "We have the last known coordinates it transmitted and a blurry image the operator managed to get before it went offline, but we disabled the tracking signal to keep hostile forces from reaching it first. We have a general idea, but the terrain is rugged and mountainous. No roads around there, boys. Mostly goat trails and gaps in the vegetation. When you go in, bring your hiking boots."

Burning disappointment and sorrow hit Greg's gut as they continued to go over details about the upcoming op. He wouldn't be going with them. The rest of the squad didn't know it, but he did. The doc would send her report to Whittleton and that would be the end of it. He wanted to hate her for it, and his heart ached, but he couldn't blame her.

A weakened SEAL who didn't have all his physical resources in top form could get the entire Team killed. Greg hated to be left behind, but putting the rest of Beta Squad at risk would be worse. He'd seen guys with survivor's guilt and wanted to stay the hell away.

"All right, any other questions?" Whittleton addressed the whole room and Greg came back to the present. "No? Good. We go wheels up at thirteen hundred, gentlemen. Dismissed."

As the men around him gathered up their notes, Whittleton met his gaze. "Killian, I need to see you in my office."

Here it comes. "Yes, sir."

No one else said anything, but Retro, Magic, Rimshot, and Deli sent him wary looks. *Yeah, guys, I'm right there with you.* He nodded his head in acknowledgment and followed Whittleton to his office.

"Close the door, Killian." The lieutenant commander settled behind his desk. "Have a seat."

"Yes, sir." Greg dropped his weight in the chair in

front of the metal desk and tried to ignore the feeling he'd be offered a death sentence.

Whittleton sighed and his hazel eyes filled with compassion. "I'm sure you know what this meeting's about and that Dr. Meecham sent over her report this morning."

"Yes, sir." Greg nodded.

"So you know she recommended you do not resume active duty in the Teams."

The bile threatened to come up, but he nodded again. "Yes, sir."

Whittleton nodded in response. "Yeah. I'm not gonna give you any platitudes about how the weakest link can harm the whole squad or that this is a new chapter for you. You know the first and the second is bullshit in the eyes of a man facing medical retirement. In all honestly, this fucking sucks and I don't like it any more than you do, Killian."

"Yes, sir." What else could he say? The lieutenant commander was right, but it still didn't change things.

"However, Meecham's report did hint at the possibility of full recovery over time with therapy and conditioning. Did she mention that?"

Greg blinked. "No, sir. She said it was possible, but not guaranteed."

"The way the report reads, she's confident you'll get feeling back in your hand, just not in the time frame needed to be an active SEAL." Whittleton set the report down on his desk. "As far as I'm concerned, that's a helluva positive diagnosis. Are you still going to the physical therapist?"

"Yes, sir." Surprise and hope bloomed in Greg's chest. Meecham had made it clear she couldn't give him confidence in complete recovery, but it sounded as if she thought it was possible. "I haven't missed a session."

"Good. Keep going with that."

"So, what now, sir? I know I'm out of the squad and off active duty. Does this mean I'm officially retired, sir?"

Whittleton sat back in his chair and tilted his head. He reminded Greg of a kestrel eyeing a field for potential prey.

"That's up to you, Petty Officer. But I might have another choice for you."

Before Greg could ask, someone knocked on the door and Whittleton called, "Come in."

"Sorry, I'm late, sir."

Greg stiffened. He knew that voice, although he hadn't heard it in a few months. Turning his head, he met the warm gaze of Lieutenant Junior Grade Christiana "Ghost" Hunter, the first and only female SEAL to have made it into the Teams, and his erstwhile squadmate.

"Good morning, Bam-Bam."

"Lieutenant." He rose and saluted as she limped to the other chair beside him.

She returned the salute, snorted and waved him back into his chair. "Let's throw that rank business out the window right now. Lieutenant Commander Whittleton invited me here because I heard you might be medically retired. That true?"

"Yes, ma'am." Greg sat down in the chair, surprised at how glad he was to see Ghost. She looked happy and confident despite her limp. They'd almost lost her a couple years earlier when an ambush destroyed her leg. But she'd come through that and the ensuing kidnapping by terrorists with flying colors. He respected the hell out of Lt. Hunter.

She swung her gaze to Whittleton. "What's the prognosis on his injury?"

"Meecham's report says he has nerve damage causing numbness in his right index and middle fingers, but otherwise the arm is sound." Whittleton closed the file. "She also says it might be reversible with therapy and time."

Chris's eyebrows rose and the corners of her mouth lifted. "Yeah? That's good news." She turned her gaze on Greg. "I've been authorized to try to convince the best damn demolitions guy to come through BUD/S in the last decade to serve the remainder of his enlistment as an instructor in the BUD/S training facility here in Coronado. What do you say, Chief Petty Officer Killian?"

"Chief petty officer?" Greg's mind hadn't quite caught up with her suggestion.

"Yep. The position comes with a promotion in rank, though given your record you weren't far from earning the next step anyway."

He shot a look at Whittleton, who nodded and smiled, before he returned his gaze to Chris. "You really want me there when my arm's not a hundred percent?"

She nodded. "You heard the doctor's report. You just have to work on therapy and give it time. No time limit to being an instructor. You'll have to do your usual PT, of course. Gotta be able to keep up with the newbies. But you only have to push them, not do the pain and misery yourself."

Greg laughed. None of the BUD/S training had been a picnic, but he'd had his favorite parts. Building explosives, both underwater and on land, had been the most fun. *That, and blowing shit up.* And learning about new ordinances as well as how to dismantle them still fired his blood. What better way to learn about new demolitions than to teach it to someone else?

"Yeah, I'd prefer not to do Hell Week again."

"Hooyah, Bam-Bam."

They knocked knuckles.

"So are you interested?" Chris tilted her head and shot him a challenging look. He remembered that from missions they'd been on together.

Greg took a deep breath. He could walk away from the SEALs and the Teams completely, or he could help the next generation of SEALs be the best of the best. *Well, when you put it like that...*

"Yeah, I'm interested. When does the next class start?"

Chris grinned, wrinkled her nose, and threw a low-key fist-pump. "Yes!" She straightened and smoothed out her expression. "Excellent. There are mounds of paperwork to get this squared away, but you'll have some time. The next one doesn't start until the first of June. That should be enough to get that arm up to speed."

He remembered the very same words from Dr. Meecham that morning. "Copy that." He returned his gaze to Whittleton. "So I guess my choice is to sign on with the BUD/S school, sir."

"Glad to hear this, Killian." Whittleton clicked something on the computer and the printer behind him chugged out some papers. "I just need you to sign these…"

"In triplicate, sir?" Greg smirked.

"SOP, Killian." Whittleton grinned. "And I'll get them filed so you can start on June first."

"Thank you, sir." He leaned forward to grasp the pen and ignored the dead feeling of his index finger as he forced his hand to sign the paperwork. It wasn't his usual sharp scrawl, but it worked well enough to do the job. "I'm grateful for the opportunity."

"I'm glad it came up. When Lt. Hunter here said they needed a demolitions guy, I offered you up on a silver platter."

Greg snorted. "With all the trimmings, sir?"

"I don't know, Killian. How's your turkey gravy?"

Greg laughed outright and slid the papers back to Whittleton. "Lumpy and damn near inedible, but I make kick-ass mashed potatoes."

"Barbeque at your place next weekend, right?"

"I'll bring the sangria." Chris grinned as she rose and stuck out her hand to Greg. "Welcome aboard the instructor's staff. I'm so pleased to be working with you again, Killian."

"Thank you, Hunter." He stood and shook her hand. It would be good to work with Chris. He expected some pecking order rearranging, but he'd at least have a friend. "One question. What am I supposed to do until June first?"

"Continue your therapy and recuperation, take the time to rest, and there will be orientation classes as well as instructor trainings you'll need to attend in the next three weeks. I'll make sure to get you a schedule." Chris counted the events off on the fingers of one hand. "I'm pretty sure Senior Chief Castle will put you in the demolitions side, but I don't know who will be your direct superior yet. It'll be part of the briefing packet you'll get once this clears command."

Greg nodded. "Sounds good. Thanks again for the opportunity. I wasn't sure what I'd do."

"You're welcome."

Whittleton stood up and they all saluted. "You're dismissed, Killian."

"Thank you, sir."

He and Chris turned as one, just like the squadmates they used to be, and filed out of his office. She accompanied him down the hall toward the door and they stepped out into the early summer sunshine together.

"I have a little time before I gotta be home. Why don't I take you to lunch down at the Channel Island Café? We can catch up since it's been forever since I've talked to you."

Greg blinked in surprise. "Yeah, sure. That'd be good, Chris." He really needed to talk to the Base Housing department, but he didn't like the idea of being on base when he was no longer an active SEAL. Sure, he'd be an instructor, but not for a while. *And I really want to spend more time with Zamora.*

"Let me get my Cruiser and I'll meet you there."

"Sounds good. See you in about fifteen mikes."

"Roger that."

They split up and Greg let the new parameters of his life sink in. Divorced, medically retired, from combat duty, homeless, and soon to be an instructor for new BUD/S recruits. *All in one fuckin' weekend.* It gave new meaning to the phrase, "the only easy day was yesterday."

He climbed into his FJ Cruiser and started the engine, letting his mind drift to his need for housing. He'd have to call Base Housing soon. *But I don't want to live there.* No, what he really wanted was to stay at Zamora's beach cottage with a view of the base. Not only was the house homey and comfortable, but she lived there, and he wanted more time with her.

Greg shook his head. *If she wants me to be there, too.* He'd tried living with MaryAnn when she didn't want him there and it became a mine field of walking on eggshells. No matter what he did or didn't do, it would set MaryAnn off. *She was probably afraid I'd find out she was fucking someone else.* He growled and drove his ass to the café, hoping to rid himself of his frustration before having lunch with Ghost.

CHAPTER THIRTEEN

Greg rolled his head on his shoulders and glanced at the clock on the dash of his FJ Cruiser. Seventeen hundred and time to get back to Zamora's place. He'd had a nice lunch with Chris Hunter and she'd settled some of his concerns about being an instructor. She'd also admitted how disappointed she'd been to be on the permanently retired list, and how she missed the camaraderie of being with the Squad.

Greg worried about the same thing, but she insisted the instructors were good people for the most part and professionals about not stepping into each other's expertise. They worked a lot like the SEAL squads, and everyone remained united in making the best damn SEALs they could in the limited time they had. He'd asked about being the only woman and how the recruits dealt with it. She'd shrugged, but a mischievous glint lit her eyes as she told him some stories about the young men thinking she was a stripper until she put a couple on the floor before they'd even known she'd moved. After that, her reputation spread and she hadn't had much trouble.

"Weeded out more of the douchebags faster, actually." She'd shrugged and smirked. "I told them, 'If you're thinking with your dick now, son, you should probably ring-out today because you won't make it through the rest of the course.'"

Greg barked a laugh as he parked in front of Zamora's cottage and got out. He could see Ghost doing it and suspected the male instructors played it up to give her street credit. He shook his head. Men were stupid when it came to women. *Can't see past the tits, most of 'em.* He'd learned to see Chris as a capable fighter, regardless of her gender, but sometimes the old habits came back.

He shook his head as he tried the door knob on Zamora's house, but stopped when he found it locked. He frowned. *Not home yet?* He shot a look over his shoulder at the garage, but he couldn't tell if her car sat inside or not. He fished out the key and turned the lock, letting himself inside.

"Zamora, you here?" He closed the door and scanned the dark house. A light in the living room gave him a beacon to follow, but old habits of checking darkened corners kept his gaze moving. "Zamora?"

He found her curled up on the couch beside the single lamp, an ereader resting on her lap. She wasn't reading, though. She stared out the windows at the sunset colors of the sky, the book forgotten. When he sat down beside her, she turned her head toward him and smiled, but it didn't reach her eyes.

"Hey, Greg. How'd it go today after the doctor's appointment?"

"Good." He frowned and studied her expression. Something was off. "Are you all right?"

"Yeah." She took a deep breath and nodded sharply as if making a decision. "Yeah. I'm good." She set aside the ereader and stood. "Are you hungry? I hadn't realized how late it had gotten. I bought some ground turkey and left it in the fridge if you still want burgers."

She headed for the kitchen and Greg followed her, his

internal warning bells clanging.

"Burgers still sound good. As long as you help me season the meat." He paused at the counter as she flicked on the lights and opened the refrigerator. "Are you sure everything's okay? You seem...distracted about something."

"Yeah. No, I'm fine. Tell me about your day." She snorted, some of her usual humor returning to her face as she opened up the ground meat and threw it in a bowl. "Well, as much as you can being a super secret SEAL guy. Did it go well on base?"

He understood she was deflecting him, but he let it go for now. "Yeah, it did. We had a team meeting and I met two new squad members. One guy's really tall. Tall enough to make me feel short."

"Damn." She grinned and pulled out spices. He read garlic, celery salt, basil, thyme, and something odd called tandoori as she set them on the counter. "Bet he'd make me feel like a midget."

Greg laughed. "Nah, just petite."

She laughed with him. "I'm anything but 'petite'. What else happened?"

He sighed, not used to sharing some of his personal events with anyone. *Not even MaryAnn.* But maybe that had been the problem. Would his marriage have survived if he'd opened up a little more? He mentally shook his head. It didn't matter now, that part of his life was done, but maybe he could try to be a little more open with Zamora. Especially now with his forced retirement from combat duty.

"I, uh, I was informed I'd be retiring from combat duty today."

Zamora stopped and rested her hands on the counter, her expression filling with compassion. "Oh, God, Greg. I'm sorry. Was that what the doctor told you this morning?"

He nodded, grateful she hadn't brought up his break down in the parking lot. "Yeah, my arm is pretty messed up. Nerve damage and all, and my fingers still go numb." He shrugged away the pain of the admission. "But the doc seemed optimistic about the chances of healing from it completely, just not in the time frame needed so I could remain on combat duty."

"Really?" She smiled. "That's great news about the recovery."

"Yeah. I told her about the Reiki and energy manipulation you did and she seemed to think that was a great therapy for my arm." He shrugged again. "She said I should continue it. You know if you're okay with helping me and all."

Her smile broadened. "Of course. I'd be happy to." She threw a bunch of different spices into the meat and mashed them around until completely mixed. "I'm sorry to hear you're done being a SEAL. What will you do now?"

"Oh, I'm not done, not really."

A strangely sad tension froze her expression. "Not really?"

"No. I got the opportunity to work with a friend as an instructor for BUD/S now. I'll be teaching the new recruits how to blow shit up in the most efficient manner possible." He grinned to dispel some of her unease, not sure where it came from. "So while I'm not on combat duty, I'll be training the new SEALs."

"That's terrific, Greg." A real smile curled her lips. "I'm very happy for you. When do you start?"

"June first is the official date, but there'll be training and orientations while I get used to my new duties."

She handed the bowl of meat to him. "I'm so glad you get to keep your foot in the game, Greg. I know how much the SEALs mean to you. Now, you said you can make some mean burgers. Have at it."

"Got a grill?" He took the bowl and set it down on the

counter.

"Hibachi. Out on the deck." She waved at the glass doors. "I haven't started it yet."

The odd distance came back into her body language and Greg paused. Something must have happened during the day to make her reluctant to go outside. She shifted around him to the fridge to take out an onion and some tomatoes to cut up for the burgers, not looking at him.

"I'll start it. Where are your matches and charcoal?"

"Here in the pantry." She opened a door and handed him the matches. "The charcoal is outside on the deck in a bin."

"Let me get this started and I'll work on the burgers."

"Sounds good."

She sounded so distant and he'd be damned before he'd let that go, but first he had to get dinner started. She sat back down on the couch with her ereader while he went out to start the little grill. The warm evening air sighed with the sounds of the ocean sliding across the sand and the rattle of palm fronds. He found the bin of charcoal and started the little brazier, trying to find the best way to ask about Zamora's unease. They were friends-with-benefits, but he didn't know if it included the right to push about her worries.

Once he had the hibachi going, he returned to the kitchen to finish prepping the burgers. Zamora set the tea kettle on to boil and settled into one of the kitchen chairs. He liked that she seemed to want to share the space with him.

"So do you want to tell me what's going on or should we just pretend nothing is?" He kept his voice carefully light, not wanting this to become a combative situation like it had with his ex.

"Going on? Why do you think something's going on?"

"Because I might not have known you that long, but I can tell when something's on your mind. Did something happen today at the shop?" Greg sliced the onions quickly and set them aside. *No use crying when I'm waiting on her explanation.*

Zamora sighed and sat back in her chair. "Yeah, something happened. My ex came by."

Greg forced himself to keep working on the condiments for the burgers despite his surprise. "That's kinda unusual, isn't it?"

"Yeah. I haven't seen him in six years." Her mouth flattened in an unhappy line.

"What did he want?" *Focus on slicing the tomatoes and washing the lettuce.* For some reason, her words made his gut cramp.

"I don't know, really. He said something about giving it another try, and that if I married him, I wouldn't have to work anymore." She shook her head. "It doesn't make sense. I told him I didn't want that life six years ago. I have no idea why he showed up now, or how he even found out where my shop was."

"Maybe he asked your parents?" Greg worked on forming patties for the burgers.

She shook her head. "Wouldn't have helped. I cut ties with my family. We've had no contact in all this time. They wanted me to be a good little Stepford Wife, and I wanted to run my own business. So I left and didn't look back."

The bitter sorrow echoed in the undercurrents of her voice and he resisted the urge to wrap his arms around her.

"I'm sorry to hear about your family, Zamora. That's tough."

She shrugged, but her body language said she still mourned.

"But it is weird he'd show up now when you've had no contact with him. He didn't have your cell number or anything?"

She grimaced and shook her head. "No. I was done and said so." She rubbed her hands through her hair. "I suppose he could've looked me up online. I haven't been hiding really, just stopped contacting them. If they Googled my name, Think Ink Tattoos would've come up. But he wants to try again, after six years and no contact? Yeah, ain't happening. And I told him I wouldn't be his perfect little wife, all 'yes dear' and dressed to the nines no matter the occasion. That's not me."

Greg set the burger patties on a plate and washed his hands as he considered her words. There was something hinkey about the timing of her ex's appearance, but he didn't know enough of the story to say what. He carried the plate around to the sliding glass door.

"Come out with me. It's nice tonight and I want to keep talking to you."

She raised her head and nodded. He ignored the warm feeling in his chest as he stepped outside into the balmy evening air. He normally didn't talk so much, he certainly hadn't with his ex-wife. But he wanted to talk to Zamora, and he wanted to reassure her. He had the feeling she hadn't told him everything and needed to know the whole story.

Why? She's not yours. No, but she was a friend and he did his best for his friends.

"So what else about this makes you nervous?"

"Why do you think I'm nervous?"

He raised an eyebrow as he set the burgers on the hibachi to cook. "You were at home with the doors locked, the lights off except a single one beside you, and you're wearing enough tension in your body to equate to Kevlar body armor. You want to tell me what's really going on?"

He expected her to bristle and bluster, but she snorted and gave a rueful smile. "You know me so well already, huh?" She rubbed her hands over her arms and shrugged. "I don't know. There was something really off about him, like he was more desperate than interested. It was like he had a deadline, but what it could have to do with me, I don't know. It's not like I have anything he'd value. But he showed up at my business on a day I was closed. I guess it wouldn't be too hard to figure out where I lived, and he gave me the creeps."

"Do you want me to stay here until we find out what he really wants or goes away?"

The question was out of his mouth before Greg thought about the implications. But he'd been thinking about asking her to let him stay longer and he wanted her to feel safe. If his presence in the house would do that, he'd happily stay.

I want to stay forever. Yeah, that probably wasn't likely, but he'd take what he could get.

Zamora raised her eyebrows as they went back inside. "What about base housing? Didn't you talk to them?"

He gave a one-shouldered shrug. "No, I was still trying to come to terms with my loss of combat status." That was mostly true. He rooted around under the counter to hide his chagrin and look for a small skillet. "I'd planned on talking to them tomorrow. But I can hold off if you'd feel safer with me here."

She tilted her head, rolled her eyes, and sighed. "Oh, who am I kidding? Yes, I'd feel safer with you here. Yes, I'd like you to stay longer, and yes, I like sharing the house with you."

"You do and you would?" He resisted the urge to do a victory dance like a football receiver in the end zone, but he couldn't stop his smile. He just hoped she couldn't read it as relief. "Well, hell, inkheart, I'm happy to stay as long as you'll have me, and provide the feeling of safety. I took an oath to protect this country from enemies both foreign and domestic. I think this qualifies."

"Thanks, Greg." She walked straight into his arms and squeezed him around the waist. "I needed that. I like this whole friends-with-benefits thing."

He laid his head against her hair and inhaled her scent. A woman in his arms hadn't felt this right since his wedding day. And MaryAnn hadn't really felt right after that day. *God, I want Zamora.* But he was just her friend and he forced himself to release her when she pulled back.

"You're welcome. Let's get dinner done and then we can sit on the couch and watch TV or something." The 'or something' he had in mind referenced the 'with benefits' portion of their friendship, but he'd let her take the lead. He wasn't gonna fuck this up now that she'd said he could stay.

"All right. And we should do more energy work on your arm. Doctor's orders after all."

"Oh, yeah. Right." To be honest, he wanted her touching him, even if it was as innocent as helping his arm. And if he was lucky, he'd get her to do far more than that.

CHAPTER FOURTEEN

Zamora crossed her arms over her chest and raised her chin. "What do you want, Stan?"

"Come on, Zamora. Don't be like that. I just wanted to take you out to dinner tonight. Surely you can spare one night?" He gave her his slick smile.

It curdled her stomach. It had been three weeks since he'd first shown up, and now he made a point to come every couple of days, pushing for them to get back together. She'd told him no every time, but he never gave up. And he always came on days when no one else was at the shop with her.

"No, not one night, not one dinner. I'm not interested, Stan. I made it clear six years ago and for the last three weeks." She shook her head, preparing to close up shop. Toby had gone home early with a stomach bug. "I have to close up the shop early and get home. But thanks for the invitation."

"You know, you work too much. If you married me, you could have more time to relax." He reached toward her face to tuck a lock of hair behind her ear.

She lurched backwards and caught his hand, holding it away from her face. "What the hell are you doing?"

His brows lowered and he tried to jerk his hand free, but she held fast. "That's not very lady-like, Zamora, and you need to let me go. I was only pushing your hair aside."

"My hair doesn't need your help and neither do my manners. You don't like them, get out." She released him and stepped out of reach as anger clouded his expression. She'd seen the look enough times in the past to know his temper boiled just under the surface. "I'm serious, Stan. I'm done. You need to leave and not come back. I've told you enough times I'm not interested in you, in your proposal or lack thereof, or anything else you have to offer. You need to go."

"You can't talk to me like that." His voice had dropped and his expression grew thunderous.

A niggle of fear snaked down her spine and she wished Greg had stopped by that afternoon. But he'd attended one of his orientation trainings as a new BUD/S instructor that day and God only knew how long it would go. Still, she needed back up and slid her phone closer to her on the ledge below the front counter. She kept her movements subtle to keep Stan from seeing what she did as his hands clenched into fists at his side.

"I don't want to talk to you like that, but you're not listening to me. I'm done." She didn't want to bring up the past as she tapped out a quick S.O.S. message and sent it to both Toby and Greg. Hopefully one of them could send someone to back her up. "You need to go, Stan."

She'd only seen Stan lose control once, and he'd beaten the living daylights out of a maid for having mis-laundered his shirts. Of course, he'd denied everything and the family covered it up, but she'd been horrified at his rage. She'd gone to her parents and called the engagement off immediately. By the time Stan caught up to her, he'd been back to his affable self and seemed completely astonished at her change of heart.

They hadn't believed her. Called her a liar and an

alarmist, but she remembered the rage. Like now.

He took a deep breath and some of the anger retreated. He smiled, but it was ugly and twisted. She prayed one of her friends had gotten the text.

"Really, you can't speak to me like that, Zamora." He stepped closer to the counter and she slid the phone into her pocket, glad she'd put it on vibrate while working. "I came here to see you and reconnect with you. And to release you from having to work all the time. Can't you see that? You don't have to work. You'll never have to work again if you marry me like you were supposed to six years ago." He held up one hand as she opened her mouth to protest. "I know, you think you saw something and accused me of it, but we both know you were overreacting and I didn't do what you claimed."

Dear God, did he really believe what he said? Had he changed history to fit his own claim of innocence? The maid had been bruised, bleeding, and wheelchair-bound for the rest of her life. She'd had no one and that had spurred Zamora's need to visit the injured in the hospital, particularly those without family.

"I wasn't overreacting, Stan—"

"Yes, you were!" He slammed his fist on the top of the counter, making her step back in retreat. "There, now, see what you've done? You've made me lose my temper. You really shouldn't do that, Zamora." He dredged up another twisted smile. "You were just overreacting, but it's all better now."

She cleared her throat as she stared at him, considering her words carefully. "I was going to say, I realized back then I needed a different path. I wasn't meant for marriage and children and parties and being someone's arm-candy. I had too much I wanted to do on my own. I didn't want to hurt anyone, but I needed to do my own thing."

"But you hurt me, Zamora. You hurt me by your selfishness. We had a good thing back then." Stan gripped the edges of the counter, his knuckles white, and she swallowed against the fear clawing up her throat. "We can be good again, I know it. Just have dinner with me and you'll see."

He's lost his mind. Everything about Stan screamed unhinged, but while she'd had some martial arts a few years before, it had been a long time since she'd used her skills and they were rusty. She tried taking a deep breath to calm herself down, but her heart hammered in her chest and her gut tightened.

"I can't tonight, Stan." She tried to keep calm, but her voice shook as she wracked her brain for an excuse. "I–I–I have a Reiki session in forty minutes and I have to get home to prepare."

That sounded plausible. She performed energy manipulation on Greg most nights and his arm had improved over the last three weeks. *What I wouldn't give for Greg to show up right now.*

As if by magic, the doors to her shop opened and Greg strode in, his sharp gaze taking in the tableau with Stan. He wore blue digital camouflage fatigues and shiny black combat boots, but neither disguised the pure menace he wore like a second skin. Relief hit her so hard she damn near sagged against the wall, but she straightened and smiled.

"Hey, good to see you, Petty Officer. I'm afraid I'm about to close soon."

Some of the threat left Stan's posture and his smile smoothed out to gentle affability. Zamora didn't buy it for a moment and she suspected Greg didn't either. He stopped beside Stan, standing a good three inches taller than the slighter man and looked over the counter at the scheduling book. She suspected he didn't miss her white knuckles against the "cherry" wood composite counter.

"Aw, that's okay. I just wanted to make sure I got in here to schedule a tattoo. I've had a big promotion recently and I wanted to commemorate it."

He met her gaze and smiled, but it never reached his eyes. He wore his warrior face, the one she suspected filled the mirror when he prepared to head out on a mission. She'd never seen him prepare, but the cold eyes made her swallow hard.

"Oh, okay. Let me see what we have available." She clicked on the computer to open the schedule as Stan eyed Greg.

"You really think a tattoo is a good idea?" Stan sounded genuinely interested, friendly and curious.

Greg shifted his gaze to the shorter man. "Yeah. Isn't that why you're here?"

Stan shook his head. "Oh, no. I'm just here to see my girl."

Zamora clenched her jaw to keep from spitting or laughing outright, she wasn't sure which. She was no more Stan's "girl" than she was a Buddhist monk. She wanted to scream it at him, but she kept her mouth shut as Greg raised his eyebrows.

"You mean Brianna? She's nice."

"Brianna? No." Stan frowned. "Zamora." He shot a sticky-sweet smile at her as he reached for her hand over the counter. "We have a history together."

She moved her hand before he touched her, his nearness giving her the creeps.

"I told you, Stan. We're not together and I'm not interested. And we're also closed." She shot a look at the clock, relieved it read after six. She could legitimately close early. "I appreciate your efforts in stopping by, but I'm serious when I say no thank you. Now I really need to get this tattoo scheduled before I go home." She almost added 'out you go now' as she flapped her hands at him, but stopped herself before she made the situation worse.

Stan's expression darkened and some of the rage seeped in before it cleared as if the dark emotion had never been. He patted the counter and nodded.

"You have a good night, now, Zamora, and I'll see you tomorrow." He gave her a smile, nodded to Greg, and sailed out the door.

She held on to her composure until he disappeared out of sight down the street, but her heart galloped in her chest and tears threatened. She took a deep breath and refused to meet Greg's gaze as she walked around the counter and deliberately locked the doors. She needed the thin barrier of glass and steel to give her some protection from the man who refused to leave her alone.

"Are you okay, Zamora? I got your text." Greg's voice held concern, but she still couldn't look at him.

"I am now. Thank you for coming. Do you still want me to put you down for a tattoo?"

"No, thank you. I haven't found something I want yet. Are you sure you're okay?"

"Yeah. Let me close the computer and turn off the lights. Then I'll talk about it, okay?" She finally raised her gaze, grateful she could keep it steady.

"Roger that."

She logged off and locked the computer, her fingers shaking against the keyboard. She took a deep breath to keep from trembling and strode around the front, turning off the lights and switching off the OPEN sign. Greg melted into the darkness of the back as if he didn't exist and she appreciated his stealth. Something told her Stan might still be watching.

Thank God for SEALs. She never thought she'd say that, ever. But having Greg at her back shored up her deteriorating courage. She followed him into the back and headed for the office, her heart still thundering in her chest. *Deep breaths, Z. It's gonna be okay.*

Her phone vibrated with a text message as soon as she stepped through the office door. Greg slipped in behind her and closed it. She nodded to him as she checked the message. Toby's worry came through clearly in capital letters. *ARE YOU OKAY?*

She texted him back that she was fine now and would call later.

Despite her response, the phone vibrated with an incoming call. "Hello?"

"What the hell happened, Zamora? Are you really okay?" Toby sounded worried.

"Yeah, I'm fine. Greg came just in time."

"What was going on?"

"My ex Stan Lords came by again tonight. He insisted we're getting back together and pushed the issue. It was intense." She grimaced. Intense was an understatement. *Fucking scary is more like it.*

"You need to call the cops on him, Zamora. I'm serious. He's been harassing you for the last three weeks." Toby groaned in pain and she remembered his stomach bug. "You gotta let someone do something about him."

"And what will they do, Toby?" She snarled into the phone. "You know the cops around here don't give a shit about a tattoo parlor, much less one owned by a woman. You know how disdainful they are of both women and ink."

"Yeah, but if you have a complaint filed, at least there's a history."

Zamora sighed. "I'll think about it."

"Hand me the phone, please." Greg extended his hand.

"Why?" She raised an eyebrow.

"I'd like to talk to Toby since you texted both of us for help tonight." He didn't smile, and she handed him the phone, but clicked it on speaker. Greg nodded. "Toby? Yeah, I got here just in time. Lords was coming on pretty strong. You could smell the crazy on him."

"You gotta get Zamora to call the cops."

Greg raised his gaze to Zamora, who pursed her lips and shook her head.

"I'll work on it. She's safe at the moment."

"Is she still letting you go home with her tonight?"

"She is forced to."

"Say goodbye to Toby right now, Greg. I need to talk to you." Zamora reached for the phone.

"Good." Toby sounded relieved. "I'll talk to you both later after I've died. This stomach thing is kicking my ass and the stress of that asshole showing up isn't helping."

Greg handed her the phone. "Feel better, Toby."

Zamora took it off speaker phone. "I'm gonna close early and take off, Toby. Take care of yourself and I'll talk to you tomorrow."

"I'm serious about the cops. They have to know about this guy." Toby groaned again.

"Go take care of yourself before you throw up on the phone."

"Yeah, okay. Later, Zamora."

"Later, Toby." She ended the call and fixed Greg with a narrow-eyed gaze. "I'm forced to let you go home with me tonight?"

"Well, yeah." He gave her a relaxed smirk. "I'm staying at your place and have nowhere else at the moment. You're not that heartless."

"You seem pretty confident of that." She threw the phone into her purse.

"I have faith."

"You take a lot on faith." She flung the purse strap over her head and grabbed her keys. "I'm going home for some chocolate and some tea. You coming?"

Greg nodded, his face going back to the hard-warrior look. "Yeah, I'm going to tail you home and see if anyone else tries to do the same. I don't like the idea of Lords following you."

She grimaced as she headed out the door of the office. "Yeah, I don't like that idea, either."

Greg followed, at least, she thought he did. She

couldn't hear him at all, but he caught her shoulder before she headed toward the back. "Let me out the front."

"Why?"

"I want him to see me leaving that way."

She swallowed hard. "You think he's watching, too."

"Oh, I know he is. I don't want him to make the connection between us yet."

"Yet?" She raised her eyebrows as she headed for the front doors.

"Yeah. The time will come when I make it obvious he's dealing with more than just you."

She stopped him with a hand on his chest. "Just me? 'Just' me? I think I can handle a guy like that pretty well, thank you."

"Zamora." He grasped her shoulders in his hands. "You're the object of his focus. Whether it's obsession or something less disturbing, either way, he's fixated on you. And the crazy is strong with him. While I know you to be very capable, with crazy, it's always best to have a team at your back."

Her gut sank. "You think he's dangerous? Do you think Toby's right and I should call the cops?"

Greg shrugged. "He might be, but I want to do some digging first. So let me out and I'll tail you home. We'll see if we can get to him before he gets to you. Keep your phone on and I'll call if I think you need to take the long way home."

Zamora's stomach curdled, but she nodded and let him out the front doors. He didn't pause or kiss her goodnight, trying to appear like just a customer. She pasted on a professional smile as she locked the doors behind him and retreated into the back. *God, I don't even want to walk out to my car alone. Fucking asshole, Stan. I don't need a stalker.*

She paused at the back door, took a deep breath, and pushed it open. Her unease made her hesitate and scan the back lot. Nothing moved. *Grab your courage, Z. Greg is out front. You'll be fine.* The words sounded good, but her heart galloped as she locked the door behind her and scurried to her car.

Once in the driver's seat, she could breathe again. *This is ridiculous.* It was, but somehow she'd make it through. She set her phone on the console beside her in case Greg called and turned the ignition. All she had to do was get home safely and Greg would be covering her back. *God, I hope so.*

****

Greg watched Zamora's car slide into the evening traffic and pulled out after her at a discreet distance. He alternated between watching her vehicle and looking for another making the same turns. So far everything seemed quiet, but there was 'quiet' and 'calm before the storm.' He didn't want to get this one wrong.

Shoving his Bluetooth into his ear, he scrolled through his contacts until he found Master Chief Gabe Szellem's number. His return to light duty and the training as an instructor had brought him back together with his squad and its new members. And while Gabe was new to the team, Greg had connected with him immediately. They shared the same dry sense of humor and a love of rugby. They'd become friends while cheering on the Aussies.

"Szellem." The smooth voice picked up on the second ring.

"Hey, Gabe, it's Greg Killian. How was Peru?"

Gabe snorted into the phone. "Wet, cold, and snowy. What's up, Killian?"

"I need a favor. I got a guy harassing a friend of mine, a tattoo parlor owner, and he says he's got a past with her." Greg believed Lords, but still wanted some ammunition against the creepy bastard. "I need to take a look at his background. I want to know more about him like his financial status, if he's been in the psych ward ever, what his favorite color is, et cetera. Think you could give me a hand with that?"

Up ahead, Zamora turned left and Greg slid to a stop with his blinker on as he waited for oncoming traffic to pass. No one else sat in front of him or pulled in behind, but he still scanned the cars around him as the sun painted the buildings in its orangey sunset glow.

"This an official investigation?" Gabe's voice sounded more curious than censorious.

"No, sir. This one is on the QT. I need to know what I'm facing. He accosted her today in her own shop and if I hadn't showed up when I did, it could've gotten ugly."

"Did you file a police report?" Before Greg could do more than take a breath, Gabe added, "I know the cops are often slow to act on harassment issues, but this is civilian jurisdiction, and they can do a better job keeping an eye on things in their daily routines."

Greg sighed. "Yeah, I know, but she's reluctant to talk to them. Says the cops don't give a shit about tattoo parlors or women. Something about the bad element who comes into such places."

"Oh, yeah, that fucking stigma. As if cops are pure as the driven snow." Greg could almost see Gabe shake his head. "You should still try to convince her to file a report. If she gets in trouble while we're on duty, we'll be the last to know."

"That's a concern, definitely." His gut clenched as he watched a black Beemer with tinted windows pull out and follow Zamora for a few blocks. "But I need to know if this guy has a history we can point to, and if we need to take more precautions than just the usual. It'll also help me convince her to file the report."

"I don't know how fast I can get you the information, Killian, but I'll see what I can dig up. What's the guy's name?"

"Stan Lords, don't know if that's his full name or just short for Stanley, but he looks like a pretty rich boy, if you ignore the cloak of crazy he wears."

Gabe snorted. "Yeah, he sounds like a creep. Just watch your six and go to the civilian authorities if it gets squirrely out there."

"Copy that. Thanks, Gabe."

"You're welcome."

Greg ended the call and breathed a sigh of relief as the Beemer pulled into a strip mall. No one else tripped his concern and Zamora made it home safe. Greg took his time pulling up in front of her house and thought over what Gabe had said. He wished he could take the scary bastard out, but in truth he had to convince Zamora to go to the cops. He might be a big bad SEAL, but they didn't operate on domestic soil and technically, he couldn't do anything.

Greg shot a look at the last of the sunlight creeping on the edge of the ocean then scanned the neighborhood around her cottage. Nothing seemed out of the ordinary and his gut didn't scream a warning, but he planned on sleeping light that night. He'd be damned before he let Lords hurt Zamora.

After several minutes of domestic peace, he exited the Cruiser and headed into the house. Vegetables of various kinds sat cut up on the table with a small bowl of dipping sauce. The lights blazed in the kitchen and living room, and the curtains to the ocean lay open. But there was no sign of Zamora. Greg closed and locked the door behind him, listening hard. He searched the house as he headed for his room, finally hearing the sound of the shower. He stopped at her bedroom door, debating.

We're only friends-with-benefits. Yeah, but he'd steadily fallen for his roommate over the three weeks he'd stayed with her, and he'd caught himself wanting much more than just casual fuck-buddies. *I want what I didn't have with my ex.*

Finally he stepped into her room and headed for the bathroom, hoping she'd buy the 'with-benefits' explanation for his presence. He pushed open the bathroom door and stuck his head inside. Steam filled the space in the updated bath with a stand-alone shower and made it difficult to see. He'd prepared to joke with her about seeing her naked, but his smile dropped from his face the moment he caught sight of her curled up in a ball beneath the cascading water.

She rested her head on her upraised knees and her shoulders shook with sobs disguised by the sound of the spray. Her tears undid him and he yanked off his combat boots and emptied his pockets before opening the door to the shower. She looked up at him without surprise, just dull sorrow, and her face crumpled.

He ignored the water sheeting down on him as he sat beside her and gathered her into his arms.

"I've got you, inkheart. I'm here." He'd never been good at comforting anyone, particularly women. But he remembered her words when he'd first found out he was done with the Teams, and used them on her now. "You're safe."

"But your uniform…"

"It'll dry." He bowed his head over hers as he cuddled her to his chest. It killed him to see her crying and made him want to beat the living shit out of Lords for causing her this much distress. "Right now, you need me more than I need to be dry."

To his surprise, she gave a watery chortle. "Nothing like having a hot, wet man at my disposal."

He couldn't stop his grin. "Not just *any* hot, wet man, a SEAL."

"Are you going to sit up, clap your hands together, and yelp, *arrt arrt arrt?*"

"Not if I can help it. Any SEAL who does that should seek professional help. But I might be persuaded to do that if it makes you laugh." He tucked a finger under her chin and lifted her face. "Would it make you laugh?"

"Probably." She didn't smile and his heart ached. So he did the next best thing and kissed her.

The soft warmth of her lips and her sweet flavor crashed across his awareness and he couldn't help but deepen the kiss. *I love you.* The words echoed in his mind as he stroked his tongue across hers, holding her wet, slippery back with his good hand. He wanted to tell her how he felt, but he didn't want to scare her off, especially since they'd agreed on friends-with-benefits. Too bad his heart had bypassed that little directive.

He pulled back long before he'd had his fill of her. "Why don't I let you finish your shower and I'll have some coffee and a warm towel waiting."

"No, don't go yet." She clutched him tighter. "Just hold me a little longer. Please, Greg."

"Zamora..." He met her glorious green-gold gaze and felt his resistance melt a little more. "I'm afraid if I do that, I'll step well across the friends-with-benefits line into something more."

She blinked up at him, her expression thoughtful. "And you don't want that?"

Holy shit, was she tacitly giving him the go-ahead? He definitely wanted more, but he didn't want her to shut down. *But she asked the question. Doesn't that mean she's interested?* God, he had no idea. He'd never been very good at deciphering clues to women, especially with his own ex-wife. And he could storm a fortress full of insurgents armed with automatic rifles without a qualm, but admitting his heart interests scared the living daylights out of him.

Almost as much as the idea of living without Zamora.

Man up, Killian, and tell her, or ring out. He swallowed hard, inhaled a deep breath, and took the plunge.

"I want it more than I'd like to admit. But I suck at

relationships, and I don't want to screw this up at all." The hope in her face died and he scrambled to come up with something to set it ablaze again. "But if you're willing to take the chance on me, I really want more than just friends-with-benefits."

She smiled up at him, the water plastering her crimson hair down around her face, and he thought she'd never looked so beautiful. "I'm willing to take the chance. I want that, too."

"Hooyah." He'd never said it with such relief before as he took her mouth for another deep kiss.

At which point, the hot water ran out.

Zamora yelped and scooted out of the spray, knocking the door open. Greg swore and lurched to his feet, his wet pants tightening around his thighs as he lunged for the taps. His feet slid out from under him and he ended up hanging by his arms as the showerhead dripped the last few drops on his head. Zamora lay beside him curled in a ball, laughing hard.

"Easy for you to say. You're not wearing any clothes."

She sat up and wiped her face. "I can help you with that." She got to her feet and held out a hand to him, the water sliding over her lovely tattooed skin. "Come on, SEAL. Let's get you out of that wet uniform."

"And into something more comfortable?" He chuckled as dragged his feet under him and took her hand.

"Who said anything about getting into clothes? I'm rather partial to seeing you without them."

He grinned and carefully lowered himself to his knees to get his balance before standing up. "I didn't say anything about clothes, but I would like to be dry."

She laughed as she stepped out into the room. "Me, too. Let me get some towels."

Greg enjoyed the play of her ass and legs as she padded across the hallway to dig out more towels. He sat on the toilet and unbuttoned his uniform shirt, peeling back the wet fabric. *Damn, I'm gonna have to wring these things out.* Thank goodness they were summer weight. He'd be dragged to the bottom of the ocean if he wore his winter uniform. *Not that it gets cold enough for that here in California.*

"Here. It's the biggest towel I own." Zamora returned wrapped in a colorful beach towel with large red hibiscus flowers on a white background. She held out another beach towel with sailboats at sunset on it. "I think it should do the trick."

He pulled off his undershirt and dropped it with a sharp *splat* on the tile floor before reaching for the towel. Zamora watched his movements, her gaze stuck on his chest as he rubbed the towel over his head. When she didn't move, he slid it down over his chest and abs, watching to see her reaction. She licked her lips and swallowed hard as her gaze followed his hands. Her scrutiny warmed him from the inside out and hardened his cock.

"I'd forgotten how beautiful you are." She raised her gaze to his and smiled.

"I didn't know men could be termed beautiful."

She shrugged. "They can in my world and you definitely are. Even with your battle scars." She reached out to drag one finger over his abs where a kid with a machete had slashed his ribs during an op in Nicaragua. "They tell a story of your experience and survival. And they only add to your beauty."

He nodded, trying to ignore the ugly scars on his arm. "I'm glad you think so."

"I do."

She met his gaze and they both froze. It was an innocent phrase, and merely meant agreement in this instance, but Greg swore he heard wedding bells in the back of his head. *What the fuck?* When the hell did he start thinking anything about marriage? He'd only just gotten out of one a month earlier. Except, he'd been out of his marriage long before it became official, and he'd known Zamora a lot longer than just a month.

But marriage?

"Uh, thanks." He blinked back to the present. "Let me get out of my pants and let's at least make some coffee. I'm chilled."

She laughed again and reached for his waist band. "I can help you get out of your pants."

His cock cheered that idea, but a shiver worked its way up his back and his balls complained about the cold.

"Thank you. Tell you what, I'll get undressed and you can warm me up any way you see fit." Then his stomach growled. "After we eat."

She chuckled and nodded. "But I can watch you get undressed, right?"

"You want to watch me get undressed?"

"Hell, yeah. It's like my own private peep-show." She winked and crossed her arms over her ample chest. "I'll sit back while the 'Navy SEAL'"—she raised her fingers in air quotes—"strips and gives me a lap dance."

He snorted, but inside his heart fluttered like a kid at Christmas. "You want me to sit on your lap? You do know I'm close to two hundred and thirty pounds, right?" He unbuttoned his pants and tugged at the material.

She tilted her head and winked. "Okay, so I'll sit on your lap after you strip."

"Now we're talking." He grinned and worked his pants and underwear off his hips. The wet fabric took some finagling and made for a decent strip tease simply because it stuck to his skin.

Zamora sighed happily and his cock stretched to half-mast.

"Yeah, really beautiful." She met his gaze and her smile softened. "I'm glad you're here, Greg. I love..." She hesitated and her gaze flicked to the side then back. "I love having you in the house with me. It feels like a home for the first time in years."

Home.

That was a word he didn't use often, though he'd used it more in the last month than he had in the last seven years previous. He hadn't had a home, even with his ex-wife, until now. And he wanted to stay, wanted to be with Zamora in this house, make it their home, rather than just a place to crash.

SEALs didn't get many guarantees, but having a place he could come back to where he could decompress was the ultimate dream. He wanted it more than he wanted to remain in the Teams, and he wanted it with Zamora. *Because I'm falling in love with her.* Although if he was completely honest, it was already a done deal. She'd snagged his heart in the hospital when she came back each week with her treats.

"Zamora." He wrapped the towel around his waist, constraining his eager cock, and reached for her. "I like being here, like it so much I don't want to leave. It feels like my home, too. I..." *Man-up and tell her, jackass.* "I think I'm falling in love with you."

CHAPTER FIFTEEN

I think I'm falling in love with you.

The words did strange things to her insides. On the one hand, she'd warned herself not to fall for a Navy SEAL. They were heady and intense, but they were secretive out of necessity and regularly disappeared for weeks, even months, at a time. And sometimes they didn't come back at all. On the other hand, having Petty Officer Greg Killian in her home, knowing he'd be there when either of them got off work, sharing her days off with him, and even just sitting next to him reading while he worked on homework for his instructor's training made her yearn for more.

And the sex with him rocked her world. *Hell of a benefit.*

But to hear he loved her, even the beginnings of the emotion, only encouraged her raging inner romantic. Her heart wanted to throw caution to the wind and give its all to Greg. Could she do that? She'd seen many military marriages and relationships implode. And Greg had just concluded his divorce. But she'd learned over the last few weeks his marriage had ended at least a year before the hearing made it official. *That means he might be ready for another permanent relationship, right?*

"Say something, please."

Zamora blinked and dredged up a smile. "I'm sorry."

His eyes widened. "You're sorry?"

"No, no, that's not what I meant." What the hell was wrong with her? Had she completely lost the ability to communicate? "I'm sorry I was daydreaming."

"You were daydreaming." It wasn't a question as his brows lowered into a frown.

"Oh, God, I'm so not saying things right." She shook her head and rubbed her hands over her face. "I didn't mean to daydream, but I was fantasizing about what your words meant."

She sent him a pleading look, hoping he wouldn't shut down after her botched confession.

"And what did they mean to you?"

She sighed. *Lay it out for him. He took a chance on you.*

"Okay, don't laugh." She bit her lip and took a deep breath before meeting his guarded gaze. "They mean I'll have someone to come home to. Someone who'll help me when I'm stuck or scared, someone to cook dinner with, and a movie-buddy on Saturday nights. They mean I'll have backup when I need it and I'll have someone who depends on me backing him up. They mean walks on the beach, pizza on nights we both don't want to cook, and someone to hold up the world when it's too heavy for me to carry on my own."

The frown on his face lightened, but she wasn't done. "Your words make me want to happy-dance like a six-year-old with her first tiara and plastic heels, and fist pump like a heavy-metal fan. They make me hope for both romantic cuddling in front of the fire, and hot, kinky sex in a king-sized bed." She winked and he grinned. "But they also make me want to take the chance that this isn't a fling or a fluke. That my clean-cut Navy SEAL can actually love me in all my inky, big-boobed glory and funky quirkiness."

She swallowed hard and squared her shoulders. "They mean I'm not alone in how I feel about you."

He took a step closer to her, his cock pressed against her belly in a terrycloth ridge. "And how do you feel about me?"

"I..." Despite her determination, her courage faltered. She mentally shored it up with the last vestiges of her romantic 'white-knight' armor. "I love you, Greg. I tried not to. I tried to just be your friend and fuck buddy, but I saw you, here, in my house, and realized you're so much more than just a SEAL."

"You saw me? I'm kinda hard to miss." He raised an eyebrow.

"I saw you." She poked his chest with one finger. "You, the person who lives in this beautiful male body full of scars and muscles. And that's the person I want. Being a SEAL is part of who you are, and despite the dangers that come with loving a SEAL, I'm gonna do it anyway."

"You love me?" He cupped her face in his big, callused hands.

"Yeah. I love you, heart and soul. God help me."

"Fuck, yeah."

The relief in his voice made her inner romantic cheer just before he crushed his mouth to hers and kissed the hell out of her. His taste and the slide of his tongue against hers electrified her, and she wrapped her arms around his broad chest, holding him against her breasts. She loved the feel of the hard muscles under his warm skin and the heat of him permeated her body.

She gave as good as she got, tilting her head to take his tongue deeper, and he moaned. God, she loved that sound. It turned her on to know she gave him pleasure.

He broke the kiss and stared down at her, a wealth of emotions filling his gaze.

"Holy shit, I've wanted to do that since I saw Lords standing in your shop. I wanted to go all caveman on his ass, beating my chest and staking my claim. But I didn't know how you felt and I knew you wouldn't put up with Neanderthal behavior in your place." Greg smirked ruefully. "But is it okay if I stalk around like a male lion, glaring at everyone for a little while? I want to make it clear that you're mine."

"I'm okay with that, but you know you don't have to."

"I don't?"

"Oh, no. I'll make it very clear that you're mine, and I don't share." She reached down and squeezed his ass. "I plan on grabbing your ass in front of men who want me and in front of women who want you."

"I think there'll be far more men who want you than women who want me."

"Don't sell yourself short, Navy. And what about the men who want you and the women who want me? I want to be sure everyone knows we're off the market."

He looked so surprised she laughed. "Now, you promised me coffee and food, and then I have plans for you."

His eyebrow went up again. "You have plans for me, do you?"

"Oh, fuck yeah. I want to celebrate our new couplehood in style." She released him and headed for the door. But she looked over her shoulder as she wiggled her butt more than normal and winked. "Copy, Navy?"

"Roger that, inkheart." He snapped off a sharp salute and grinned.

God, he's so fucking sexy. She loved the salute, and the man, and everything about him. She wanted him, and she wanted it long-term. *Hold up there, Z. Start slow. He's just come out of a bad relationship, for which he's partially responsible.* She wanted what they had to be perfect and last a long time, but if she rushed into it, it'd crash and burn like the Hindenburg. *Just start with coffee and go from there.*

She'd gotten the coffee machine set up and happily burbling when Greg appeared in the kitchen in a snug black t-shirt and sweats sitting low on his hips.

"Aw, what happened to just hanging out in towels?" She gave him a mock frown.

"I got cold, but I'm okay with you just being in your towel." He winked and let his gaze slide over her body in her hibiscus towel. *Holy shit, does he have to look like sex-walking?* Despite his injury, he'd kept up with his physical therapy and gym workouts, and the man remained beautiful. *Which reminds me, I need to do energy manipulation on his arm.*

"We should work on your arm while the coffee brews." She wanted to make sure he was strong. She needed him to be in good shape. This world had gotten out of sync with her sense of safety and she needed to do something to reestablish it.

Greg stopped in front of her with his hands on her arms. "Hey, this is supposed to be about taking care of you. Why don't you sit down on the couch, wrap up in that fluffy blanket, and I'll bring you your coffee. Let me take care of you."

As much as she wanted to curl up in a ball and do nothing, she needed to keep herself focused or she'd melt down like she did in the shower.

"Working on your arm keeps me focused and is taking care of me." She smiled to take the bite out of her words. "I need to touch you, to reassure myself you're here and I'm safe."

"Oh, inkheart. Come here." Greg wrapped his arms around her and she let herself be cuddled to his chest. He smelled like heat, clean cotton, and the special musk that was all Greg. "I've got you. I'm here, and you're safe. I'll always have your back."

Oh, she wanted that. She wanted to wake up every day and have him in her house, drinking coffee, strutting his hard-bodied stuff around like he belonged there. *I want him as my permanent partner.* She wouldn't say marriage because he'd just come out of one, and she didn't think a traditional marriage would work for her. But having him there every day to talk to, to cuddle with, to fuck. *God, I so want that.*

She pushed back from him and throttled her wishful thinking. "Come on, let me work on your arm."

The coffee machine dinged its completion and he nodded. "I'll pour us some coffee and we can get started. Then I'm pampering you."

"Heh, you already do."

"You ain't seen nothin' yet, inkheart." Greg winked at her and poured two cups of black gold into matching mugs. "I figure you can work on my arm, then I'm going to lay your bones so well, you won't be able to remember your name."

"I thought the line was 'jump your bones'." She smirked as she took her coffee to the couch and set it down beside the candles already on the table.

"I'm supposed to be recovering from an injury. Jumping isn't an option tonight."

He sat down beside her and arranged his body so the couch held him up while he relaxed against the cushions. She rubbed her hands together, warming them, and took deep breaths, trying to ignore his musky scent. Her heart pounded with increased awareness of him as she grasped his arm, but she firmly told it to take a back seat while she worked on the injury.

This time her view of the colored ribbons showed much more vibrancy. She'd untwisted some of the yellow lines until they turned green and enlivened some of the gray and black lines stretching down his arm. The worst of them still showed yellow trending toward brown, but the ones stretching across his chest and massing around his heart had shifted into pale greens and blues. *Has his heart actually healed?* She could help it more with just a push of her own energy.

Focus on what you're supposed to be doing!

Zamora withdrew from his chest region and focused on unraveling the yellow and brown energies of his arm, but her attention kept drifting. She wanted to help his heart, make it strong and whole again. She wanted to make him love again.

Don't be ridiculous. This isn't a fairytale romance.

But the energy lines around his heart and chest were too sensual to resist and she spared a few moments to boost their function until the green showed a vibrancy resembling beryl crystals in the sunshine. The blue lines deepened to sapphire and even his arm energies shifted more to a greener yellow. She gave him a little more of her energy, pouring her love and attraction for him into his ley lines.

She slowly settled her energy and his as she pulled out of his aura and took a deep breath in. When she opened her eyes, he watched her with a hooded gaze, and her nipples hardened under her towel. She wanted him more than she'd ever wanted anyone in her whole life, but she held back. Taking advantage of him after having shared something so sacred seemed gauche.

Fortunately, Greg took the decision out of her hands when he twisted and grasped her head in his hands, tilting his head to take her lips in a hot, sensual kiss.

Oh my God, I need him.

Her yearning and arousal exploded from her tight grip on them, and she whimpered as she fell into his kiss. He slipped his tongue between her lips and caressed hers, ramping her need up higher. He tasted like hot summer nights and sexy man, and she couldn't get enough of his sensual tongue.

But he pulled back and continued his assault on her senses by trailing kisses down her neck to her collar bones. She threw her head back as he feasted on her skin, licking and kissing as he pulled back the towel to expose more of her chest. He kissed across her exposed chest while one hand cupped her breast and she gasped.

"Oh my, that feels so good, Greg."

He growled with approval. "I love your skin, Zamora. Not only is it colorful, but it's so soft."

"I give you permission to explore all of it."

He chuckled darkly against her neck. "Naughty minx. I'm definitely gonna take you up on that." He let go of her and stood. "I'm taking you to bed. Now."

She loved the growl in his voice as he held out his hand to her and she leaned over to blow out the candles before she stood up. He grasped her wrist and pulled her after him as he strode for her bedroom. Once he got her inside, he closed the door and tugged her gently to the bed.

"Let me take this towel off. I want to see and touch you, skin to skin."

The heat of his words made her pussy clench with need and she whimpered, but damn near tore the towel off herself. She tossed it away and he pulled his shirt over his head. She admired the broad chest and flat little nipples with a light dusting of hair around them. He had large pectorals, large enough to match her breasts.

Zamora had never had a small chest, but his palms were big enough to cup her breasts and he thumbed her nipples as he nibbled on her neck. Arousal roared through her, lighting fires under her skin until it tingled. He dropped his head to suckle one of her areolas while his other hand slid down her belly to cup her mound. She gasped as his fingers tangled in the curls between her thighs, skimming her nether lips with just the tips.

"Damn, Zamora. You're wet for me here." Amusement and pleasure filled Greg's voice. "I think I need to taste your sweet flavor again. Lie back on the bed and let me see your pretty pussy."

She sat down on her bed and scooted back with a sultry

smile as she spread her legs. She let the pillows prop her up as she ran her hands over her thighs and stroked herself with her fingers.

"This pussy right here? You want to taste it, Greg?"

"Oh, fuck yeah." He crawled on to the bed and lay belly-down between her legs. He glanced up at her with a sexy smirk. "You know I'm hungry, don't you?"

"Oh, that's right." Some of her arousal faded and she dropped her shoulders. "Would you rather eat?"

"Oh, I'm gonna eat. I'm just going to have my dessert first."

He dropped his face to her pussy and licked slowly between her lips. Hot, slick pleasure flooded over her and stole her breath. She fell back against the pillows as he took his time, tasting and licking her folds. He used his thumbs to part her labia and licked the creases between them. Each swipe of his tongue sent waves of pleasure sweeping through her until he fastened his mouth on her clit.

"Oh my God, Greg." She gasped and writhed under his sensual assault, but he took his time, tasting and suckling her sensitive flesh. "Ohhhhh."

He laved and teased her lips before turning his oral attention to her clit again, suckling with enough pressure to make her eyes roll back, but only enough to ignite her arousal. He seemed content to take his time, tasting and touching and tickling her pussy lips with measured motions to build her pleasure slowly.

Her vagina clenched and wept with his attentions, and she whimpered her pleasure as he increased the sensitivity of her flesh. He licked and sucked her lips, raising her arousal to a screaming pitch then backed off and let her settle a little before he rubbed her clit with his nose.

"You're so fuckin' wet for me, Z." He whispered the words against her soaked flesh and licked her cream from her nether lips. "I love your wet pussy and I'm going to drink all your sweet cream."

He fastened his mouth around her clit and sucked hard just as he thrust a finger into her clenching slit.

Zamora couldn't hold back. Her orgasm hit her like a rockslide, crashing over her and tumbling her along with its immense power. She flew as the powerful pleasure exploded from the center of her chest and filled her whole world. Greg moaned in approval from between her legs and lapped up her release, the stubble on his cheeks gently abrading her sensitive skin. The extra friction sent her higher and she whimpered with the last of her breath.

At last she came down when he pulled back from her and shucked his sweats onto the floor. His glorious cock rose from a nest of golden curls and his balls had drawn up tight against the base. He crawled onto the bed again, pausing long enough to place a gentle kiss on her mound before he continued up her body to fit his hips between her legs.

She keened a low wail when his hard, hot shaft pressed against her sensitive flesh. Despite the euphoria rippling through her, her pussy spasmed with desire at the contact. Oh, she wanted to be filled with his hard cock. She wanted him to fuck her deep into the mattress until she couldn't tell where he began and she ended.

"I'm going to make love with you, Zamora." His voice was no more than a low growl. "I'm gonna slide my cock deep into you and fuck you slow. You're going to take every hard inch of me and I'm going to take my time until you can't hold back. Do you copy?"

"Oh, God, copy that, Navy."

He grabbed a condom and slipped it over his straining flesh before positioning the tip at her weeping entrance. Zamora wriggled with her returning need. She wanted to feel that hot, heavy cock sliding in and out of her aching pussy.

"Permission to come aboard."

"Granted."

He thrust in slowly, achingly slow, each inch a torturous expansion inside her. She rocked her hips to increase the friction, but he lifted himself off her with measured ease. The muscles in his chest and arms flexed as he held himself over her, and she tried to admire them. But the exquisite sensations of his hard, slick shaft sliding between her nether lips made her eyes roll back in her head.

He rocked back and forth between her legs in a measured, steady rhythm. His expression turned intensely inward as if he concentrated not only on her pleasure but his own. She wanted him to go faster, to build up the ecstasy with fast and furious motions, but he wouldn't be swayed from his steady pace no matter how much she moaned and writhed beneath him.

In a last ditch effort to make him lose control, Zamora clenched her inner muscles around his shaft, and Greg's eyes closed as he groaned. His cock flexed in her pussy and sent shock waves of pleasure through her.

"Oh, yeah, I love it when you do that."

He groaned. "Do what?"

"When you fuck me slow and your cock flexes inside me."

"You mean like this?" He met her gaze and smirked as his shaft twitched against the walls of her vagina.

"Oh, God, yes." She threw her head back. "Just like that."

He grinned as he flexed his cock again and thrust into her aching flesh. When he pulled out again, he let the shaft slide against her clit and the smoldering arousal flared. She whimpered her pleasure and thrust her hips to get the most out of his slow, steady motions.

"Just fuck me, dammit. I need you." She snarled at him as he took his time and teased her.

He laughed. "You need me?" His expression and voice tightened as he thrust in again. "How badly do you need me, inkheart?"

"I need you so much, Navy. I need you to fuck me hard and deep."

"Copy that."

His thrusts increased in speed and force until he was pounding her into the bed, his grunts mixing with her whimpers. The pleasure and arousal ignited into a conflagration of ecstasy and she grabbed his ass as he pounded into her.

"Yes, Greg. Fuck me hard. Oh, God, yes."

He reached between their bodies and strummed her clit with his thumb. "Come for me, inkheart."

His words and touches set her on fire and she shot out among the stars with her orgasm. She wailed her joy and he roared his agreement as his cock hardened to stone inside her and he came hard. His body stiffened over hers and she tried to enjoy the sight of his release through the filter of her own.

At last they came down and he tumbled to the bed, taking her with him. He tucked her against his side as he caught his breath, his chest rising and falling like a bellows. She closed her eyes and rode the last of her pleasure down into his arms, settling with a soft bump back into reality.

Zamora cuddled against Greg's chest, her heart slowing down to normal as she reveled in the euphoria of making love with him. This was the man she wanted, for however long he'd be willing to stay. She didn't need riches, or perfect clothes, or to be seen as the 'best of society.' She needed this kick-ass SEAL, a man as soft-hearted as he was hard-bodied. That made him perfect for her.

Unlike Stan Lords.

The thought threw ice water on her pleasure and she groaned.

"What? What's wrong? I didn't hurt you, did I?" Greg tipped her head up to meet his gaze.

"No, not at all. It was fucking amazing, and I enjoyed

every minute of it." She shook her head and grimaced. "I'm just wondering what to do about Stan. He said he'd be back tomorrow. I don't want him to come back. I want him to leave me alone."

Greg sighed. "Yeah, not much likelihood of that. You really should file a report with the cops." When she stiffened, he squeezed her reassuringly. "At least there'd be a record and a history of complaints. They'd have his name and description, and an "I told you so" if anything does happen."

"I don't want anything to happen." A frown pulled the corners of her mouth down.

"I know, Zamora, but it's always good to have a backup plan, and proof. As they say in the Navy, if it ain't written down in triplicate, it didn't happen." He stroked her cheek with his thumb. "File a report tomorrow. Please. For my peace of mind."

"The cops here won't take it seriously, Greg. They'll say I'm just overreacting. Or worse, they'll cite my shop as a place that attracts bad people, and if I wanted to be safe, I shouldn't sell tattoos." She grimaced and looked away. "I've seen it before in this town."

"They don't have to take it seriously, we will. But we need a record of occurrence so we can point to it when things escalate."

"You think they'll escalate?" Her gut sank. *Please, God, why won't Stan leave me alone?*

"With the kind of crazy he showed? Yeah, I think so."

"Shit."

"Hey, don't worry. I've got your back." He smiled. "I'm already working on a solution with some of the members of my old squad. We'll come up with something to keep you safe. In the meantime, let's get the local LEOs involved so there's a record."

"Leos?" She snorted. "Are we talking lions or horoscopes now?"

"LEOs." He laughed. "Law Enforcement Officers. Cops to civilians." He sobered as she lost her smile. "Please, inkheart. They can be there when I'm not."

She swallowed hard and laid her head against his chest, listening to his strong heart thump away under her ear. He sounded so confident and strong. It was easy for him, he was a SEAL. He'd seen the worst of the world and come through it. Not unscathed, but still through. She was just one human woman, unable to leap tall buildings in a single bound. This kind of shit scared the daylights out of her, particularly when faced with the jaded indifference of the cops.

But both Toby and Greg were right. It definitely paid to have a history logged with the cops. They might not believe anything was really wrong or be convinced of her innocence, but she had to make a case for why she thought so. She'd just have to buckle on her mental armor and hope the cop taking the report was more open-minded than most.

"Okay, Greg. I'll call the cops tomorrow and file a report on him."

"Thank you." He sighed and all the remaining tension left his body. "And I have some good news for you."

"Oh yeah? I could use some at the moment."

"Well, first of all, I love you, and I really like fucking you."

A laugh bubbled out of her. "That *is* good news."

"Second, we've been invited to a Memorial Day party at a squadmember's house. You'll be able to meet some of the team I used to work with."

"Oh. That should be fun, right?" Would they like her? She wasn't anything like his ex-wife—*That's probably a good thing, on second thought.* But would they think her an interloper?

"Don't worry, they'll love you. And even if they don't, I do." Greg tipped her head up again.

"Damn, how did you know what I was thinking?"

"I've seen the movie 'Meet the Parents', and Beta Squad is the equivalent of my family." He shook his head. "They aren't like that, and to be honest, most of the men in my squad didn't like my ex, even when she was my wife. Besides, only three of the other guys are married so there isn't a wives club or anything."

Zamora sighed. "Anything else?"

"Yeah, one last thing. I have tomorrow and the next day off from training so I can hang out with you at the shop if you don't mind."

She gasped. "Mind?" She tightened her grip on him and hugged him. "I don't mind at all. That means I can spend all day with you." But she pulled back and narrowed her eyes at him. "You won't get bored, will you?"

"Nah. Besides." He gave her a lazy smirk. "I have reading I need to do for the instructor's course, and if I get tired of that, I can watch your ass and boobs while you work."

"Slut!" She slapped his chest.

"Bet your ass I am." He laughed as he tightened his arms around her. "But only for you." He kissed her forehead. "I love you, Zamora."

His words warmed her heart and soul. "I love you, too, Greg." She reached up to turn off the light before snuggling up to him again. "Thanks for staying in my bed with me."

He chuckled. "If I have my way, I'll never leave your bed again."

That suited her just fine.

CHAPTER SIXTEEN

Sunday came faster than Zamora expected, but it dawned warm and she woke happy. Greg loved her, and meant it, and he'd spent the previous week with her at the shop. Stan had shown up that first Thursday, but stayed away the rest of the week and she'd relaxed. Greg had been jovial and downright talkative while at the shop, keeping Toby, Brianna and other customers laughing when he wasn't reading his 'homework.' He even expressed an interest in getting some ink, and she'd secretly hoped he wanted it on one of his glorious pectorals.

But he had some errands to run on Sunday and said he'd be back to pick her up when she was done for the day. She missed his presence, but Brianna remained up front so she had some company.

"I think we've ordered too much red ink. I counted three boxes full up here." Brianna stretched as she came down off the stepstool. She'd organized the ink supplies and replacement parts for the ink guns.

"Yeah, I think it's because I can never find it when I'm looking for it so I write it down to order it. How are we doing with India ink black?"

Brianna bit her lip. "We're a little low. I think we can

make it through this week if we don't have too many folks coming in, but we definitely need to order some."

"Okay. I'll put it on the list." Zamora wrote it down on her pad.

Someone opened the front door and came in as Brianna folded up the stepstool. "I'll get that and put this away."

"Sounds good."

Zamora frowned at her list, trying to remember all the things she'd thought she needed while Greg had been at the shop. Nothing came to mind as she heard Brianna greet someone. She didn't hear the response, but after a moment of silence, Brianna called out to her.

"Hey, Zamora?"

"Yeah?"

"Can you come out here a moment?"

Zamora paused and looked toward the front, the hair standing up on the back of her neck. Nothing looked out of place, but she had a bad feeling creeping in her stomach. She'd done as Greg and Toby asked, and reported Stan to the police. As she predicted, they weren't very concerned with her problem, but at least she had the complaint filed. She grabbed her phone and stuffed it in her pocket as she headed for the front. *Just in case.*

"Sure. What's up?" She came around the partition wall and stopped.

"Hello, Zamora."

All the blood froze in her veins as she looked into the dead eyes of Stan Lords. *Damn, why did he have to come back now when Greg's not here?* She almost smacked her own forehead. *Because he's been waiting for Greg to be gone, dumbass.* Yeah, she was a little slow on the uptake, but her mind tended to short-circuit when she had a large caliber handgun pointed at her.

"Stan. What are you doing here and why did you bring that?" She pointed to the gun. "Are you planning to rob us?"

He scowled and snorted. "I'd never be so crass. I have plenty of money. Or I will. Come over here beside your little tramp of an assistant."

"Hey!" Brianna scowled right back at him. "I didn't call you a preppy prick. You don't get to call me names."

"Brianna." Zamora dropped her voice and kept her gaze on Stan. "Not now." Her turquoise-haired friend snapped her mouth shut, but anger radiated throughout her body. "What's this about, Stan? Why are you here with the weapon?"

"We're going to talk about a few things and how life is going to be better for both of us." He waved the barrel at Brianna. "Now go lock the doors and turn the sign to CLOSED like a good girl."

Oh please don't let Brianna do anything. Zamora knew the younger woman was a raging feminist and didn't take shit from anyone, but she didn't want either of them to get hurt. *Please let her just do as he demands.*

Brianna scowled, but her lips remained shut as she went to the doors, Stan watching her the whole time. Zamora took advantage of his distraction to text Toby the SOS message again. Fortunately, the top text box held both Toby's and Greg's names, and she was able to add Stan's name to the message along with "GUN" before Stan turned around. The last thing she did as she stuffed the phone back into her pocket was set it on vibrate.

"Good job, tramp. Now, into the back. Both of you." Stan waved the gun's muzzle at them and Brianna tromped over to Zamora with a sullen snarl. "Let's go have a nice little chat about the future, shall we, girls?"

He gestured for them to proceed into the back room ahead of him. Zamora felt Brianna's fury, but from Stan she got nothing but calm satisfaction. What the hell did he want? She and Brianna headed for the futon, but Stan stopped them before they could sit down.

"Uh-uh, both of you into different torture chairs."

"Torture chairs?" Zamora raised her eyebrows. "We sit together or not at all?"

Stan shook his head, *tsking* with a pitying look before he swung the pistol toward Brianna. "Sit in one of the chairs or I shoot her."

"What?" Had he lost his mind?

"Sit down, Zamora, or I shoot your little tramp and let her bleed out all over the floor." He shot her a pleasant smile and she shivered. Now she understood what Greg meant when he said they could smell the crazy on Stan.

"Fuck you, asshole, I'll sit where I please."

Oh, sweet God, not now, Brianna. Stan didn't do anything more than widen his smile before he took two steps toward Brianna and pistol-whipped her across the face. Brianna cried out as she went down and Zamora shrieked her fury, but stopped moving when he swung back toward her.

"Ah ah ah." He shook his head. "No, no, she had it coming. She shouldn't talk to her betters like that. She's just an inked-up little whore and good for nothing more than a quick fuck to scratch an itch."

"Oh my God, Stan. What the hell? She's my friend. You can't hit her!" Zamora made to duck past him to help Brianna up, but he cocked the hammer back on his pistol and aimed it for Brianna's head.

"She'll be fine, but not if you don't go sit down." Stan stared at her, his lip curling into a sneer.

She swallowed hard and backed off toward one of the tattoo chairs. Her phone vibrated with an incoming text, but she couldn't pull it out to read it while Stan watched her.

"That's a good girl, Zamora." He reached down and yanked Brianna to her feet. "Now, you go sit down and learn from Zamora's goodness, and maybe there'll be hope for you yet."

Brianna glared fire at him, but said nothing as he roughly shoved her into one of the other chairs. She held her face with her hand, a bruise already forming on her check and temple. Stan produced a roll of duct tape and tossed it into Brianna's lap.

"Be a good girl and wrap that around one hand, please."

She opened her mouth to protest, but Zamora caught her eye and gave a quick shake of the head. She didn't know what Stan *wasn't* capable of, but she knew he'd get violent, and she didn't want Brianna hurt any more than she'd been already. Stan turned his back on Zamora as he watched Brianna wrap the silver tape around her forearm and the chair's arm.

Zamora slipped her phone from her pocket and swiped the screen. Toby had responded to her text with all capital letters.

HOLY FUCK. CALL THE COPS.

Yeah, she concurred. She wished she could respond, but Stan shifted his stance and she shoved the phone back into her pocket. Hopefully, Toby would do it for her. She couldn't even answer him as Stan fixed his gaze on her and gave her a benevolent smile.

"Now then, Zamora. I need you to secure her other hand with the tape so we can talk like civilized people." Stan waved the weapon at her. "And don't get any violent ideas, pumpkin. I have the gun."

"Yeah, that just makes you a big man, doesn't it?" Zamora clearly caught Brianna's mutter as she stood. Her own fury made her shake, but she moved to Brianna's chair.

"Now tape her down. There's a good girl."

Zamora thought fast as she met Brianna's gaze. Pain and rage filled the other woman's eyes, and Zamora wished she could communicate what she had in mind. Instead, she mouthed "I'm sorry" and pulled a length of tape off the roll.

Keeping her back to Stan, she tore the length, but

folded the loose end onto itself before wrapping it around Brianna's wrist. Brianna's eyes filled with surprise when the non-sticky side rested against her skin. Zamora gave a short nod as she pulled it snug and wrapped the rest of the sticky tape under the arm of the chair and back over the first loop of tape. She wanted it tight enough for Brianna to appear to struggle, but still loose enough she could work one hand free.

When she'd finished, she stood and turned to face Stan. "Done. Now put the gun down so we can talk."

"Oh, aren't you sweet, Zamora. But no, I'll be keeping my weapon until we're done with our discussion." Stan shook his head and waved her back to the other tattoo chair.

She returned to her own chair, but she shook her head. "No. I'm not talking until you put down the gun. And here's the thing, you can shoot me with it, but then I'm definitely not saying anything. So put the gun down and we'll talk. But until then, mum's the word."

Her phone vibrated in her pocket just as Stan barked a harsh laugh and his expression turned dark. "Oh, I won't shoot you, Zamora." The muzzle of the gun swung to face Brianna. "I'll shoot her so we won't be interrupted."

You sick sonovaprick! Outrage stung the back of her throat and her eyes narrowed. She'd be damned before she let him kill her friend, but she'd run out of options until Brianna could free her hands. And Zamora had to keep Stan's attention on her until that happened. *Or until the cops get here.* She hoped Toby had called them when she didn't answer his text. Her phone buzzed again and she wished she could read the incoming texts. *Anything to get some good news.* But Stan waited for her to respond.

"Fine. Have it your way." She shrugged and gestured for him to continue, grateful she remained unbound. "Go ahead and talk." *Doesn't mean I have to answer.* Except she had to keep Brianna safe until the cops got there or they got the gun away from Stan. *And he always was a chatty*

182

bastard.

"Good girl."

Holy fuck, if he keeps calling me that, I'm definitely gonna find a way to clobber him.

Despite his approval, the weapon never wavered from Brianna's chest. "Now we can make our plans for the future."

Zamora blinked. *Future? What future?*

"First things first, we'll fix your hair and make you pretty again, and we'll remove those horrible marks on your skin." He waved his free hand at her tattoos, his expression determined. "Can you imagine how happy your parents will be when they see you all cleaned up and us together?" He smiled with benevolent condescension. "They'll be overjoyed at your change of heart."

Change of heart? What the hell is he talking about?

"You'll see. We'll be perfect together. The perfect couple, Mr. and Mrs. Stan Lords."

Zamora blinked and shot a look at Brianna. The other woman looked just as surprised, but she crossed her eyes and stuck her tongue out to indicate her opinion of Stan's sanity. Zamora had to agree.

"We'll have to change your friends, of course. You can't been seen with degenerates like these." He waved at Brianna with his free hand. "Or that swaggering sailor." Stan thrust his face into her space, almost nose-to-nose. "I saw him kiss you, Zamora. You, my fiancée! You shouldn't be kissing other men when you're meant to be with me." He shook his head and *tsked.* He stroked his fingers across her cheek before grabbing her chin in a tight grip. His eyes gleamed with the fires of insanity as he stared at her. "You won't kiss anyone other than me from now on."

She couldn't move her head with it in his grip, but caught Brianna wiggling her wrist out of the corner of her eye. *God, I hope she gets free.* Brianna had once told her she'd started taking self-defense classes to ward off some of the drunk Navy guys while heading home at night. Zamora hoped the training would prove useful to attack someone because they'd have to overpower Stan, and insanity often made people exceptionally strong. Add to that his possession of the pistol, and they had a particularly hard challenge.

"Do you understand me?"

Zamora blinked back into the present and the scents of Stan's cologne mixed with the "minty freshness" of his breath. He squeezed her chin hard and shook her head for her attention.

"Do you understand me, Zamora?"

Do I understand you're a crazy sonuvaprick who ought to be locked up or put down? Yes, sir. She locked her lips together and nodded once.

"Good girl." He nodded sagely and released her face with one last stroke of his fingers down her cheek. She tried not to shudder. "You'll see. It'll be perfect and so full of joy. Just imagine how happy your parents will be when they see us together again. Everything will be back to the way it should be."

Behind him, Brianna worked her left hand free of the tape Zamora had wrapped around it, her glare on Stan as hot as a laser sight from a sniper's rifle. *How the hell is she gonna get free of the other tape?* It would make too much noise. Somehow Zamora had to keep Stan focused on her.

"Why?"

Stan frowned. "Why what?"

"Why do you think my parents would be happy to see me? To see either of us?" Her intent was to needle him, but the question was legitimate. "They wrote me off, Stan. They wanted nothing to do with me when I left. They even cut me out of their will." She had no idea if the latter was true, but it didn't matter to her. She didn't want their money.

"Oh, honeybun, I know that hurt you, but we'll make it

all better." He gave her a placating smile. "You'll see. When they see us back together, they'll be so happy and they'll take you back in a heartbeat. We'll just clean you up, get rid of the delinquents around you, and show you're my perfect wife, and they'll love you again. Okay?"

No, not okay. Nothing would ever be okay with Stan Lords, even if he could get her back to her family. But in truth, she'd written them off when they only valued the money and the appearance of perfection over their daughter, and that was a betrayal she couldn't forgive.

But she'd gain nothing by resisting the sick bastard, so she nodded. *I just hope Brianna gets free or Toby sends the cops.* Either way, it would be a long, scary night.

CHAPTER SEVENTEEN

Greg grabbed the coffees from the barista with the flirty smile and retreated to the table where Gabe Szellem waited for him. They agreed to meet at The Navy Bean Coffee shop since their activities weren't strictly on mission. Or legal. But Greg didn't trust Stan Lords to keep his crazy in check and he needed to know as much as he could before he faced the bastard again.

"So what'd you find out?" Greg settled into the chair opposite Gabe as he tapped on the keys of his tablet's keyboard.

Gabe shrugged and grimaced. "Not much in my initial search. He comes from a wealthy family out of Palo Alto. Looks like they made their money through social media site ownership."

"Social media sites? Like Facebook and Google?"

"Yep, although they were mostly investors, but it's definitely paid off."

"Damn, I bet."

Gabe nodded. "So while they're not 'old money', they move in the wealthy circles, and wealthy people don't like scandals. They often get swept under the rug and people get bribed to keep quiet."

Greg sipped his coffee and leaned his elbows on the table. "What scandals have the Lords swept away and paid under the table?"

"Oh the usual. Illegitimate children, shady money, but one stands out." Gabe clicked away on the keyboard. "Apparently about six years ago, your man Stanley Willard Lords the Second—"

"Yeesh, that explains a lot." Greg grimaced and shook his head.

"Yeah, I believe it. SWL Two beat a woman within an inch of her life. Kicked her ass so badly she had to have reconstructive surgery on her face and breasts, and she never walked again."

"Holy shit. And this was the guy Zamora was engaged to?"

"I dunno. Did she say this was her ex?" Gabe raised his gaze from the computer.

"Yeah. She said they had history. I wonder if the sonuvaprick hit her." Anger rose in Greg's chest and settled into a cold seething lump. He didn't tolerate men who hit women, who saw them as less.

"If he did, I'll help you hide the body, and make sure his finances get distributed to domestic abuse shelters." He read a little more on the screen. "Hell, I might do that anyway."

Greg's phone buzzed with an incoming text, but he ignored it to read more on good old Stan.

"Scratch that. I don't think he has any finances to redistribute." Gabe shook his head.

"What? Why?"

"It looks like it's all tied up in trusts and he only gets an allowance of ten grand a month."

"Ten grand is an allowance?" Greg shook his head. "Fuck. I'd like that kind of allowance."

"Well, considering his folks probably make more like a

million a month, it's not very much." Gabe typed on the keyboard. "But I could divert that to the domestic violence shelters if you ever need me to."

Greg shot him a raised eyebrow. "That's not exactly legal, is it?"

"Hell no. None of this is legal, but sometimes playing by all the rules doesn't get the job done." He grimaced and shrugged one shoulder. "But it's something to keep in mind when dealing with the assholes of the world."

"Yeah." Greg nodded and fished out his phone when it buzzed again. "That's for sure." He would've liked to do that to the guy fucking his wife, but maybe that asshole had actually done him a favor.

He swiped the screen and blinked at the capital letters marching across the screen.

SOS STAN AT THINK INK GUN

It took Greg several seconds to translate the unpunctuated words, but his gut tightened and his heartbeat increased. *Oh holy shitballs.*

"I have to go."

"What's wrong?" What he liked about Gabe was the man's ability to get straight to the problem at hand.

"Mr. Lords has shown up at Zamora's place with a gun."

"Aw shit." Gabe powered down the computer and threw it in his bag. "I'll follow you."

"You're coming with me?"

Gabe gave him a raised eyebrow. "Ever heard of a single SEAL going into a situation when he has a teammate nearby?"

Greg snorted. "Nope."

"Good. I'll follow you."

"Sounds good." Greg nodded and opened the text message to find Toby's number. He dialed as he strode out of The Navy Bean and headed for his FJ Cruiser. "Toby? It's Greg Killian."

"Oh, thank God. Stan came back to Think Ink." Toby sounded panicked.

"I know. Are you there?" Greg unlocked his vehicle and slid behind the wheel.

"No. I had today off, but Zamora and Brianna are there, and neither are answering my texts."

Greg's gut clenched, but he pushed the fear aside. He couldn't worry about what he didn't know.

"They probably can't get to their phones with Lords there. Did you call the cops?" He pulled out of the parking lot and headed toward the tattoo shop.

"Yeah, but I have no idea when they'll get there. Do you think they'll take it seriously?"

"A man waving a gun? Yeah, they won't mess around with that.

The sky opened up overhead and rain sheeted down in a summer downpour. Greg swore as his SUV fishtailed on the wet and greasy pavement when he turned onto the main drag through Coronado. Gabe's crossover SUV slid in behind him.

"Are you okay? Are you driving?" Toby's voice took on disbelief.

"Yeah, almost to Think Ink."

"What are you gonna do, Killian? You can't go in guns blazing."

"SEALs rarely go in 'guns blazing' unless we have to, Toby. We're more subtle than that." He got the Cruiser under control and slowed down as he passed the Surf 'n Turf bar near Think Ink. "How fast can you get to the tattoo shop?"

"Why? I don't have the skills to take down a gunman."

"No, I wouldn't expect that of you." He scanned the front of Think Ink Tattoos, but the door was closed, the entry dark, and the OPEN sign off. "But you do have a key to the back door. Otherwise I'd have to pick the lock."

Toby's voice hardened with determination. "I'll be

there in ten minutes."

"Roger that."

Greg disconnected the call and stopped at the red light at the next intersection as he considered his options. If the cops didn't take the threat to Zamora's place seriously, she'd need backup from outside the police. While Greg and Gabe weren't armed and Greg wasn't an active SEAL, they both had the ability to take down an armed terrorist, even one-handed. And Lords had become a terrorist when he decided to threaten Zamora's place of work.

Turning left, he found a place to park in a small parking lot of a local market. Gabe pulled in beside him and they both got out.

"What's the plan?" Gabe pocketed his keys as he locked up his vehicle.

"Let's see if we can spot anything as we walk by before we swing toward the back entrance. Toby, Zamora's business partner, said he'd meet us there with keys."

"Since when do SEALs need keys?" Gabe snorted as they headed across the street.

"We don't. But we might be able to get him to be a distraction through the front while we come in the back." Greg hunched his shoulders against the rain and slowed his steps as they approached the front of Think Ink Tattoos. "Let's take a look and see what shows up."

Gabe fell into step with him, his own head down as the rain matted their hair against their skulls. Greg's leather jacket sloughed off most of the water, but some found its way down his neck. He pushed his discomfort to the back of his mind and ambled past the front of Think Ink Tattoos.

The room beyond the doors sat dark and quiet. He took hold of the handle as if he planned to enter, but only tugged a little to be certain the doors were locked. Not many other people walked the sidewalk on Sundays, but with the rain, it made the town pretty empty. Gabe stopped beside him, casually scanning the room behind the glass.

"I can't see anything, but if they're in there, they'll probably be in the back where passersby can't spot them." He pressed his face against the glass, his hand shielding his eyes to look within. "Still can't see much, but there's a light on in the back."

"Roger that. Let's head for the back door." Greg turned on his heel and strode toward the alley between the Surf 'n Turf and Think Ink. "We'll wait for Toby and see if we can make a distraction work in our favor."

The sky darkened as the sun slipped toward the horizon and the rain pattered on the alley floor in front of his toes. The smells of wet cement and rotting garbage from the Dumpsters filled his nose, but he sniffed deeper, hoping there'd be something to give him a clue about Zamora. Unfortunately, he suspected Lords had kept the women inside and left no traces where they could be easily found. Greg forced himself to walk, not to bring any attention to the tattoo shop before he was ready, but anger and concern beat a steady rhythm in his chest as they rounded the corner to the back of the building.

A solid Navy blue awning covered the door to the tattoo shop, leaving a little pocket of dry against the brick building. Zamora's car sat a few spaces away with a Harley parked beside it. *Brianna rides a Harley? Damn.* He might have to revise his opinion of the turquoise-haired woman. A couple other vehicles sat in other spaces down the way, but otherwise nothing moved in the parking lot.

Greg stepped into the cover provided by the awning to wait for Toby. Gabe settled against the wall beside him, but said nothing. Greg tried to remember the layout of the back of the shop as he set his mind to the question of how he'd tackle this problem. Lords had a weapon and that meant someone could get shot. He'd much rather it was Lords or himself. He didn't want either of the women hurt by this asshole.

He listened carefully for sirens to tell him the cops

were on their way, but besides the wind and the rain, no other sounds reached his ears.

Come on, Toby. Zamora needs us to get in there.

He just hoped it wouldn't be too little, too late.

CHAPTER EIGHTEEN

Zamora wanted to scream, but she sealed her lips together as Stan paraded around her tattoo shop, waving his pistol to emphasize his points. She'd tuned him out when he launched into his version of how their life together would be and scanned the room for possible weapons. What could she use to distract him enough to get the gun away from him? She was so engrossed in her thoughts, she missed his question.

"Isn't that true, Zamora sweetheart?"

"Isn't what true, Stan?" She blinked up at him as he stopped in front of her, the muzzle of the pistol pointed at Brianna.

"Weren't you listening? It's not good to ignore your man when he's talking to you." Without warning, he raised his free hand and slapped her across the cheek.

Pain exploded throughout her face and she cried out as she slammed back in the chair. Tears sprang to her eyes and anger unfurled in her chest as she turned her outraged gaze on him.

"Aw now, see what you made me do? I wouldn't hit you if you didn't ignore me. Don't cry, sweetheart. As soon as we have our wedding, it'll be all better. You'll see." He reached out to cup her cheek, but she jerked away and he paused with a frown. "Don't you like my touches, sweetheart?" His expression cleared and he nodded sagely. "Ah, I see. You're a blushing, virginal bride. I understand. Don't worry. It'll be so good on our wedding night."

What the fuck is he talking about? Zamora definitely had to get out of here with Brianna. She blinked back her tears and scanned the room again, catching Brianna's eye. The other woman had been steadily working her hand free of Zamora's tape-job while Stan strutted about, but even if they both rushed him, he still had the gun.

"Yes, we'll clean you up and dress you in virginal white, and you'll be the most beautiful bride, Zamora. Just like we dreamed." He spun on them and pointed at Brianna, who froze. "Not like that little painted whore over there. She's only good for taking dick in her cunt and being left in the dirt."

The sneer on his face was ugly, and his sickness blazed from his eyes. Brianna's eyes narrowed, but she didn't make a move until he turned back to Zamora with a sickeningly sweet smile. "But you're not like that, are you, sweetheart?"

God, if he calls me sweetheart one more time, I'm gonna hit him with my tablet.

She blinked and shot a look toward the nearest table. She'd been carrying the tablet when he herded them into the back. It might not be a baseball bat, and it might ruin the electronics, but she remembered how hard to swing an object to bring down an assailant from her martial arts classes. *And if I hit him in the head with one of the corners...*

She could kill him. Part of her wanted to. Her anger had settled into her gut and solidified into determination. He'd gone well beyond help and prison seemed too good for him. But the other part of her didn't want his death on her hands and she refused to be judge and jury, even if he seemed to deserve it.

All I need is a little distraction and I can grab the tablet. She'd whack him over the head and grab the pistol then she and Brianna could truss him up like a BDSM doll. Zamora returned her gaze to Brianna. The turquoise-haired woman watched Stan, biding her time until he turned away again. Zamora's phone vibrated in her pocket with new text messages and she ached to pull it out to read them, but she didn't want Stan to take it away.

"But you're prefect for me and we'll be perfect together, Zamora." Stan turned his back to Brianna and she wiggled her left hand free of the tape. "Don't you agree, sweetheart?"

I'm not your sweetheart, you asshole.

Stan stopped and frowned. "Zamora?"

She must have scowled because he cocked his head like a curious dog. "You don't think we'd be perfect together?"

She opened her mouth to say something when the front door opened and Toby's voice rang through the shop.

"Zamora, Brianna, are you in here?"

Stan turned toward the front and the world erupted into motion.

Brianna tore her right hand free of the tape and lunged out of the chair for Stan. He spun back toward her, but she collided with him too early to get a bead on her with the pistol. Zamora took the opportunity to bolt for the table to grasp the tablet and turn back to the scuffle going on in the room.

Brianna groaned as she struggled with Stan for the weapon, their arms straining over their heads. Zamora advanced on them as Toby called from the front again. She didn't have time to answer as Stan jerked his gun hand down and forced the muzzle toward Brianna's head. Brianna snarled and ducked just as Stan pulled the trigger.

The gunshot cracked through the space loud enough to

make Zamora instinctively duck, but Brianna jerked and let go of Stan. Zamora watched her fall, blood on her chest and shoulder, and fury burned away all the fear.

"You hurt my friend, you sick sonovaprick!" Her roar accompanied three steps and swinging the tablet at his head with all her weight behind it.

The backdoor banged open just as Stan turned toward her and he caught the tablet in the side of his head. He staggered and fell, releasing the pistol and crashing to the floor beside one of the chairs. Zamora dropped the tablet and ran for the gun as two large men burst into the room. Neither of them said anything, but one tackled Stan and the other headed straight for Brianna as Zamora scrambled to grasp the weapon before anyone could get up.

"Oh my God, Zamora, are you okay?" Toby skidded to a stop in the room as Stan spat curses and struggled against the taller man's hold.

"Fine. Brianna's been shot." Zamora flicked the safety on the pistol and turned to scan the room. An unfamiliar man crouched over Brianna, his t-shirt off and wrapped around Brianna's shoulder in a make-shift bandage. "Toby, get the gauze bandages from the cabinet."

"And call 911. She's bleeding." The voice belonged to a man Zamora didn't recognize, but he seemed just as concerned with Brianna's health as she was.

The other guy who'd tackled Stan had both the asshole's arms folded up behind him with one knee in the small of Stan's back. It took her several heartbeats to realize Greg held him down with effortless power.

"Oh, God, Greg." Relief made her voice come out in a whine and he shifted to look at her.

"Yeah, I'm here, Z. Hand me the duct tape, will you?" He nodded to the silver tape roll on the table.

She set the gun down and handed the tape to Greg, resisting the urge to kick Stan in the face as he lay on her floor, snarling. Greg wrapped Stan's wrists together behind his back as easily as wrapping a mummy and eventually handed the tape back to Zamora.

"You can't do this to me! I'm an important man and that's my fiancée! You release me now!" Stan ranted from the floor and Zamora pulled off an extra strip of tape.

"Roll him on his side, please."

Greg raised an eyebrow, but did as she asked.

"What are you doing? Leave me alone! I demand—"

Zamora stretched the tape over his mouth and the sound shut off immediately. She nodded in satisfaction.

"Much better. Now get him off the floor into a chair and the cops can deal with him." She shifted her attention to Toby as he returned with the bandages. "You did call the cops, right?"

Toby scowled. "Of course. You'd know that if you checked your phone."

"Oh, I would've loved to, but it's hard to do so when the one waving a gun around might shoot you if you do." She grimaced and swallowed back tears of frustration and fear. "I'm just glad you came anyway."

"Of course I'd come." Toby shook his head then paused as sirens sounded in the distance. "And so will the cops."

"Thank God." Zamora rubbed her arms as her body started to shake in reaction to the adrenaline pumping through her body. "I think I broke the tablet." She scanned the room and remembered Brianna. "Oh, God. Brianna!" She skidded over to where the half naked man crouched beside her bleeding friend. "She's gonna be okay, right?"

He nodded his silver head. "Yeah, it looks like a through-and-through. It doesn't seem to have hit anything vital."

Brianna moaned and hissed. "Nothing vital? Holy shit, you gotta be fuckin' kidding me. Everything on my body is vital."

Toby snorted. "She's gonna be fine if she can still

swear at you."

The silver-haired man grinned. "Swearing is fine, but you better hold still until the paramedics show up. You don't want to make the bleeding worse."

"I don't need the paramedics." Brianna sounded sullen.

"Yes, you do, Brianna, and it's too late anyway. I called them and they're on their way, so just zip it." Toby crossed his arms over his chest and stared her down.

"Great, just great. And who are you?" Brianna shot a look at the man holding the bandages to her shoulder.

"Master Chief Petty Officer Gabe Szellem at your service, ma'am." He nodded as he kept an eye on her injury. Brianna's expression shifted toward interest.

"Master Chief, eh. So would you be another SEAL like Zamora's house guest?"

"Yes, ma'am." He said it with a hint of a smile, but without any trace of accent.

"Oooh, maybe I will get a quick lay with a SEAL after all."

"Brianna." Zamora rubbed a hand over her face.

"What? You think I'm going to let a serendipitous opportunity like this go? Ow!" She hissed and closed her eyes as Gabe pressed the bandages to her wound. "Motherfucker, that hurts."

"How 'bout I take a rain check on that suggestion, Brianna?" Gabe's voice held amusement.

"Just as long as you cash it in when I'm better."

"Yes, ma'am."

New pandemonium broke out as the police made their entrance into the tattoo shop and Zamora had to direct them. They took Stan into custody and threw handcuffs on his wrists before cutting off the tape. She suggested they leave the tape over his mouth, but they didn't listen. That gave them the opportunity to hear him rant and rave about his being entitled to reparations for being treated so badly.

She, Toby, Greg and Gabe gave statements about what

happened. Brianna wanted to add her own testimony, but the paramedics bundled her into the ambulance and headed to the medical center. Zamora made copies of the security footage of both the front and back rooms of her shop and gave them to the detectives. It was a long, repetitive process that lasted well after her regular Sunday business hours and she had to go down to the precinct to give her statement.

By the time everything was said and done, the sun had set and they had enough evidence to put Stan away for a long time. Still, Zamora worried his family's penchant for sweeping away scandals might get him free before he saw jail time. *Maybe Lady Justice will turn a blind eye to money this time around.* It was disheartening to think that might not be the case.

She stepped outside into the night air and rubbed her arms again. She just wanted to go home and hide for a week. She ran her hands over her face, scrubbing her eyes as she tried to decide what to do. Thank God the shop was closed on Mondays.

She took her hands away from her face and realized she no longer stood alone. Greg wrapped his arms around her from behind and the other SEAL, Gabe he said his name was, stood silently beside them. She didn't say a word, just leaned back into Greg's warmth and closed her eyes.

****

Greg relaxed for the first time since he read Zamora's text and reveled in the feeling of having her safe in his arms. His heart ached at the exhaustion wreathing her mouth and eyes, but she was safe.

He thought his heart would stop when he heard the gunshot and Zamora's resulting roar through the backdoor of the tattoo shop. He thanked his lucky stars Toby had unlocked it because he would've broken something going through it. He caught the tail end of Zamora's two-handed blow to the side of Stan's head before he saw red. It was a good thing Stan had already been taken down because Greg would've beaten the living shit out of him.

"I've got you, Zamora. You're safe."

"Yeah, but for how long? I'm sure his family's fancy lawyers will get him off on some technicality like insanity and he'll be free to wreak havoc."

"Only if the lawyer does *pro bono* work." Gabe turned his head and smiled benignly. "Mr. Lords won't be able to afford a fancy lawyer."

Zamora shot a look at Greg then back to Gabe. "How do you figure that?"

Gabe shrugged. "I was checking his financial history and it seems he recognized his problem. In a moment of lucidity yesterday, he authorized a donation of ninety percent of his monthly stipend to the Coronado Battered Women's Shelter. It was verified and notarized by his attorney, and should go into effect on June first this year, withdrawn automatically. The payment is locked for at least a year."

Greg eyed the other SEAL, but Gabe's expression never flickered or changed. *Damn, remind me not to play poker with this guy.* He suspected Gabe had done some fancy finger-work with his keyboard and hacked into SWL Two's bank records. He didn't know how Gabe had done it and frankly didn't want to, but setting up an automatic donation to a charity seemed fitting for the bastard.

"Well that was unusually kind of him..." Zamora narrowed her eyes at Gabe, but he never lost his benign innocence. "Why would he do that? It doesn't make any sense."

Gabe turned his hands palm up. "Maybe he had a 'come to Jesus' moment and did something for the greater good when he still had all of his sanity."

Greg made a mental note never to piss Gabe off if he wanted to see his Navy pension. Zamora didn't look convinced but after a few more moments, she sighed and her shoulders sagged. He held her tighter and wished he could take all her worries from her. He would if he could. She was his heart and soul, and he wanted to be with her through all her tomorrows.

When he thought he'd lose her to a psychotic lunatic, his love and need became crystal clear.

I want her forever.

He'd sworn to himself that he'd never marry another woman after his marriage to MaryAnn fell apart. But when he thought Zamora might die at the hands of Stan Lords, he suddenly wanted to wake up each morning looking at her crimson hair mussed from sex and sleep. He wanted to discover all her favorite foods and learn her favorite movies. He even wanted to revel in their shared coffee snobbery.

"Come on, Z. Let me take you home."

"Okay."

He led her to his FJ Cruiser and opened the passenger door. She climbed in without comment and slumped against the seat as he shut her in. Gabe had followed them and leaned against the hood near the driver's door. Greg nodded to him.

"Thanks for the help, Szellem. It's much appreciated."

"Yeah, not a problem. Besides, I'll hit you up whenever I need some of your special skills." Gabe shrugged and grinned.

"You mean when you need some shit blown up?"

"Yeah, or a tattoo." Gabe winked. "That might come in handy." He sobered and nodded his head toward Zamora. "She's a helluva woman."

"Yeah, she is."

"Can I offer you a word of advice from someone who lost a helluva woman?"

Greg raised his eyebrows, but nodded. "Sure."

"Devote your attention in your down time to her like you do when you're on an op, and you'll never lose her."

Greg nodded slowly. "Hard lesson learned?"

Gabe shrugged, sorrow flashing across his face before benign mask returned. "The only easy day was yesterday, right?"

"Hooyah, Master Chief."

"Hooyah." He gave a sharp nod and headed off toward his own vehicle.

Greg watched him go as he settled behind the wheel of his Cruiser. Zamora followed his gaze and grunted with surprise.

"Is he really a Navy SEAL?"

"Yep." Greg nodded and started the engine. "The most average looking guy you'll ever meet, but he can still sneak up on you and kill you before you even realize he's there."

She shifted her gaze to him. "You like him."

"Yeah, I do. I'm kinda sorry I'm off the squad now that he's here. Would've been nice to work with him in the field."

"Maybe you'll have a chance to work with him anyway. Can't be in the SEALs forever."

"That's the truth. And he's a Master Chief, which means he's a lot closer to retirement than I was." It was still a bitter pill to swallow, but he had the training of new men to look forward to.

"Are, Greg." Zamora's voice and expression turned firm. "You're a SEAL, you're not retired." She turned her head to look out the window. "You'll always be a SEAL to me. My SEAL."

Her voice grew so quiet he had to strain to hear her. Had she said what he thought she had? That he was *her* SEAL? The thought warmed his chest from the inside out and sparked more certainty in his determination to be with Zamora forever.

But first he needed to take her home and pamper her.

He pondered Gabe's words about keeping his woman as he made the drive home. Once there, he helped Zamora out of the Cruiser and led her into the house, listening hard for anything amiss. *Old habits die hard.* She didn't seem to notice his extra vigilance and switched on the lights in the kitchen.

"I'm going to make some tea."

"Sounds good. I'm going to run you a bath."

"No thanks, I don't want one." She shook her head.

"What?" Some of his pampering plans slithered away. "Why not?"

"I don't like soaking in my own filth. I'd rather take a shower." She set the kettle on the stove and rubbed her arms with her opposite hands.

"Tell you what, why don't you go start the shower and I'll join you in a bit. I have a few things I need to do. Then I'll wash your hair. Okay?"

She blinked. "You'll wash my hair?"

"Yeah. And your body if you let me." He smiled before he reached out to kiss her lips in a tender greeting. "Go start the shower, inkheart, and I'll be there in a bit."

She sighed and leaned into his chest. "Say that again."

"What? Inkheart?"

"Yeah. That's it. Stan kept saying 'sweetheart' and it sounded so wrong, so gross. I'm not his sweetheart."

Pride and pleasure made him want to puff out his chest, but he resisted. "No, you're my inkheart, my beautiful, strong, amazing woman, my friend with more than just benefits."

"Thank God." She hugged him and he wanted to stay there forever in her arms, but she pushed back. "I'm gonna get in the shower."

"Roger that. I'll be there in a few."

She nodded and retreated toward the bedrooms. He watched her go, his mind already cataloging what he needed to do before he joined her. *Make tea, set out her robe, light candles, throw the towels in the dryer.* He heard the shower start just as he found the matches for the candles. The kettle whistled by the time he'd set out her robe and he trotted back to the kitchen to pour the water into the teapot. He threw the towels in the dryer and shucked his clothes on the way to her bathroom, ready to take Gabe's advice. *Devote your attention in your down time to your woman.* Hell yeah, he would. Zamora was worth it.

He found her leaning against the tiled wall, her shoulders shaking as she sobbed in reaction to the events of the day. Greg's heart ached and he stepped into the shower with her, gently gathering her in to his arms. She didn't resist and he held her as she wept.

"I-I'm sorry." Her voice came out watery and she tried to wipe away the tears along with the shower water.

"Shhh, no need for that, inkheart. Let it all go. I'm here. I've got you."

She sobbed for a little longer and he reveled in her trust. He wanted to be there for her no matter the events. And now that he'd become an instructor, he could be there for her. He could devote his full attention to her and her needs of him. *Thank God.* He'd never valued that before and it occurred to him MaryAnn hadn't inspired him to give up his selfishness. He thought he'd loved his ex-wife, but really he'd loved the idea of a pretty woman waiting for him.

Zamora was more than just a pretty woman waiting. She didn't need him, not the way MaryAnn had, but she wanted him. She could manage on her own, especially after she took care of Stan with one skilled blow to the head, but she seemed to want Greg around. Want his company and his attention. And Greg wanted to give it to her.

Eventually her sobs wound down, and he was able to step back enough to pour some shampoo in his hands. He scrubbed her scalp in gentle circles, lathering up the soap to coat her silken hair. He loved her crimson tresses and the softness of it. He helped her rinse, added conditioner, and reached for the puff to wash her body. He'd been aching to get his hands on her, to feel her supple curves under his palms, and know she was safe and alive.

Greg kept his ministrations purposeful and gentle. As much as he wanted to make love with her all night long, he didn't want her to believe he only wanted her body. He let her rinse off and kissed the back of her neck.

"Finish up and I'll be waiting for you."

"You're not going to wash up?" She turned drowsy, tear-swollen eyes on him.

"Not at the moment. Take your time." He kissed her again and stepped out into the cooler room.

He toweled off quickly and hurried to his room to throw on shorts and a t-shirt before heading for the kitchen. He'd feed her, take care of her, and hold her through the night. It was something he'd often wished for after a mission and something he missed when his ex seemed less than interested. But he was done thinking about that woman. He wanted only Zamora and her comfort.

By the time she'd finished her shower, he had an omelet burrito made and waiting in the oven, her robe set out for her, and he held a dryer-warmed towel in his arms. When she opened the door he extended the towel and she took it, blinking in surprise when she felt the heat.

"Why is it warm?"

"I threw it in the dryer. I figured you could use a warm towel after your shower."

She nodded slowly. "Yeah. It's wonderful. Thank you."

He smiled, desperately wanting to gather her into his arms again, but biding his time. "You're welcome. There's food waiting, and hot tea, and I set your robe on the bed. Come on out to the living room and have some food."

She grimaced and shook her head. "I'm not hungry."

"Yes, you are, you're just dealing with the mind-fuck from the stress. But your body needs it." He reached for her hand and pulled it to his lips, kissing her knuckles. "Give your body the fuel it needs to process the stress, and you'll feel a lot better."

"But it won't change Brianna's health." She scowled and retrieved her hand from him.

"No, it won't. But she needs you to stay strong so she doesn't have to worry about you." He left the bathroom to grab Zamora's robe. "Besides, she has a whole hospital of people to watch out for her and you can go visit her tomorrow."

"He hurt my friend, Greg."

"I know he did, inkheart, but he's not getting anywhere near you—or her—for a long, long time." He hoped that was true, and if he and Gabe had any say, it would be. "Now, let's get some food into you before I tuck you into bed."

"Will you be coming to bed with me?"

The question warmed his heart along with the hopeful look on her face.

"Yeah, inkheart, I'll hold you all night long."

CHAPTER NINETEEN

The last week of May sped by faster than Zamora expected. While it was rough without Brianna, she and Toby managed to still get inkwork done as well as man the front of the shop. Surprisingly, her tablet had weathered the attack on Stan's head and she took that as a good sign.

She made a point to visit Brianna in the hospital every day and even found time to take treats to the injured soldiers in the recovery ward. Several times she found Master Chief Gabe Szellem visiting Brianna as well and she noticed her turquoise-haired friend seemed to blush a lot more than usual while he sat with her. Gabe had at least ten years on her. *Talk about a May-December relationship.* She shrugged it off. It wasn't her business, but she hoped it would work out between Brianna and the SEAL.

Speaking of SEALs, she had her own and one who had become so much more than a friend. She found herself looking forward to seeing him at home when she was done with work and doing chores became fun with him in her house. They'd fallen into a routine of dinners together each night she didn't stay late at her tattoo shop. He'd started giving her dreamy, pensive smiles when he thought she wasn't looking, and she wondered what he was up to.

"You're still okay with being closed this Sunday for the party, right?" His question held notes of uncertainty .

"Yeah, why? Has it been cancelled or something?"

"No, no. I just wanted to be sure you were okay with it."

Her mind kept running over the conversation all through the rest of the week. She could tell he had something important in mind because he seemed distracted, but he insisted everything was fine whenever she asked him about it.

At last the day arrived and they packed root beer, mashed potatoes, and fruit salad into the back of his SUV before heading off to the Memorial Day party. Greg said the whole squad would be there with their wives and he seemed excited to see them all. She suspected he'd been relieved to hear they'd all come back from their latest "training" mission alive. She didn't blame him at all.

They pulled up in front of a well-maintained ranch style home with a wide porch and parked.

"Wow. Who lives here?" She got out of the Cruiser and headed for the back to retrieve the food.

"Christ and Todd Hunter, and Jim Waters. All SEALs."

"Wow. It's beautiful. Are they, uh, gay or just roommates?"

Greg laughed as he picked up the mashed potatoes and the root beer. "No, Chris is the first female SEAL to make it through BUD/S."

"Wait." Zamora held up a hand as he closed the hatch. "I heard about the first woman SEAL. She was in *your* squad?"

He nodded. "Yep. She was a helluva SEAL. Now she's an instructor. Keeps those boys on their toes."

Zamora snorted. "I just bet she does."

They knocked on the door and were greeted by a tall, blond man who had a sweet Texas accent. He ushered them inside and gave Greg a back-slapping man-hug. Greg introduced her to Chief Warrant Officer Todd Hunter and his wife Chris.

"Awful nice to meet you, Ms. Zamora." Todd shook her hand, but Chris elbowed him.

"Stop hamming up your accent, Magic. She's not a spooked horse."

"I dunno. She looks nervous as a cat in a room full of rockin' chairs. Could be she's enterin' a nest of SEALs and she finds that a bit intimidatin'."

"Well, when you put it that way, hell yeah, I'd be scared, too." Chris rolled her eyes as she held out her hand. "It's nice to meet you, Zamora."

"Don't let her fool you, Zamora." A dark-haired man came up beside Chris and wrapped his arm around her. "She's not afraid of anything. But you are welcome. I'm Jim."

"That's not helping, Retro." Chris elbowed him. "We're all big softies when we're home."

Zamora laughed out some of her nervousness. "Yeah, sure you are. I can tell."

Chris grinned. "Well, *I* am, at least. There's no accounting for these geniuses." She elbowed the men affectionately. "Come on in and meet the rest of the crew. Bam-Bam's been talking a lot about you and I'm pretty sure everyone is curious about the woman who's healed his heart after his divorce."

Zamora blinked and shot a look at Greg. "Healed your heart?"

"Oops, did I let the cat outta the bag?" Chris's smile dropped so fast Zamora wasn't sure it had ever been on her face. "Damn, I'm sorry. I didn't mean to be a blabber-mouth."

"Come on, darlin', let's at least let her into the house before you give away all the secrets." Todd kissed his wife and Jim dragged Chris away from the door with an indulgent smile.

"Healed your heart?" Zamora whispered to Greg.

"Would you buy 'healed your arm'?" He shot her an apologetic look.

"No, she seemed pretty sure."

Greg sighed. "Yeah, she did. Let me introduce you to the rest of the squad before we talk more, okay?"

"Wait, Greg." She stopped him with a hand on his chest. "Tell me this isn't going to be a thanks-for-everything-but-we're-done party."

"What? Oh, God, no, Zamora. No way. Not even close." He grabbed her hand and held it against his chest as he met her gaze. "No, I wanted to introduce you to my family, the men and women who have my back when things get tough emotionally. I want them to know who you are because you've become part of my emotional squad."

Some of her fears bled away and her shoulders relaxed. "I'm sorry. I'm just really nervous. These folks are your family, like you said, and they're all so clean-cut, like you. Their opinions matter to you, and therefore, they matter to me."

"They'll love you because I do. I had a clean-cut woman once, and they weren't impressed." Greg squeezed her hand again. "You're authentically you, and that's what matters. To them, and more importantly, to me." He winked. "And don't let their looks fool you. None of these people are what society thinks they should be. Trust me."

She took a deep breath and straightened her shoulders, lifting her chin. "Okay." She dredged up her smile as she shoved her misgivings away. "Bring it on, SEAL."

"Hooyah, inkheart."

His nickname for her strengthened her confidence and she faced the rest of the people in the house with a smile. Greg pulled her over to a couple, the woman roundly pregnant.

"Zamora, I'd like you to meet Lindsey and John

Andrews. John retired from our squad because he's gonna be a dad soon, and Lindsey is a retired undercover cop."

"Wow, a retired undercover cop? Where?"

Lindsey smiled. "Las Vegas. It's where I met John."

"I bet that's quite a story." Zamora dropped her gaze to Lindsey's belly. "One you can tell your kids about someday."

Lindsey laughed. "At least the edited Disney version." She winked at John before turning back to Zamora. "I understand you're the one who put Greg up that first weekend. That was very kind of you."

Zamora shrugged and nodded. "He looked like he could use a little help and I've been there. I figured I could pay the help I'd gotten forward."

"He was lucky to have met you, then." Lindsey wrapped an arm around her husband's waist and leaned into him. "I swear these big, bad SEALs actually need rescuing from time to time."

John chuckled. "I didn't mind being rescued by you. You were my knight in a little black dress."

"I didn't really rescue Greg." Zamora shrugged.

"That's not what I heard." Lindsey wiggled her eyebrows. "But now I need to use the bathroom." She sighed. "Pregnancy sucks."

"Excuse us." John led his wife off, and Zamora took a deep breath.

"Wow. Are all your friends that intense?"

Greg laughed. "I don't know. They don't seem intense to me. Come on. Let's put the food down and get some beers."

"Yeah, okay, good." She followed him through the house to the kitchen and they set down the food while she tried to get a grip on the incredible people around Greg. The women were strong, beautiful, and smart. The men were unbelievably handsome. *Where the hell did they find all the handsome guys to be SEALs?* It wasn't statistically possible, but all the men would've caught her eye if they'd stopped in her shop.

Greg handed her a root beer. "Ready for a little more? I have a couple of other people I want you to meet."

"Yeah, okay. Let's do this."

He laughed. "Hey, it's not like running a gauntlet. It'll be fine. Just be the woman I met at the hospital all those months ago."

"I would, except I don't have my wagon full of treats to share as peace offerings." She shot him a dry look to take the sting out of her words and he laughed again.

"I promise not to let them eat you." He leaned close to whisper in her ear. "That's my job."

Zamora laughed, letting the worry go. These people were his family, but she had his heart. *I hope.* He pulled her over to the couch where two more men sat watching a baseball game on TV. One was short, dark, and compact, with scruff on his cheeks and piercings in his ears. She also caught a distinct New Jersey twang to his voice when he yelled at the game.

The other man was tall, broad, hair graying at the temples, and had tattoos up his left arm from his wrist to where his t-shirt strained across his biceps. He had a quiet voice and watchful eyes, but the laugh lines ran deeply grooved around his mouth.

"Deli, Bones, I'd like you to meet Zamora Hart, my woman." Greg winked at her as Deli stood up, the top of his head about equal to her nose.

"Not your girlfriend?" Deli raised his eyebrows and smirked.

"Does she look like a girl to you?"

"Hell no." Deli held out his hand. "Petty Officer Eugene Rubenovich, but you can call me Deli."

"Nice to meet you, Deli." Zamora nodded, turning to the older man. "Bones is an interesting nickname. How did you get that?"

"What, you don't believe that's my real name?" Bones chuckled at his own joke. "Petty Officer Martin Skelling, ma'am. Bones came from everyone mistaking my last name for Skeleton, including the U.S. Navy for a time."

"That's not what you said first, Skellin'." Another man slid up to them as silent as an owl. "You said it was 'cause you were so good at breakin' them."

"What else was I gonna say to a new squad full of guys wanting to test the 'old man', Rimshot?" Bones pointed to his silvered hair. "Even if I am the same age as the rest of you mutts."

"He does have a point, Kevin." An auburn-tressed woman with freckles across her nose thumped the newcomer in the shoulder before holding out her hand to Zamora. "Hi. I'm Jaime Hensen, Kevin's fiancée. You must be Zamora, right?"

"That's me. The tattooed, pierced, single woman who's ruining his clean-cut reputation." She winked at Greg, hoping he'd laugh.

"Who's clean-cut?" Kevin asked, his eyebrows rising into his shaggy hair. "Bam-Bam? Clean-cut? You gotta be shittin' me."

Zamora blinked and smirked. "Bam-Bam? They call you Bam-Bam?"

"Yeah, it's a long story." Greg shrugged, but his cheeks turned pink with his blush.

"I'm willing to listen." She bumped his shoulder with hers. "You haven't told me this one yet."

"You know I'm a demolitions specialist." Greg shrugged.

"Yeah, he loves to blow shit up," Kevin added helpfully.

"And he used to eat Flintstones vitamins like candy," Deli put in with a grin.

"Flintstones vitamins? You mean, like the kids' vitamins?" Zamora snorted.

"Yeah, they tasted a helluva lot better than the adult multivitamins the Navy supplied." He shrugged again. "I used to keep them in my bunk kit."

Deli leaned close. "He liked the cherry flavored ones best. Just sayin'."

Zamora couldn't hold in her laugh. "I'll have to keep that in mind and make sure I have them on hand at the house."

"Oh, man, I'm never gonna live this down, am I?" Greg rolled his eyes.

"Nope. We're gonna make sure she knows all your quirks, Bam-Bam." Deli punched him in the shoulder.

"Great. Zamora, can I talk to you?" Greg shook his head and headed out the back door to the deck where the grill chugged savory-scented smoke into the air.

"Oh dear, I better go with him. But I'll keep that in mind, Deli. I do want to know his quirks." Zamora smiled and hurried after Greg as the others chuckled behind her. "Greg, wait. I think your nickname is cute, especially the story that goes with it."

"I'm glad to hear that." He nodded, but wouldn't look at her and her gut clenched.

Had she insulted him in front of his friends? *Way to go, Z. Maybe you could launch into the old 'baby killer' rant to make the insults complete.* She followed him as he stepped off the deck and headed for a little arbor set between some tall palms and hibiscus plants. She had no idea what was going through his head, but tension sang along his shoulders. When had this party gone from nerve-wracking to utter crap?

"I'm sorry, really. I didn't mean to make fun of you." She trotted to catch up to him. "Greg, seriously. I'm sorry. Please wait."

He stopped under the arbor, his gaze trained on the palm fronds swaying in the afternoon breeze. His shoulders remained tight and she moved to stand in front of him, pressing her hands to his chest.

"Greg, please, talk to me. I'm sorry. I don't know what I did to embarrass you, but it wasn't my intention." She bit her bottom lip. "Please, look at me."

He dropped his cerulean gaze to hers and the intensity there took her breath away. She loved his eyes and how they could convey so much without him using his voice. But at the moment, the intensity was hard to read and she hoped he hadn't shut himself off to deal with his anger at her mistake.

"I'm sorry I embarrassed you."

"What?" Greg's gaze sharpened and he blinked. "When did you embarrass me?"

Zamora drew back, her brows lowering. "Back there in the house, when you left. Isn't that why you walked away from me and your friends? Isn't that why you're out here?"

"Oh, oh. No, shit, screwed up already." He shook his head and took a deep breath. "No, I just wanted to get out of the house and be with you alone for a few moments."

"You did? Why didn't you say anything?"

"I did, I said I wanted to talk to you." He blew out his breath. "But I didn't say it very well. I guess it's because I'm nervous."

"You're nervous?" She blinked at him, her stomach rolling. *Oh, God, what is he going to do?* "Why?"

"Because..." He bit his lip and shot a look at the house. When nothing seemed to give him the answers he wanted, he rubbed the back of his neck with his hand and returned his gaze to her. "Do you remember when Chris said you'd healed my heart and Lindsey said she'd heard you rescued me?"

Zamora nodded slowly. "Yeah. What about it?"

"They were both right."

She tilted her head. "Did you tell them I rescued you?"

He nodded. "Yeah, I did, because it's true. I think you started your rescue campaign when you came to the hospital that first time. I'd never seen anyone like you with your beautiful hair, eyes, and ink. You were so different from anyone I knew or had met, and you didn't take shit from any of the guys in the ward. Hell, they looked forward to your visits." He gave her a shy smile. "I did, too."

She couldn't help but smile back at him. "Would it make you feel better to know I always went to your room first, just to see you?"

"Oh, yeah?" His grin widened.

"Yeah. It was your blue eyes and the need to ink that lovely chest of yours."

He laughed. "You want to ink my chest?"

"Not necessarily. I just remember thinking your pectoral could use some sexy designs."

"Hmm, maybe I'll take it under advisement." He nodded with a thoughtful smile. "But what I wanted to say was, when you offered me a place to stay, even after I came to your shop all shit-faced and stupid, you made me realize how very special you were. You're sexy, smart, and so damn kind, you slowly healed my heart from the damage done to it by my ex, and you rescued me from a life of utter misery."

"Oh, come on, Greg. Utter misery?" Zamora smirked.

"I'm serious, Zamora. I wasn't happy, and I hadn't been happy in years." He grimaced and shot a look toward the house before dragging his gaze back to hers. "I liked my job, and I liked the idea of coming home to someone, but I didn't particularly like the person I'd chosen. As it turned out, she didn't particularly like me, either."

"I'm sorry, Greg." She grabbed his hands.

He shook his head. "Don't be. She taught me a lot about what I didn't want and what I was doing wrong in a relationship. And she prepared me for meeting you."

He paused and seemed to be gathering his thoughts as he let his gaze slide over the yard and the house again. She wondered what he had in mind as he let go of one hand to dig around in his pocket for something.

"I know we haven't talked about anything more since the whole 'more than friends with benefits' discussion, but living with you and spending time with you made me realize just how much I want to be with you. I know I've said I love you, but I didn't understand how much I loved you until Stan Lords put you in danger a week ago." Greg met her gaze again. "I couldn't lose you, not when I hadn't had the chance to tell you how I felt, how things had changed. I had to protect you and save you from bastards like Lords."

Greg gave a self-deprecating laugh as she tilted her head again.

"Yeah, I know. It turns out you don't need saving, or rescuing, you just need me to make sure the bastards stay down when you clobber them."

Zamora laughed. "You did a great job, though."

He snorted. "We're not paid the big bucks for nothing." Then he sobered. "But I wanted to be there for you, whenever you needed me, and with my career shifting toward the instructor's side rather than a front-line operator, I can be there. You make me want to be there, to make an effort to pay attention to life at home, with you, in that fantastic cottage on the beach. You make me want to be a better man than I've been, work harder on our relationship, be smarter and stronger for you. You've healed my heart, Zamora, and rescued me."

He dropped to one knee in front of her and held up a little maroon velvet box with brass details. Her heart thundered in her chest as he tipped the lid back with a soft squeak.

"Will you marry me?"

CHAPTER TWENTY

Holy shit, did he just ask me to marry him?

Zamora lost her voice as she gazed at the rainbow of square cut sapphires set in a flat white-gold ring nestled in maroon satin. She'd wanted to be with him, but he'd been an active SEAL, and active SEALs often didn't come home. She couldn't handle that. When he'd stopped being combat-ready, she dismissed being with him because SEALs didn't talk to their partners, couldn't talk to them about their jobs, and she needed clear communication. But though he hadn't given her details about his training, he had shared little tidbits about his days on base with her.

Still, she'd braced herself for the inevitable. She'd have to let him go because he couldn't do relationships, as evidenced by his failed marriage. *Emotionally unavailable.*

But Greg had given her his insecurities, had admitted vulnerabilities to her. Hell, he'd even wept on her shoulder after the doctor told him he was out of the Teams. That wasn't exactly emotionally unavailable.

And now he asked her to marry him. *Oh my God, what do I do?*

Say yes, you dumbass. The snarky voice sounded remarkably like Toby.

"I..."

Greg's smile faltered and he swallowed hard. She hated putting the uncertainty back in his body language and raised her chin as she screwed up her courage.

"Yes, I'll marry you as long as I don't have to wear heels."

His smile returned to its brilliant wattage as hope and joy spilled into his eyes. "Fuck no, Z. You don't have to wear heels." He plucked the ring out of the box and she held out her hand so he could slide it on her ring finger. It fit perfectly.

"Wow, how did you do that?" She stared at the ring as Greg stood up. "And how did you know I've always wanted a rainbow ring?"

Greg's smile turned smug. "Research."

"Research?" She narrowed her eyes. "How long have you been planning this?"

"I told you, since last week."

"And you figured out my favorite kind of ring and the right size in the last week?"

"Well, I had a little help." He winked. "I asked Toby." He ran his thumb over the ring on her finger. "It looks good on you."

She nodded. It looked freakin' fantastic on her hand, but his looked naked. "What about your hand? When do I get to see a ring there?"

"Do you want me to wear a ring?" He looked surprised.

"Hell yeah. Even if it's a tattooed ring. You know, so it doesn't snag on anything while you're working blowing shit up and everything. Bam-Bam."

Greg threw his head back and laughed. "That's right. I'll have to think about that. Would you do the work?"

She rose onto her tiptoes to kiss him. "Yes, sir."

"Hot damn."

He took her mouth with enthusiasm and her pussy

clenched with the need to celebrate their new status as engaged. But uncertainty about what his family would think soured the moment and she pulled back from the kiss with a sigh.

"What is it? What's wrong, inkheart?" He ran his thumbs over her cheeks as he searched her eyes.

"Are you sure your SEAL family will be okay with this, especially after your last marriage?" She grimaced. "I'm not exactly like the other women who've married into your squad."

Greg raised his eyebrows and gave her a half smile. "No one is like you, that's for sure, but if you're referring to your non-traditional appearance, I think you fit in pretty well."

"Oh, really? How do you figure?"

He squeezed her hands. "You know this is Chris and Todd's home, right?"

"Yeah. They're a nice couple, even if they do have a roommate."

"They are, but he's not just a roommate." Greg tilted his head, waiting for Zamora to catch on. "That's her other partner, Lt. Waters."

"Partner...Wait, she has two guys?"

Greg laughed. "Yep. She fell in love with two men, and lives with them in a permanent ménage relationship. Not traditional at all."

Zamora let her breath out in a laugh. "Lucky lady."

He raised an eyebrow. "Hey, are you saying you'd want more than me?"

She shook her head. "No. Like I said, I don't share. But I'm envious that so many men see her as capable and strong and kick-ass without giving up being feminine."

"Zamora, look at me please." He waited for her full attention. "I've never seen you as anything less than yourself. You're smart, capable, beautiful and feminine."

"But not SEAL-capable, not like her." She shot a look

at the house.

"No one is like her and I'm grateful for that. She's not my type. Too tough. Why would you want to be a SEAL?"

"I don't. But I want to be respected like one. No one doubts a SEAL's abilities. Ever." Zamora grimaced. "But a woman business owner and tattoo artist is open for debate all the time."

"Not to me, not ever. You're perfect for me exactly as you are."

"But the other ladies, Lindsey, an undercover cop, and Jaime. You didn't tell me what she does, but they're both strong, and elegant. I'm never going to be that way, Greg."

"Thank God." He grinned at her wide-eyed stare. "Zamora, I don't want perfectly coifed. I had that before and it didn't suit me at all. I want hot, passionate, authentic, and honest. I want you, Zamora, just the way you are with your crimson hair and rainbow tattoos. I don't want you to change unless you want to."

He tilted his head. "My question for you is, am I, as an injured SEAL with a failed marriage in my past, good enough to be your husband?"

She wanted to laugh at the silly question, but she raised her gaze to his, taking her time. She thought of the old woman who'd tried to dissuade Greg from being with her and a happy smile curled her lips.

"Roger that, Bam-Bam. You're my badass SEAL, and I want you to have my back."

"Copy that." And they sealed the deal with a hot kiss.

THE END

AUTHOR'S NOTE

You can find out how John and Lindsey met in BRONCO'S ROUGH RIDE, Book 0.5, how Chris, Todd, and Jim got together in THE NAVY'S GHOST, Book 1, and how Greg got injured in RIMSHOT'S HARD TARGET, Book 2 in the Bad Boys of Beta Squad series. Happy reading!

Siobhan

BRONCO'S ROUGH RIDE
BAD BOYS OF BETA SQUAD, BOOK 0.5
SNEEK PEEK

What happens in Vegas, stays in the heart...

Chief Petty Officer John "Bronco" Andrews only meant to stay one night in Vegas for a little R&R before resuming his duties as a US Navy SEAL in Coronado. But someone slips him a mickey in the bar and he finds himself in Madame LeBeau's sex trade. As the product. Doped up on ketamine to keep him docile, Bronco has no choice but to let it ride.

Detective Lindsey Jarvis has been undercover in LeBeau's sex slave racket for two years and she almost has enough evidence to take it down. Between abduction, prostitution, and murder, she has LeBeau by the short hairs. All she needs is a "product". John is the perfect witness if she can get him out before the drugs shut down his heart. Then she'll be free to start a normal life.

Lindsey doesn't count on her overwhelming attraction for Bronco or her need to see him through detox. But she's a cop in Vegas and he's a Navy SEAL, two lifestyles with too much unpredictability to maintain a relationship. Neither have time for more than one wild rough ride, and what happens in Vegas, stays. Forever.

THE NAVY'S GHOST
BAD BOYS OF BETA SQUAD, BOOK 1
SNEEK PEEK

A SEAL is strongest with her Team…

Ensign Christiana "Ghost" Brickman is the only female SEAL to survive BUD/S training, a real Navy Jane. But when an ambush ends her career as an active SEAL, she's free to pursue other interests. Like her two best friends Lt. Jim "Retro" Waters and Chief Warrant Officer Todd "Magic" Hunter. She's wanted them for over a year, but never dared to approach them while in the squad.

Retro has fought his dark desires since high school, certain the need to share a woman unnatural. Magic had never considered sharing before Ghost mentions it, but it solves his dilemma of choosing between his best friend and his woman. But Retro balks at Ghost's offer to share and retreats from both when she marries Magic.

Everyone feels Retro's loss, but he ignores the ache of their broken connection in favor of living 'normal.' When Ghost and the other wives of Beta Squad are kidnapped, Retro must reevaluate how much both Ghost and Magic mean to him. And he must decide how far he's willing to go to save the woman he loves, before she becomes the Navy's ghost.

OTHER BOOKS BY SIOBHAN MUIR

Her Devoted Vampire (from Three Lakes Books)
Queen Bitch of the Callowwood Pack (from Siren Publishing)
Not a Dragon's Standard Virgin (from Siren Publishing)
Second Chance Succubus (from Three Lakes Books)
Darwin's Evolution (from Amazon)

Cloudburst Colorado Series
A Hell Hound's Fire (from Three Lakes Books)
The Beltane Witch (from Three Lakes Books)
Christmas I.C.E. Magic (from Three Lakes Books)
Cloudburst Ice Magic (from Three Lakes Books)

Rifts Series
Take the Reins (from Three Lakes Books)
A Centaur's Solstice Wish (from Three Lakes Books)
In Death's Shadow (from Three Lakes Books)

Bad Boys of Beta Squad Series
Bronco's Rough Ride (from Three Lakes Books)
The Navy's Ghost (from Three Lakes Books)
Rimshot's Hard Target (from Amazon)
Bam-Bam's Inked Hart (from Three Lakes Books)

The Ivory Road
A Walk in the Sand (from Three Lakes Books)
Outback Dreams (from Three Lakes Books)

Triple Star Ranch Series

Rope a Falling Star (from Three Lakes Books
Star Light, Star Bright (from Three Lakes Books)

Warbler Peninsula Series
Order of the Dragon (from Three Lakes Books)
The Valkyrie's Sword (from Three Lakes Books)

Coming Soon
Deli's Take Out (Bad Boys of Beta Squad #4)
Wildfire's Heart (Elemental Hearts #1)
Loch'd Hearts (Elemental Hearts #2)

ABOUT THE AUTHOR

Siobhan Muir lives in Cheyenne, Wyoming, with her husband, two daughters, and a vegetarian cat she swears is a shape-shifter, though he's never shifted when she can see him. When not writing, she can be found looking down a microscope at fossil fox teeth, pursuing her other love, paleontology. An avid reader of science fiction/fantasy, her husband gave her a paranormal romance for Christmas one year, and she was hooked for good.

In previous lives, Siobhan has been an actor at the Colorado Renaissance Festival, a field geologist in the Aleutian Islands, and restored inter-planetary imagery at the USGS. She's hiked to the top of Mount St. Helens and to the bottom of Meteor Crater.

Siobhan writes kick-ass adventure with hot sex for men and women to enjoy. She believes in happily ever after, redemption, and communication, all of which you will find in her paranormal romance stories.

Connect with Siobhan online at:
http://siobhanmuir.com
http://www.facebook.com/siobhan.muir.35
http://twitter.com/SiobhanMuir
http://siobhanmuir.com/siobhans-blog
http://pinterest.com/siobhanmuir.35